**"One of my patients is going to have an exorcism instead of continuing therapy."**

Megan started to tell the story, but halfway through she had to stop. Greyson was laughing too hard for her to continue.

"Exorcism? Darling, your patients never cease to amaze me. Exorcism, of all things."

"Ted could really get hurt."

"And if Ted wants to do something incredibly stupid, that's his prerogative. I somehow think we have more important things to worry about right now, don't you?"

Megan opened one eye—opening both seemed like too much effort—and glared at him. As much as she could with one eye anyway. "I'm trying not to think about it."

"Enjoy one last night of not thinking about it, then, because tomorrow we need to get to work. In more ways than one."

"The meeting." She sighed.

"The meeting," he said. "And the fact that whoever it is who's trying to kill you will probably be there."

"A fun, scary, and sexy ride on the paranormal express!"
—award-winning author Carole Nelson Douglas

"Fun, scary, exciting, and everything in between."
—*Fantasy SciFi Book Review*

# DEMON POSSESSED

## STACIA KANE

Pocket Books
New York   London   Toronto   Sydney

The sale of this book without its cover is unauthorized. If you purchased this book without a cover, you should be aware that it was reported to the publisher as "unsold and destroyed." Neither the author nor the publisher has received payment for the sale of this "stripped book."

Pocket Books
A Division of Simon & Schuster, Inc.
1230 Avenue of the Americas
New York, NY 10020

This book is a work of fiction. Names, characters, places, and incidents either are products of the author's imagination or are used fictitiously. Any resemblance to actual events or locales or persons, living or dead, is entirely coincidental.

Copyright © 2010 by Stacey Fackler

All rights reserved, including the right to reproduce this book or portions thereof in any form whatsoever. For information address Pocket Books Subsidiary Rights Department,
1230 Avenue of the Americas, New York, NY 10020.

First Juno Books/Pocket Books paperback edition March 2010

JUNO BOOKS and colophon are trademarks of Wildside Press LLC used under license by Simon & Schuster, Inc., the publisher of this work.

POCKET and colophon are registered trademarks of Simon & Schuster, Inc.

For information about special discounts for bulk purchases, please contact Simon & Schuster Special Sales at 1-866-506-1949 or business@simonandschuster.com.

The Simon & Schuster Speakers Bureau can bring authors to your live event. For more information or to book an event, contact the Simon & Schuster Speakers Bureau at 1-866-248-3049 or visit our website at www.simonspeakers.com.

Design by Dave Stevenson

Manufactured in the United States of America

10 9 8 7 6 5 4 3 2 1

ISBN 978-1-4391-6761-8
ISBN 978-1-4391-6764-9 (ebook)

*This one is for Stephen.*

# Acknowledgments

Aside from my family, my husband and daughters, I have to thank Corinne Knell and Caitlin Kittredge, Stacey Jay, Mark Henry, Richelle Mead, Synde Korman, Todd Thomas, Kaz Mahoney, David Bridger, and all the pals who were so patient with me while I finished this book and completed an international move. Additional, huge thanks to Paula Guran, Jennifer Heddle, Chris Lotts, and Erica Feldon.

# DEMON
# POSSESSED

# Chapter One

The woman shifted on the ivory leather couch and smiled. "Thank you for seeing me at such short notice, Dr. Chase."

Megan nodded and forced herself to return the smile, just as she would if the woman were a patient.

But the woman—Elizabeth Reid—was not a patient. Elizabeth Reid was an FBI agent.

Eleven months before, the idea of a federal agent having any reason to talk to her, to question her, would have surprised Megan enough to make her spill her cocktail, had she been drinking one. Not so now. Damn it. She was only surprised the feds were being so blatant this time, that they were actually speaking to her openly.

"Of course." Megan folded her hands in her lap, decided that looked too prim, as if she had something to hide, and rearranged herself into a more relaxed pose, arms resting on the arms of her chair, ankles crossed. Casual. She hoped.

At least Agent Reid didn't seem to see a problem. Her mind, when Megan reached into it as stealthily as she could, seemed totally focused on her objective, and seeing what it was put some much-needed steel into Megan's spine.

"You haven't asked me why I'm here, Dr. Chase."

"I assume you'll tell me, Agent Reid."

The woman smiled. "I suppose I will. We were wondering if you knew anything about the Bellreive Hotel."

Okay. This had not been in the woman's head a few seconds ago. Good thing Megan had had some practice lately in keeping calm, in not letting her own emotions and feelings show. Something she'd always considered herself pretty good at; now she figured she'd just about graduated from the Masterclass.

"I've heard of it," she said. "I've never been there. I wouldn't be able to afford it, I don't think. Why?"

Agent Reid gave her a sunny smile, as if this was the answer she'd expected. Which it probably was. She pushed a strand of ink-black hair behind her ear and leaned forward, her black-suited body a deep crack against the pale couch and walls. Everything in the room was light, an attempt to counteract the darkness of the windowless space in the dingy little strip mall.

Maybe not as bad as that. It was a big space. It was in a nice part of town. But it still wasn't . . . wasn't what she'd dreamed of when she'd thought of having her own practice.

It was good enough, though. And she couldn't have everything. The rest of her life certainly held little cause for many complaints.

"Since you asked, we've received some interesting information," Agent Reid said. "And I think you'll be especially interested, as it concerns you."

"I assumed it did, since you're here," Megan replied, "but I can't imagine how this could have anything to do with me."

"We've received information that a meeting is due to take place at the Bellreive next week. Attending that meeting will be one or two . . . persons of interest to us."

"I'm afraid I don't know anything about that."

"You haven't taken next week off? According to your schedule—"

Megan stood up. Done. "Next week is my birthday. As I believe you know. Yes, I'm taking some vacation time. I have every right to. So?"

"So you're confirming the meeting?"

Megan just stared at her.

"Dr. Chase, I'm trying to . . . I'm offering you a deal. Immunity. Full and total." Elizabeth reached into the sleek black briefcase resting like a coiled viper at her side. "If you'd read over these papers—we know you're not involved. But your testimony, if you would—"

"I'm sorry. I have a patient due here any moment." Megan dodged the papers and pushed past Elizabeth to open the door. "Thanks for your time, but I have no idea what you're talking about."

"Perhaps Greyson Dante does." Elizabeth didn't move; neither did her eyes, focused intently on Megan's face. "Greyson Dante? You are involved with him, right? Don't bother denying it. We already know."

"Thank you for your time," Megan said again. She raised her eyebrows, glanced at the open door and the bare little room beyond. The office's arrangement was one of its chief charms; it may not be the greatest place in the world, but it did provide her patients with privacy. Those exiting left through that little room. Those waiting sat in the furnished waiting area with magazines and a water cooler. Neither saw the other.

She'd never thought the arrangement would be of such benefit to her. It wasn't as though Agent Reid had "FBI" printed across her forehead in big block letters or anything, but just the same . . . Well. If it weren't for the separate exit, Megan could hardly stand there with the door open, could she? Not when her two o'clock was bound to be already waiting, and her two o'clock was a notorious shadow-jumper.

Agent Reid finally gave up. She sighed and stood, shoving the papers back into her briefcase. "I do wish you would think about it. It's only a matter of time, Dr. Chase. Someone with your public image . . ."

Had Megan thought the woman had given up? Ha. No, she'd just been waiting for the opportunity to turn the screw tighter.

But Megan's skin was pretty thick. So she let the implied threat fall to the ground between them and refused to pick it up. "If you don't mind, I do have another appointment."

"Of course." Agent Reid slipped a stark white business card from the black depths of her suit jacket The blue FBI logo seemed to glow against the background. "Take my card, though, please. And call me if you change your mind. Or if you find yourself at the Bellreive next week."

Megan took the card. No point in appearing uncooperative. Or rather, more uncooperative than she already appeared.

It didn't really matter; she hoped it didn't anyway. But that bothered her too, didn't it? Hoping it wouldn't matter? Hoping that Agent Reid and her fairly odd attempt to get whatever information she thought Megan might have were no more important than the few casual words Megan exchanged with the checkout girl at the grocery store and no more likely to stick in anyone's mind later?

Yes. It did. But there was very little she could do about it at that moment, save utter a quiet "Fuck" under her breath when Agent Reid finally closed the exit door behind herself.

Meanwhile timid taps at the other door told Megan she'd been exactly right. Her two o'clock—Ted Anderson—was there, and even if she wasn't really watching the clock, he certainly was. He always did.

She shouldn't be so hard on Ted, though. He'd followed her over from Serenity Partners the winter before, and that loyalty meant something to her. Sure, most of her patients had come along. That didn't make their loyalty any less valuable.

The door opened with an almost imperceptible squeak. She'd have to oil those hinges again. The office plaza now housing her practice wasn't old, but apparently the previous tenant had run some kind of family-encounter group that involved lots of slamming doors.

Ted stood just past the threshold in his typical hunched pose, like Sisyphus trying to push his worries up a hill. The overhead lights shone through his thin hair and made his scalp beneath glow pinkish.

"Come on in, Ted." Megan stepped back. Usually he practically knocked her over in his haste to enter the room. Not a surprise, really. Ted's wife ignored him. So did his children. Those years of neglect seemed to have erased him somehow. Sad. But it was something Megan usually felt she was doing a decent job of counteracting, encouraging Ted to speak up at home, to get out into the world more.

Today, however, he didn't move from the doorway. "Dr. Chase, I just . . . I just came to tell you I won't be coming anymore. I thought I owed you letting you know in person."

Oh, for fuck's sake. First the FBI showed up and made vague little threats and offered vague little deals, and now this. Losing a patient wasn't exactly a joy. "Ted, I . . . Is something the matter? Please, at least come in and sit down."

He hesitated.

"Come in, please. Whatever decision you've made is your decision, and I respect that. I won't try to talk you out of anything. But if you wanted to tell me in person, you obviously thought there was an explanation to be made, right?"

Still he waited, like a golf ball teetering on the edge of a hole. Finally he nodded and edged past her.

"Okay." She sat back in her chair and plastered what she hoped was an understanding smile on her face. "What's up?"

"You can't help me anymore," he mumbled. A piece

of paper she hadn't noticed before tumbled in his hands; he folded and unfolded it as though performing the motions incorrectly would result in the destruction of the universe. "What's wrong with me . . . it's not something you can fix."

"It's not a matter of 'fixing.' I don't think there's anything wrong with you, or that you're broken in some way. You shouldn't feel—"

"I'm possessed."

"No, you're not," she said, before she thought, *Okay, double what-the-fuck.* Possessed? Where the hell would Ted get an idea like that?

Especially since it wasn't true. Not remotely. She could still read him; had he been possessed, she couldn't have.

He glared at her. It surprised her almost as much as his previous utterance had. "That's what he said you'd say."

"He?"

"Reverend Walther. He said you'd say that. You people are just desperate to keep us on a string, to keep taking our money."

"Where in the world—"

"All these years I've been coming here, thinking something was wrong with me, and it wasn't me. It was these demons."

"Ted. You are not possessed by demons." And she should know. She was, in fact, probably the only human being in the world who could tell him definitively that his problems had nothing to do with demons. Or at least very little to do with them. Ted's personal demons—his little Yezer Ha-Ra, that was—numbered only two, and they were fairly content with that.

At least they were now. Since Megan had assumed the leadership of the local Yezer "family," there'd been a few sticky moments. At one point she'd almost lost them completely, along with her life.

But that had been months before. Now her relationship to and rules for the Yezer had reached a level of equilibrium, and if the Yezer weren't growing fat off the misery of humans, they weren't starving either.

But none of that was the issue at the moment. She seriously doubted Ted was talking about Yezer, especially since Yezer didn't actually possess people. They merely sat on people's shoulders and tried to persuade them to commit . . . well, if not evil acts, then certainly not good ones. Selfish acts. Mildly cruel acts. Depending on the person, of course.

"I don't expect you to believe it, Dr. Chase. But all this therapy, psychology . . . what you do . . . it can't help people. It's demons making people unhappy and demons making us do wrong, and Reverend Walther can help me. So I won't be coming back here. Just thought I should tell you."

Eep. He'd never know how right he was about demons making people unhappy, even if he was wrong about how it actually worked. Possession . . . Walther . . . A bell rang somewhere in the back of Megan's head. Yes, she'd heard of him, hadn't she? Seen something recently on one of those newsmagazine shows. Her memory of it was rather vague but clear enough for one thing, at least.

"Are you talking about an exorcism?"

Ted nodded. Shit.

"Ted, please. I really have to strongly advise you against this. It could be dangerous, I don't know—"

Ted stood up. Megan could say one thing for whoever Reverend Walther was, he'd given Ted more strength than she'd ever seen from him.

Of course, that strength was based on falsehoods and the promise of a quick fix and so was more akin to zealotry than any actual strength, but why quibble? There didn't appear to be much she could do about it either way.

"The only dangerous thing is to go on living the way I am," he said. "To let these demons grow and take over. No, thank you, Dr. Chase. I know there's a solution to my problems, but it requires faith. And faith I've got."

"You need to have faith in yourself, Ted, you don't need an exorcism, you just need—"

"Thanks, Dr. Chase, but I have to go. Lily's waiting for me in the car, and we're about to head over to see the reverend." He stood up and held out his hand.

Megan took it and, with it, the visions that came when she lowered her shields: Ted's wife, Lily, convincing Ted this exorcism thing was the answer to their problems. Why had Ted never told her how deeply religious Lily was becoming over the last six months? The shadowy face of a man—Reverend Walther, she assumed. A face she instinctively disliked, but whether that was because she thought he was a charlatan, because he was lying to one of her patients, or because of some other reason, she didn't know.

And at that moment she didn't particularly care. It was barely quarter past two on a beautiful July day, and all she wanted to do was go home, crawl under the covers, and stay there.

"If you ever need anything . . . you can always give me a call." She dropped his hand. "I'll still be here."

"Well, thanks again," he said.

They stood for an awkward moment, unsure how long to keep shaking hands or if they should do more or what. Rather like greeting a long-lost cousin you'd never really liked. Should you forget the time he locked you in the basement and kiss him anyway because he was family, or did you treat him like any other stranger? How thick was that blood anyway?

Not so thick in this case or, rather, nonexistent. Ted let go of her hand, nodded, and let himself out the little exit door, leaving Megan with an open forty-minute window and plenty to think about during it. Including the FBI.

# Chapter Two

Her first instinct was to reach for the phone, but she stopped herself before her fingers closed over the receiver and slumped back in her desk chair instead. Greyson wasn't available today anyway, right? In meetings all day.

Sure, he'd still answer if she called or if she texted and said it was an emergency. But it wasn't an emergency. Having a shitty day—or a decent day that had suddenly plummeted into the depths of shittiness—wasn't an emergency. Neither was the FBI agent, although the "We have a deal for you" angle was new.

The information about the Bellreive . . . now, that might be important. Extremely important. Contrary to what she'd told Agent Reid, there was indeed a meeting there the following week, one which Megan was absolutely attending.

She had to. All of the Gretnegs were attending, and that meant her. Taking over the Yezer Ha-Ra family—more technically known as a Meegra in the demon tongue—meant more than simply an unusual and sometimes awkward situation for a psychological counselor to find herself in. It meant learning to work with the other Gretnegs, trying to balance friendly relations with them against the desire to keep herself removed from some of their . . . well, more interesting activities.

What Megan did not enjoy about dealing with demons was exactly what they lived for: fucking with humanity, leading them astray, and in most cases making a damned good living from it. The Meegras were like the Mafia, only with a lot less trouble hiding the bodies; a fire demon could reduce a corpse to ash in less time than it took her to sear a steak.

Which was probably not the best analogy to use, now that she thought about it, especially not as she'd planned to have steaks with *her* fire demon that very night.

Sort of. Sort of hers.

The less she considered that question, the better.

She rested her head on her forearms on the desk. Only one appointment left; she was closing early on this particular Thursday and taking Friday off. She was off for the next week, although technically her birthday was an excuse rather than the reason. The reason was the meeting, and the meeting was now in jeopardy. Oh, who was she kidding? They wouldn't cancel it. They certainly wouldn't change the location. The Bellreive was the most expensive and luxurious hotel in the city, and the other Gretnegs would just as soon slice off their own heads as stay in an inferior hotel.

Seemed rather silly to her, to stay in a hotel for a week when everyone involved had perfectly nice homes right nearby. Well, no. *She* had a perfectly nice home. The other Gretnegs had mansions.

But the politics behind who hosted what on which day and how many servants and assistants everyone needed and would be allowed or whatever had proved too frustrating, and thus the Bellreive was being used as a compromise. Everyone could make their own arrangements and stay in whatever suites they liked. It had taken almost two months to get everyone to agree and to get everyone booked, and now . . . shit, where would they go?

Maybe they'd cancel the damn thing altogether, which wouldn't bother her. It wasn't as if she had a lot to do there, since she refused to get involved in Meegra money schemes. In fact, she'd prefer them to cancel, since she knew one topic of discussion was bound to be the Haiken Kra ritual and why she hadn't done it yet.

They all wanted her to. Wanted her to allow the piece of demon inside her, nestled by her heart, to grow. Wanted her to magically somehow become demon, or at least more demon than human. A demon majority, as it were, right there in her body.

She didn't want to do it. She'd come close to it back in December, when she'd had to allow the demon—not just the demon but the part of her that connected to the Yezer—to grow. She'd thought at the time that might have actually been the Haiken Kra and that the decision had been made without her actively having to make it, but no. It had consolidated the demon, had set its power on a direct path, but it hadn't physically made her a demon.

It had simply defined her. Psyche demon. A demon

with mental powers, not physical ones. It had turned her own gifts into something far more intense, but it hadn't gone farther than that.

A happy medium, in her opinion. Not so in those of the other Gretnegs. Why doing the ritual was so important to them she had no idea. And she liked it that way.

"You don't look very happy."

She raised her head, every inch an effort, like hand-winching up a drawbridge. Oh, good. Just what she needed when she was feeling down. "Hi, Roc."

"I thought you had an appointment with Ted." The little demon's eyes darkened for a second, becoming little more than marbles in his dark green face. Rocturnus, who was both her assistant—for lack of a better term—and her own personal demon, liked Ted. Or liked Ted's problems. For him it was the same thing.

"Ted's not coming anymore."

"Oh?" Another little flash in the eyes. Not because of Ted this time but because of her.

"Would you not do that, please? Not while you're looking right at me. It bugs me."

Roc shrugged. "We have a deal. I help you, and in exchange I get to feed off you. You're upset, that's food for me. I'd think you'd be used to it by now."

"You think that because you have all the empathy of a piece of newspaper. I mean it, Roc. Feed off me if you must, but do you have to let me see you do it? It's weird."

"You feel it anyway. What difference does it make?"

Her arms tightened around her, an unconscious hug that she stopped the moment she realized what she was doing. Yes, she did feel it now. She hadn't before, but now she did. One of the dubious joys of her new . . . demon-ness? Whatever. "I just wish you didn't enjoy my personal problems so much."

"Hey, it's not like you've been awash in misery lately. I take it where I can get it."

"I watched *Schindler's List* for you the other night! And cried. Which I hate doing. Just because you said you were feeling light-headed."

"Yeah, that was good. Maybe tonight we can do it again?"

He was impossible. No, he wasn't; that wasn't really fair of her. Roc was what he was, and, in a way, so was she. As she looked at him, a little warmth that could only be fondness stole over her heart.

He frowned. "You're not playing fair. That's useless to me, you know."

"Fine. I'll think about Ted some more, if you promise not to look at me. He's gotten himself mixed up with one of those exorcists. A faith-healer type."

Roc giggled. "Really?"

"It's not funny, Roc. He could get hurt. He honestly believes he's possessed, that some demon is, I don't know, stealing his strength or whatever. When I read him, he seemed to think it was dragging him down somehow."

Roc's wizened little face wrinkled even further as he fought his grin. "You do realize—"

"Yes, but not like how you guys do it. He thinks of it as something inside him that controls him. He thinks he doesn't have a choice."

Roc finally stopped smiling. "But choice is the most important part. If there's no choice there's no victory, and if there's no victory it's like . . . like cookies without frosting."

Not exactly the tack she was hoping he would take, but at least he was getting the point. Mostly. "Right. But I've seen these guys on TV before. It can be really dangerous, even without the psychological damage it can do. Some of those men tie their subjects down, they don't feed them or give them water for hours on end . . . I think people might have died, if I remember correctly."

She was sure she did. Something else she'd seen on that TV newsmagazine? Perhaps that was why they'd done the story to begin with?

She'd google it later. Thinking about being tied up without food or water made her think of torturous interrogations, which made her think of the FBI. Which didn't make her happy, which also caused the slight shiver down her spine that told her Roc knew she wasn't very happy and was having himself a nice little snack. Ugh. The less she thought about that, the better.

Having Roc around was rather like eating nothing but fast-food French fries and ice cream for dinner. Not a problem until she really stopped and considered it. Then it made her want to scour out her insides with steel wool. Which wasn't appealing either.

"What else are you thinking about?"

"A—an FBI agent came here. Right before Ted. She wanted to ask me about the meeting next week."

"An FBI agent? Really? Did she have a big shiny badge like the last one? Did you see her gun? I—"

"Yes and no." Agent Reid had certainly had a gun, but Megan hadn't seen it. She hadn't looked. On purpose. "And that's not the point. The point is, she knows about the meeting. The FBI knows about the meeting."

Roc tilted his head to the side. One papery ear moved faintly in the current of air from the vent; with temperatures outside approaching one hundred, the air conditioning was working overtime. "What did Lord Dante say?"

"I haven't told him yet."

"Why not?"

"Because he's working all day, and I don't want to bother him. It's not an emergency. I'm going to see him in a few hours anyway."

"Oh, right. You're taking tomorrow off. I forgot. Should I go pack your bag?"

"No. I have to pack for the whole week, so I'll do that tonight."

"Suit yourself. Is Erica coming today?"

"Yes, in . . . half an hour."

"I'll stick around. I wanted to check in with Altarus anyway."

She nodded. Altarus was one of Erica's demons, one Roc seemed to particularly like. Megan had a sneaking suspicion Altarus was female, but frankly, she didn't want to think too much about how her demons reproduced. It was enough to know they did and that when they did, she had to congratulate them. The mechanics of the process were not her concern, and she was exceedingly glad of that.

Of course, that might not have been the reason Roc wanted to check in with Altarus. He often did hang out during her appointments, pulling her patients' demons aside to chat with them and see how things were going, then reporting to her later. As much as she hated to admit it, it was a big help, a way to keep track of her demons and make sure they were obeying the rules while still having some freedom and enough to eat. If "eat" was the correct term, which it really wasn't, but "feed" still gave her the willies. Especially as it related to her patients.

Her cell phone buzzed from the depths of her purse, distracting her from the narrow and pitted little alley of her thoughts. It took her a minute to dig the damned thing out, especially after she banged her forehead on the edge of the desk.

"Hello?"

"Oh, hey, Megan. I thought I'd be leaving a message."

Her spirits rose. A little. "Hi, Brian. No, my patient—my appointment got canceled. What's up?"

Silence. Hmm, that probably wasn't good. Brian Stone was an investigative reporter for the city's largest paper, as well as her friend. As well as someone with a habit of pausing and considering his words very carefully when he had bad news to impart.

"Brian?"

"Yeah, sorry. Actually, I don't really want to talk over the phone. I was thinking maybe we could meet later?"

Okay, definitely not good, then. And she had a sneaking suspicion she knew what it was about too. Brian had plenty of informants and pals in law enforcement, not least of whom was his girlfriend of nine months. "My last appointment ends at four. If you want to be at my house around four-thirty?"

"Will Greyson be there?"

She sighed. "Does it matter?"

"Well . . . not normally. But this time, yeah."

A lie. It always mattered, and she'd given up. "He won't be there."

"Okay. I'll see you around four-thirty, then."

After they'd hung up, she stared at the phone. Bad news from Brian. At least she assumed it was bad news; it was entirely possible it wasn't, but she didn't think he'd be so damned cagey on the phone if it was. People didn't usually refuse to share things like "I just won the Pulitzer!" over the phone. And they especially didn't check to make sure one would be alone when they imparted such news. Hell, if Brian ever won a Pulitzer, he'd want to make sure Greyson was there, so he could rub it in a little.

That wasn't entirely fair. The two men didn't hate each other. They just didn't like each other much. Silliness.

If Brian was going to tell her about the FBI agent or that there was some sort of big investigation happening . . . that could be a problem.

Her previous FBI visits had been taken care of easily. She told Greyson; Greyson sent someone—she didn't know who and she didn't want to know—over to "discuss" the situation with the agent. Which probably involved hypnotism or some other sneaky psychological trick if it didn't involve outright bribery, but did not, as far as she knew, involve any bloodshed.

But her previous FBI visits, and the ones she knew the other Gretnegs dealt with on a semiregular basis, involved one or two agents acting on a tip or a hunch or whatever. Easy to tie up the loose ends when only a few people were involved. If this was getting big enough for Brian to have heard about it, it probably wouldn't be so easy to clean up.

Not to mention that Brian was psychic too, which meant Brian was not easily hypnotized. Brian wouldn't forget the investigation. And Brian hated her involvement with the demon world.

Because Brian was sensible. Because Brian was able to be objective. So Brian could see how the merest hint of impropriety could destroy her career. She had a public image to protect; she had a weekly radio show. She didn't particularly enjoy the radio show but it certainly provided her with much-needed income, or, rather, the income from it enabled her to charge her patients based on *their* incomes rather than a flat rate. Which she enjoyed. The radio show also enabled her to provide at least some form of counseling to people who really needed it and wouldn't have gotten it any other way.

All that could crumble if the public discovered she was involved with a criminal.

The sensible thing to do would be to end that involvement. Well, no. The sensible thing to do would have been to end that involvement back when it started. Back when she really realized what she was getting into, back when she really realized she wasn't just having fun, wasn't just enjoying a casual and extremely satisfying physical relationship but was . . . emotionally involved. And that those stupid emotions could destroy everything she'd worked so hard for.

So much for sensible.

# Chapter Three

Brian shifted in his seat. "So . . . yeah, I thought you should know."

"Thanks." Damn. Damn, damn, damn. And one more for good measure. Yes, Brian was there about the FBI investigation, and worse. Brian was there because in this instance, at least, it seemed the FBI was working casually, getting background information, from local law enforcement.

In the person of Brian's girlfriend, Sergeant Julie Richards, among others.

"Megan, I'm really sorry."

"Yeah. I know you are." She managed a smile, one that almost made the furrow in his brow disappear. He looked tired, she noticed; shadows lurked beneath his blue eyes, and his light-brown hair stood out in little tufts at the back of his neck. He needed a haircut. "Brian . . . Julie wouldn't exactly be pleased if she knew you told me this, would she?"

"No."

"Right. So why, then? If you don't mind me asking."

He shrugged. Looked away. "You're my friend. And it really isn't about you, you know. I mean, nobody thinks you're—"

"Yeah. I know." Oops, that came out a little too sharp. Why did the idea that everyone thought she was some sort of innocent bystander bug her so much?

Especially when that's what she was. She didn't know what sorts of crimes were being investigated. She didn't know what sorts of crimes were committed, at least not beyond minor ones like the casino.

But she wasn't involved in them. She wasn't some sort of moll. The very idea was laughable. She wasn't busty enough to be a moll. Oh, and she doubted most molls had PhDs, although she supposed it was possible.

Perhaps that was it. Everyone assuming she had no idea whom she shared a bed with, who he really was, was basically the same thing as them all patting her on the head and telling her they knew she was just a silly little woman, easily taken in by a handsome face, a flashy car—although that wasn't fair; Greyson's Jaguar wasn't really flashy—and some expensive gifts.

She did know who he was. She'd never been under any illusions about that, not ever.

But she knew who she was too. Part demon. In charge of a gang of little personal demons who spread misery everywhere they went, or at least tried to. Someone not perfect, in other words. But someone who felt perfect when she was with Greyson.

"Hey, I'm not trying to—" Brian started, but she cut him off.

"I'm sorry. I shouldn't have snapped at you. This whole thing just puts me on edge."

"I guess that's understandable."

"Yeah, but it's not fair of me to take it out on you, especially not when you're trying to help. It's just been kind of a shit day, really, what with— Hey. Do you know anything about exorcists?"

Brian's eyebrows shot up. "I think if you're planning on breaking up with Greyson, you could find a less dramatic way to do it, don't you?"

"Ha ha. No, I mean for real. Or not real, I guess."

"Oh, it makes so much sense now."

The laugh felt good, and sharing it with someone felt even better. Laughter wasn't a rare occurrence in her life, it had just been a particularly bad day. "One of my patients thinks he's possessed. Apparently he's found one of those faith-healer guys, you know the ones I mean?"

"Oh. Right. That kind of exorcism. Not Catholic."

"No. Sorry, I probably should have said." She'd actually forgotten for a second that Brian was Catholic, a regular mass-goer and everything. Of course he'd be picturing chanting and pea soup or whatever.

Brian leaned forward, grabbed his almost-empty Coke can and twisted it in his hands. Without speaking Megan got up, opened the sliding patio doors, and handed him the heavy glass ashtray she kept in the liquor cabinet.

He blinked. "Oh. No, that's okay, I—oh, what the hell."

Megan smothered her smile and sat back down as he pulled a pack of cigarettes and a cheap plastic lighter out of his pocket. Brian claimed not to smoke. And true, he didn't smoke a lot; she'd spent entire days with him in which he didn't even reach for a cigarette. But she'd never met an actual nonsmoker who smoked as much as he did.

Still, she let him have his illusions. She, of all people, understood what it was like not to want to admit things to oneself.

"I don't know a lot about it," he said after he'd lit up. "Catholic exorcism is an ancient ritual. I mean, it's been around almost since the beginning of the church. But it's—well, you know, I'm sure. It's not something they do on a whim or anything. I don't think what you're talking about has the same kind of caution behind it."

"No. At least not this guy."

"I remember something about it, a few years ago, maybe? Someone died, and it was because of a botched pseudo-exorcism."

"Right. That's what I thought."

"Did you google it?"

"Not yet."

He nodded. "Give that a try. What's the guy's name, do you know? I can ask around, check the paper's archives and stuff if I have time."

"Thanks, I'd appreciate it."

He stood up, ready to go, but she stopped him with a hand on his sleeve. "Brian . . . I really do appreciate it, you know."

"I know." He smiled. Not for the first time, she wished she'd been attracted to him. Things would have been so much easier if . . . Well, no, actually. They wouldn't have. She might not have had the FBI at her door, but Brian wouldn't exactly have been happy when she had to get out of bed in the middle of the night to deal with a problem with her demons. He certainly wouldn't have had a snack waiting for her when she got back, the way Greyson always did—some cheese and crackers, usually, or warm toast or cookies, whatever was on hand. Something light that didn't require a lot of effort, but it was the thought that counted.

Brian wouldn't have done that. Wouldn't have understood what she was doing and why. Wouldn't have hung back and only offered advice when she asked for it or held his tongue when she did things he didn't agree with—which was often.

So no. A relationship with Brian couldn't have worked. But, as always, she was glad for his friendship. In fact—she'd forgotten. "Oh, hey. Come with me."

"What?"

He followed her into her small kitchen and waited while she opened the fridge and took out a Tupperware container.

"Here." She handed it to him. "I made peanut-butter cake yesterday. Two of them."

His eyes lit up. "For me?"

"Yes, for you. Just bring back my Tupperware when you're done."

"And this is why I help you," he said, lifting the lid of the container and reaching in. "You bake."

"Such journalistic integrity."

"Hey, I'm like any other guy. I can be bought."

"No, you can't."

"No, I can't," he agreed through a mouthful of cake. "But it's tempting when you make me stuff like this."

"Just save some for Julie," she said, ignoring the little

twinge that ran through her at the mention of Brian's girlfriend. Brian's girlfriend, who was currently assisting an investigation that could conceivably put Megan's boyfriend—for lack of a better term—in prison.

She didn't think it would actually happen. But she didn't want to think about it anyway.

What she did want to think about was the packing she had to do and the week ahead. And a bit about Reverend Walther. So she closed the door behind the still-chewing Brian and headed for her bedroom.

She was still thinking about all of those things an hour later when she loaded her luggage for the next week into the car. The July night smothered her like a hot blanket; the air barely moved. A week and a half into a heat wave and no relief in sight.

She slammed the trunk down on her suitcases and turned back toward the house, only to have her blood run cold.

It was some relief from the heat but not the kind she was looking for. Someone was out there. No, not someone. A demon. She felt it, those shivers up her spine like when Roc fed off her. But it didn't feel like Roc. Wasn't Roc.

Who, then? Who was out there, reaching out to her but not speaking? Tasting her, reading her?

Trees lined her street. Silent cars hunkered like bugs in driveways. So many hiding places, and suddenly she was aware of them all, aware of the road stretching before her eyes and the houses full of people. People living their own lives, watching TV or having dinner, or whatever it was they were doing as the sky faded above them. Darkness came late this time of year, but even with the sun barely set, the shadows were long and deep.

Reflexively she lowered her shields. Yes, lots of people in their houses; she felt them all, saw what they saw, a flood of information easier than it should have been to control. Psyche demons—which the demon inside her now was, fully and completely—assimilated that information without hesitating, without thinking, and so did she.

But none of these people were responsible for that shivery feeling. Something else was out there, watching her, and threat hung heavy in the still air. It quivered against her skin. This was not just a visit. Whatever was out there wanted to harm her; it felt malevolent. Wrong.

It took every bit of strength she had to lift her foot and take one step toward the front door. Not all demons were visible all the time. Was it standing right beside her? Right behind her? She spun around, her breath loud and harsh in her own ears, searing her lungs. She couldn't get enough oxygen from the hot, thick air. It choked her.

The soft dusk light blinded her, turned everything gray in a way she normally loved. Now it was as though the street, her house, everything around her was wrapped in dusty shrouds. She wanted to see and couldn't. Wanted more light, but the sun was rapidly setting, and she was alone.

And only fifteen feet from her house. This was silliness. Summoning as much courage as she could, girded by the glow of her own windows, she took another step, trying to look unconcerned.

Another shiver up her spine. Stronger this time. Her casual act was only giving her tormentor—or whatever it was—confidence; it was getting closer to her.

Her front door was unlocked. She couldn't just get into the car and go. Even if she sent Malleus, Maleficarum, or Spud—Greyson's guards—back to lock it up, it would still be open for close to an hour. An hour in which her unknown lurker would have full access to her home. Her belongings. Everything.

A scrape, the faint tinge of metal against pavement. Again she spun around. Again she saw nothing. Her head pounded almost as hard as her heart. Whoever—whatever—it was out there had to know she knew it was there. And it hadn't spoken. Hadn't stepped forward, even though she knew her fear was strong enough to taste, to feel. Her watcher knew she was afraid and wanted her that way.

Which pissed her off, and that was a good thing. Someone wanted to lurk in the shadows as the sun went down and intimidate her? Fuck that. She straightened her spine, forced her head high. The simple act of looking unafraid grounded her.

One step toward the house, and another. The air around her thickened, pressing like a hot iron against her skin. *Danger. Danger.* The word echoed in her head, vibrated through her body.

Her flip-flops slapped impossibly loudly on the sidewalk, announcing every step she took. She tried to ignore it, just as she ignored the sweat trickling down her spine and temple. It didn't work. Hidden in that hollow flapping sound, in the too-loud beat of her heart, were whispers and giggles, the sound of her watcher's footsteps or breath.

She stopped, spun around again. A flicker of movement this time. A shape? Or her panicked imagination? She had no idea which. All she knew was at any moment a hand would close over her arm or her mouth; any moment someone would grab her and drag her down.

Pain erupted in the back of her calf, a stinging horrible pain. She stumbled. Shit, what was that? No time to look. She kept going, but her next step felt as if it was taken through seaweed, and her hands and feet tingled in a way she didn't like.

The door in front of her wavered, tilted at an odd angle. Why wasn't it upright?

Another sharp pain in her leg. She opened her mouth to try to scream, but she couldn't seem to make any sound come out except for a queer, muted gurgle.

Panic started taking over. She could feel her blood racing through her veins, faster and faster. Could feel her palms hit the hot sidewalk. She'd fallen. She'd fallen and her sweaty hair clung to her neck and her mouth wouldn't close and something icy touched her leg where it hurt. The last thing she saw was a flash of impossibly bright light bleaching the front of her house.

# Chapter Four

Why did she always have to throw up?

It seemed as though in every time of stress, every time of worry or fear, Megan's overly sensitive stomach was the first thing to rebel, spilling its contents into or onto whatever happened to be handy.

Worse than that, these days it seemed as if she always had a fucking audience. And worst of all, yet again it was Greyson.

"I'm sorry," she croaked. Sweat still dripped from her hair and into the toilet bowl, but not from the heat. At least not from the heat outside; they were safely insulated from that by the walls of her house and the low whirring of the air conditioning. No, this was from her internal temperature: boiling hot yet freezing, while her muscles quaked and her head threatened to split open. Why not? Her stomach already had. She would have been thankful it was empty if it had mattered even the tiniest bit.

"Don't be ridiculous." Greyson wiped at her forehead with the cool washcloth again; it felt so good she sighed. "*Litobora* venom is horribly poisonous. Anyone would be sick. If they survived."

"If this is surviving . . ." she started, then stopped

when the corner of his mouth turned down. Right. This was something to be taken very seriously. And she intended to, as soon as she was able. At that particular moment she was too busy and semidelirious to focus on anything.

The cloth moved around to the back of her neck. "Want to try getting in bed?"

It took her a few seconds to answer. "I'd nod, but I'm afraid to move my head too much."

His soft laugh comforted her. So did the heat of his body as he gently helped her up off the floor—her stomach gave a warning twist but held—and back into her room. Her legs felt rubbery beneath her.

"How about if I carry you?"

"No. No, I can make it."

She did, barely, and collapsed onto the bed with piteous gratitude. But the sheets were icy. The whole room was suddenly frigid, worse than standing outside in a swimsuit in the middle of winter.

"I'm cold."

A few seconds of silence, just enough time for her to wonder what he was doing, and then his bare skin pressed against hers, bringing with it the faint scent of smoke and his aftershave. Oh, that was good, both the heat and the smell. As a *vregonis* demon—a fire demon—he had a body temperature that was perpetually elevated. It had made the summer interesting and accounted at least in part for the meat-locker-esque temperatures at which she usually kept her house. She'd gotten into the habit of cranking the air up half an hour or so before she expected him to arrive, and at that moment, sick or not, she half expected to see ice crystals forming in the untouched glass of Sprite that Greyson's guard Malleus had set by her bed.

But as much as Greyson's overly warm body had to be worked around and compensated for in summer, at that moment she was eternally and ridiculously grateful for it. She almost thought she heard her own skin sizzle when it came into contact with his; some of the cramping in her muscles relaxed.

Only to tense up again when she saw, through her half-closed eyes, Greyson's second guard and Malleus's brother, Maleficarum, advancing on her with a hypodermic needle. Something clear squirted ominously from its sharp silver tip.

"Oh, no," she managed. "You are not giving me a shot."

"'Sonly under the skin, m'lady. You'll barely even feel it, honest." Maleficarum's features did not do "innocent" well; he looked like a serial killer trying to hide a severed head behind his back. Not his fault. It was simply the way he was made. Bald head, horns, large frame, beady eyes. It was a good thing he was a guard demon, because his appearance would have been an issue in most professions. Megan couldn't imagine, for example, Maleficarum as a pediatrician. Or either of his brothers. Spud, the third brother, was probably prowling around outside.

"I don't want—"

"Let him." Greyson rubbed her arm. "It's basically just an antivenom. And something for the pain."

"And that's why I don't want it. I need to tell you what happened today."

"It won't put you to sleep. Just let him give you the shot. Please?"

She hesitated. On the one hand, she wasn't at all sure she believed him when he said it wouldn't put her to sleep. On the other, something to kill the tremendous crashing ache in her head and the stabbing pains in the rest of her body sounded good.

Finally she nodded. "Go ahead, then. But if I fall asleep, I'm blaming you."

"And your vengeance will be terrible indeed, I imagine."

"Yes, it will." She squeezed her eyes shut as Maleficarum wiped at her arm with an alcohol pad and slid the needle in. It didn't really hurt—she wasn't bothered by needles much anyway—but the necessity of it . . . that, she didn't want to face.

A demon attack. A *litobora* demon, a poisonous psyche demon. Had Greyson and Malleus not shown up when they did—had they not been on their way to her place already—she would have died. As the pain in her body eased, that simple fact drilled itself into her head, crashing through every other thought and leaving her with nothing else.

"Somebody sent it, right?" she asked, dreading the answer. "I mean, that demon didn't just show up here by chance."

Damn him, and damn Maleficarum too, now sneaking out of the room. Her eyelids were getting heavy; whatever was in that shot was most certainly going to put her to sleep. But along with that came an easing of her nausea and the relaxation of her muscles, so she really couldn't complain too much.

"I would think so, yes." He snuggled her more closely to his chest. "A lion doesn't just show up on your doorstep without help. Neither do *litobora*."

"So somebody is specifically trying to kill me?"

Pause. Long pause, while his body tensed against hers. "I would think so, yes."

"Shit." Once again she knew she should care. Once again she couldn't quite bring herself to; whatever was in that syringe was powerful. "Who do you think it is?"

"I don't know."

"But you'll find out, right?"

His lips on her forehead felt like a kiss through cotton. "I'll certainly try."

"I'm not sure I like the sound of that 'try.' "

He sighed. "I'm not either."

"Why would someone want to kill me?"

"Do you really want to discuss this now?"

No, she didn't. But there didn't seem to be much choice. Despite the gentle tugging of sleep, despite the peace finally settled in her limbs and stomach, she still felt the faint sting on the back of her calf. Still couldn't quite forget the terror of those few minutes standing outside, alone but not at all alone.

"I don't. But I'm kind of thinking we should."

He helped her shift around to face him; the world spun for a second when she rolled over but settled again when her gaze found his face. Those sharp features, that dark hair and deep brown eyes, so familiar now, calmed her, but the look in those eyes didn't. He was worried, and seeing him worried shook her.

He waited for her to settle comfortably before he spoke. "I suppose there are lots of reasons someone might want to kill you. Anyone in a position of power is also in a position of vulnerability. As you know."

Yes, she knew. This was an old, old discussion. Her job—seeing patients and, to a lesser extent, the radio show—put her at risk. But what was she supposed to do?

Three choices, none of them appealing. The first was to take a piece of the undoubtedly crime-filled action the other Gretnegs offered her. Lucrative, but she had to be able to face herself in the mirror every day. The second was to let Greyson support her. Keep her. She didn't even want to think about how she would face herself if she did that, let alone how she would fill her days.

The last was doing more with the radio show. Taking speaking engagements. Appearing on television. She didn't want to do it, and she was pretty sure Greyson would practically have a heart attack if she suggested it. The semipublic nature of the show already made him antsy, she knew, although thankfully the media blitz the station orchestrated when the show first aired had died down. Going on TV, well, things didn't get much more public. And there was that whole pesky public-image-dating-criminal issue.

Three choices. None of which she wanted to make. But at some point she would have to make one, especially now. That the attack had occurred at her home didn't matter much. Neither did the fact that it was demon-related. She was vulnerable, and she knew she was, and she'd been hoping to put off having to do something about it, but it looked as though her days of putting it off were coming to a close.

But first things first. The knock at the door gave her the opportunity to veer off subject, and she was glad for it. "Come in," she said, and was not remotely surprised when Rocturnus slunk sheepishly through the door.

"Megan, I'm sorry." If he'd possessed a hat, she had little doubt he would have been turning it in his anxious fists at that very moment. As it was, he twisted his long-fingered hands together and stared at the carpet. "I should have been here."

"It's okay, Roc. You didn't know."

"You didn't call me."

"I thought it might—oh, never mind. It's not like you would have been able to do anything about it if you had been here anyway."

He straightened up, insult written all over his face. At least so she assumed. Her vision was a little bleary, haloed around the edges. "I could have helped. I could have done something."

She sighed. "Right. Of course you could have. I'm sorry, Roc."

"Do you think it's to do with the FBI?"

"No, they wouldn't—" she started, but Greyson cut her off.

"FBI?"

Oh, right. She hadn't had a chance to tell him yet. "They came to see me today."

"What, the entire Bureau?"

She would have laughed, but her body didn't seem to be capable of it. She settled for a sleepy smile. "No, just one agent. She came about the Bellreive. Offered me immunity."

"In exchange for what?"

"Testimony. About what happens at the meeting, I guess."

"What was her name?"

She told him. "Oh, and one of my patients quit because he's going to have an exorcism instead."

"What?"

She repeated it, or at least started to. Halfway through the story she had to stop; he was laughing too hard for her to continue, and Roc was practically falling on the floor.

"Stop, it's not funny. Well, maybe it's funny. But no, don't laugh, you're shaking the bed."

That plea, at least, had an effect. With obvious difficulty Greyson got himself under control; she didn't think she'd ever seen him laugh that hard. Roc continued to giggle, a subtle, bizarre backdrop as she shut her eyes again.

"Exorcism? Darling, your patients never cease to amaze me. Exorcism, of all things."

"Ted could really get hurt."

"And that's the choice Ted made. He's a grown man. If he wants to do something incredibly stupid, that's his prerogative. I somehow think we have more important things to worry about right now, don't you?"

She opened one eye—opening both seemed like too much effort—and glared at him. As much as she could with one eye anyway. "I'm trying not to think about it."

"Right. Well. Enjoy one last night of not thinking about it, then, because tomorrow we need to get to work. In more ways than one."

"The meeting." She sighed.

"The meeting," he said. "And the fact that whoever it is who's trying to kill you will probably be there."

# Chapter Five

The antivenom or antiallergen or whatever it was Maleficarum had given her was effective. Either that or the effects of the *litobora* venom were short-lived.

Either way, by the following afternoon she felt fine, at least physically. Mentally? That was another story.

Although she had to admit, feeling lousy in a luxury suite at the Bellreive beat the hell out of feeling lousy in her own home. It even almost beat feeling lousy at Greyson's place, the massive white mansion that was his official residence as Gretneg of his Meegra. Ieuranlier Sorithell was beautiful, and more than that, it was familiar, and some of her stuff was there. Not a lot of stuff, but some things, a toothbrush and bottles of all her shampoos and such, a few spare items of clothing kept in a drawer.

But hey. Some of her stuff was there at the hotel, spilling out of her suitcases, and the hotel had a stunning lake view that not even the Ieuranlier could match, especially as the sun went down. She stood on the balcony with the door open, letting the cold blast from the very efficient hotel air conditioning cool her back while the warm breeze brushed her hair from her face.

It was hard to believe, when watching the bright turquoise pool fourteen floors below with its yellow and white fringe of deck chairs and the rippling lake beyond turn pink in the sunset, that someone in this hotel was probably trying to kill her.

Movement by her side; Greyson rested his forearms on the rail beside her. Beyond his sharp profile the landscape blurred, as though he was the only real thing against a blue screen in a movie.

"What do you think?"

"I think it's beautiful." She picked up the gin and tonic Spud had made for her off the iron table beside her and took a sip. Perfect. "I still can't believe we're here, though. Especially after what Win said this morning."

He shrugged. "Nobody's particularly worried about the FBI, and everyone wants the meeting, so . . . not many acceptable options on such short notice."

"But they went to Win's house. To his wife. I can't believe he isn't more upset."

"Oh, he's upset. He just isn't going to show it, any more than the rest of us would. Remember who we're dealing with."

"Right." Demons were very into appearances. Powerful demons, Gretnegs, were even more so, and Winston Lawden—Win was Gretneg of House Caedes Fuiltean, the blood demons. "I don't suppose we could just stay in here tonight? Get room service and watch pay-per-view?"

He smiled, and the golden light hitting his skin as he did made her breath catch in her throat.

He noticed. She knew he would. Reddish light that

had nothing to do with the sunset flared in his eyes. "We have some time before dinner," he said softly, drawing her close. "It would be a shame to waste it standing here, wouldn't it?"

"I don't think I'd call it a waste," she started, but she was only joking and they both knew it. She let him interrupt her without protest, let his kiss draw her away from any other silly ideas about talking. He was right. It would be a waste of time.

And a waste of the beautiful balcony, where the breeze lifted her hair from her shoulders and neck so his mouth could find her bare skin more easily. What the wind didn't do his hand did, gathering the loose strands and twisting them gently at the back of her head.

Her own hands were busy as well, finding the buttons of his shirt and opening them one by one, slowly, savoring the unwrapping. The night before had, of course, been a chaste one; work had kept them apart for a few days before. It felt like longer, much longer.

Power rushed through her, smooth and warm like melted chocolate. Greyson's power, tinged with fire and smoke, igniting her nerve endings. She let it dance along them like tiny sparks before sending it back, colored with her own power.

His sharp breath made her push harder. Made her give him more, energy she knew smelled like her, tasted like her. The demon powers that had been a dubious Christmas gift had one clear benefit, and she used it, sending the essence of herself into him and feeling him accept it. Feeling his breath grow hotter, his kisses more urgent, his body harder as he drew more of it in.

They swayed back inside, both aware that even private balconies weren't necessarily private. He swung the French door shut behind them with his foot and pulled her hips closer, pressing her against him. Pressing more power back into her, a circuit that did not stop, until she couldn't be entirely certain whose power was whose. They didn't exist as separate entities anymore, not in her head or in any of her senses.

Orange with flame and dark with secrets, the energy they created together burned through her, sparked with desire. She gave herself over to it, pulled it into her the way her hands pulled at him and his at her.

Cold air played over her skin, goosebumps rising on every newly exposed inch of it. His palm slid over them, soothing them with heat, making her tingle in a different way when he pushed off her top, let her bra fall to the floor. His strong arm behind her was all that kept her from falling when he bent down to take her nipples into his mouth and his free hand slipped between her legs.

"Missed you," he murmured into her throat.

She wanted to reply but couldn't; she was too busy tugging down his zipper and trying to keep herself from exploding. All that energy buzzed inside her, so intense she shook from it, and when she fed it back to him, he shook too.

They shook together. Their clothes lay in heaps on the floor. His warm skin rubbed against hers, little shocks everywhere they touched. Flames glowed from the ceiling, adding their own intimacy to the blazing golden sunset light bathing the room and their bare bodies.

In the center of the bedroom stood an enormous four-poster bed, its white sheets crisp and cool. They fell onto it in a tangle of arms and legs, of searching hands and soft words.

"I missed you too," she managed to say, but he was beyond that. His body slid into hers, his power slid into hers, stronger than before. Strong enough to make her cry out and dig her fingers into his skin, strong enough to make her fight to give it back and drive him as high as he drove her.

His soft moan, the faint buzz as he took what she gave him, told her she'd succeeded. He moved faster inside her, his back shifting under her hands, and returned it.

It was her turn to be overwhelmed. Her turn to drown in him, to turn his energy into her own and keep it. To let their passion feed her. The intimacy of it, the sense of holding him everywhere in her body and mind, made both her human and demon hearts pound.

She flipped him over, looked down at him through half-lidded eyes. Over the last eleven months she'd probably spent more time looking at him than she'd ever looked at anyone else; she'd probably spent a couple of solid weeks of her life doing nothing but looking at him. It didn't feel long enough.

She shifted her weight, rocked back and forth. He reached out to cup the back of her neck and pull her face down to his, giving her more power, taking more. Her entire body tensed.

They rolled over again. No more playing. With a low,

soft sound, a few words in the demon tongue, he sent power shooting through her body, coursing through her blood. Too much for her to handle, and that, coupled with his relentless movements inside her and his mouth on hers, sent her over the edge.

Her last coherent thought was to give it all back to him; her last willful act before her body took over was to do so. They drifted together, riding the waves until the flames in the air disappeared and the world came back into focus.

Winston Lawden—or Win, as she'd grown used to calling him—was the first person she saw when they entered the dining room an hour and a half or so later, and she was glad. She didn't know any of the other Gretnegs very well, except for Greyson, and Win had always been kind to her. Had always seemed to be on her side.

"Seemed" being the fly in the ointment. She'd never had any reason to distrust Win. But that didn't mean she necessarily trusted him; she liked him, but she wasn't stupid, and in the demon world, at least, her natural skepticism stood her in good stead. If "Trust no one" was a good blanket policy for life among humans, it was doubly good when dealing with demons.

Winston greeted them with such enthusiasm Megan wondered if he'd been drinking. Or drinking more than normal, to be accurate; a roomful of demons could make liquor disappear faster than virtue.

But when he kissed her cheek, she realized he was

simply happy. Perhaps a little nervous but mostly happy. His blue eyes danced in his ruddy face. "Megan, have you met Sarita?"

"No, I haven't." She started to smile, started to hold out her hand to the lovely dark-haired woman he clasped tightly at his side. Halfway through, she realized what she was doing, realized who Sarita was.

Too late to pull her hand back. So instead she went ahead and shook hands, smiling with as much friendliness as she could muster while her stomach churned. The woman wasn't a fellow Gretneg. She could have been one of Win's *rubendas,* members of his Meegra, sure.

But what she undoubtedly was was Winston's girlfriend. Mistress. Whatever. She was not Winston's wife was the point, Winston's wife, Alvia, whom Megan knew. Whom Megan had cooked for one night when she had a little dinner party and who had cooked for Megan in her home when she did the same thing. Alvia, who knitted and made her own pasta, who had raised Winston's four children, and who had a sweet smile and looked at her husband as though he were a god.

"Nice to meet you." It wasn't the girl's fault, she tried to tell herself, ignoring the little voice in her head that said it most certainly was. Win wore a wedding ring, for fuck's sake. He was a Gretneg, he was a person—demon—of standing in the demon world. People knew who he was, they knew his sons and daughter, and they sure as fuck knew his wife.

Instead she forced herself to listen to the more effective voice that told her it was none of her business. It wasn't. How Win chose to run his personal life, who he spent time with or shared his bed with, were emphatically None of Her Business. And if a little something inside her—something that had nothing at all to do with her inner demon—squirmed at the thought of keeping a secret like that, of giving his scummy philandering her tacit approval simply by keeping her mouth shut, there wasn't much she could do about that.

What she could do something about, or at least say something about, was the warm greeting Greyson gave Sarita. The kiss on the hand. The brief conversation that made it clear he already knew the woman.

"How do you like the place, Megan?" Win smiled at her, just as if he hadn't put her in a totally awkward position and presumed her discretion without asking. What in the world had she ever said or done that would make him think she'd be okay with that?

She gave him a tight smile, didn't meet his eyes. "It's lovely."

He and Greyson said something else to each other. She didn't know what it was, because while not meeting Win's eyes, she'd caught sight of Gunnar Ryall, Gretneg of House Aquiast, the water demons. They were a smaller house—not as small as hers but small nonetheless—and they kept to themselves more than the other Meegras did.

But she'd met Gunnar. And she'd met his wife. Who was decidedly not the young woman at his side, his hand resting casually on the small of her back.

What the hell was going on?

Her attention was dragged back to the people before

her when Greyson gave her hand a squeeze. Right. She had to smile and make nice.

Especially as a new person had joined the circle. A new woman, to be more exact, and Megan almost did a double-take. That was simply her distraction, making her think for a second that Tera was standing there; on second glance the woman bore very little resemblance to Tera, the witch who was Megan's closest friend. Her only real female friend. What would Tera make of all this?

For a moment Megan wished violently that Tera were there. Then she remembered where she was. The animosity between witches and demons was ancient and seemingly insurmountable, and Tera's presence wouldn't be good for anyone.

But the woman standing at Win's side was slim and blond, like Tera, and just as pretty. More important, she had the same impeccable coolness Tera had, the same confidence. There stood a woman whose lipstick never smeared, whose stockings never ran, whose hair never frizzed. Unlike Megan's, although she had to admit that since the day she'd discovered that Malleus, Maleficarum, and Spud were incredibly talented makeup artists and hairstylists—the result of centuries of guarding high-ranking ladies—those weren't problems she had much either.

The difference was that Megan couldn't get used to that and always rather expected the smear, the run, or the frizz. Even on a night like this one, clad in a black silk evening gown with iridescent dark green feathers—

dark green was one of her House's colors—edging the irregular hems of layers of taffeta overskirt. Even with the diamond necklace and earrings Greyson had given her for Christmas. She still couldn't quite accept that she looked the way she looked.

Win smiled and put his arm around the woman. Jesus, how many girlfriends had he brought? "Megan, this is my daughter, Leora."

Right. That's why the girl looked vaguely familiar. The resemblance was there in the deep blue eyes and the fine, straight nose. Megan had met both of Win's sons but hadn't met—wait, his daughter? He'd brought his daughter along to a gathering to which he'd also brought his girlfriend?

Too unsettling. She didn't want to stand there anymore, while Leora told Greyson something about her recent trip to Washington, D.C.—his hometown—and Sarita leaned against Win. No matter how tightly Greyson held her hand or how reassuring that firm grip was, she wanted a drink, and she wanted not to have to smile politely at a man who was cheating on his wife. Publicly.

Greyson must have noticed she wasn't making much conversation. "Meg, shall we go get ourselves a couple of drinks?"

She nodded; he led her away, toward the bar but not actually to it. They stopped a little more than halfway there, by one of the large marble pillars supporting the high arched ceiling. It really was a hell of a room, a small and intimate reception area before the private dining room, but those high ceilings and the pale walls and floors gave it a sense of light and space. At the apex of the ceiling stretched grids of tiny white lights. The glow they cast reminded her of the walls in their bedroom earlier, and some of her anger drained away.

Some but not all. She didn't think a bath in a vat full of gin would be able to wash it all away.

"What's wrong?"

"What?" In trying not to speak too loudly, she accidentally hissed the word; luckily it seemed lost in the leafy vine wrapped around the pillar. She tried again, with more success. "What do you think is wrong? I just had to stand there and pretend it doesn't bother me that Win's here with some woman who isn't Alvia, and I know Alvia. How can I look her in the face after this?"

Confusion spread over his features. "Alvia? Why would you—"

"Yes, Alvia. Win's wife. You do know her. And look, they all have girlfriends with them. Am I supposed to—"

"Okay. Okay, calm down, please, before they really start to get curious." His arm slid around her shoulders, bringing their faces and bodies closer together and affording them a bit of privacy. A bit more when he shifted them around so their backs were to the small crowd.

It *was* a small crowd; aside from the Gretnegs and the girlfriends, there were assistants. That was it. Something struck her about that, but she filed it away for later.

"You can look Alvia in the face after this because she is fully aware of what Win is doing and who's with him.

You don't think he'd bring his daughter into a situation that would divide her loyalties like that?"

"What? She knows?"

He nodded. "All the wives know. It's a—a status symbol. Their husbands are wealthy and can afford to keep a mistress. The prettier she is, the nicer her home and car . . . Come on, *bryaela*. You know the story."

Uh-huh. She sure did. Appearances again. "And his daughter . . ."

"Leora's known Sarita for years. Since she was a child. They all know her. She and Alvia exchange birthday gifts."

She examined his face, tried to persuade herself to believe him. Well, no. She did believe him. She just didn't want to, because to believe him would send her thoughts running down alleys she had no desire to enter.

"These guys are the old guard, Meg. Their marriages were arranged. Win and Alvia are lucky, you know. They've always liked each other. Templeton and his wife usually had a good time. But they're not all lucky like that. It's just the way things are done—the way they *were* done."

Memory dinged in the back of her head. Templeton Black's wife, teary at his funeral. And something else too. "Your parents hated each other."

"Right. With a deep and fiery loathing." He smiled and squeezed her shoulder. "Come on, let's get you a drink. You look naked without one."

"I do not."

"Maybe I just wish you were."

She returned his smile. Returned the sentiment behind it too; she really didn't want to be there, not when that big bed upstairs was empty. "Maybe later you'll get your wish."

"Now, that," he said, taking her hand and heading toward the bar, "is something to look forward to."

# Chapter Six

Five minutes later, nicely fortified by a cold gin and tonic and a kiss, she spotted Roc sitting in a chair against the wall. Of course; everyone was supposed to have met in the room at nine, but she and Greyson had been a few minutes late.

Beside him sat Carter Slade, Greyson's assistant. Well, "assistant" wasn't quite the right word; after Templeton Black—the old Gretneg of Greyson's house—had died and Greyson had become Gretneg, Carter had taken Greyson's old job, which meant he was a sort of advisor/ assistant/second-in-command.

Both of them rose when she and Greyson approached. Only one of them met her eyes. Carter kissed her hand, made an appropriate greeting, but didn't look at her. He never did. She didn't know if it was some kind of respect thing—she'd never heard of it, but she kept forgetting to ask—or if it was a particular issue of his, but a tingle of annoyance rose up her spine just the same.

Much like the tingle when she realized what had been missing from her discussion with Greyson by the pillar.

She was at the meeting as a Gretneg, an equal. What if she wasn't? Would he have brought her anyway, even though she wasn't a demon? Or would he have brought . . . someone else?

"I have those papers for you to sign, Grey." Carter started to gesture, as if he was picking up his briefcase, only to discover it wasn't there. Just as well. It would have spoiled the perfect lines of his tuxedo, his perfect appearance in it. Carter's dark hair never seemed to grow; his olive skin never flushed. Typical for a demon, really, but still.

When had she become so surrounded by cool, immaculate adults?

Except Roc. Bless him. Or whatever one did for demons. She smiled at him. Being who and what they were, they didn't have important business to discuss that couldn't even wait until after dinner. People were unhappy; her demons fed off it; that was pretty much it.

"They're in my room anyway," Carter went on. "And tomorrow morning you have a meeting with Lord Lawden."

"Can't you delay that?"

Megan couldn't read demons, at least not very well. Since the events of the previous December, she'd occasionally been able to get flashes—usually from Greyson when they were physically close—and she'd always been able to feel demon anger like an icy breeze over her skin. But this time she absolutely felt Carter's desire to glance at her, felt him resolutely avoiding doing so. Why?

"I really think it's best you get it over with quickly," he said, and a shiver ran down Megan's back that had nothing to do with the fact that she was standing directly beneath an air vent.

"I seriously doubt it will be the last discussion I have to have with him," Greyson replied.

"No, but—"

"I'd rather you delay it. I need a few more days to prepare."

Carter shrugged. "If that's what you want."

"It is."

Megan and Roc glanced at each other. Greyson hadn't said anything to her about a meeting with Win, but then they didn't discuss his business, so why would he? It didn't concern her, and one of the best things about their relationship—one of the best things on a list she thought was rather embarrassingly long—was that they didn't invade each other's privacy.

Private business apparently dealt with, they all headed into the dining room. Megan barely managed to suppress a gasp on entering; demons were into formality and luxury and didn't believe much in the character-building powers of self-denial, but even some of the grandeur she'd seen in the last eleven months faded when compared with the room before them.

Candles floated above the table, courtesy of the air demons—House Caelaeris—led by Baylor Regis. At her feet were flower petals, strewn from ivy-covered wall to ivy-covered wall.

Ivory damask tablecloths peeked out from beneath an enormous silver centerpiece loaded with ivy and white roses; silver plates waited at every chair, surrounded by crystal glasses and solid silver cutlery. Demons liked to eat. She had no doubt this would be a meal to remember.

And it was, but not for the reasons she expected. No sooner had they sat down than Justine Riverside, Gretneg of House Concumbia, turned to her, her succubus smile spread all over her perfect features.

"So, Megan," she cooed. "We're all dying to hear about your plans for your Haiken Kra. When will you be doing it?"

Had someone dropped a pin, Megan felt certain she would have heard it. She wished someone would. It would provide some distraction.

But no one did. No one made a sound. *Shit.*

"I don't plan to do it, actually. There's really no reason for me to, at this point."

Justine's perfectly arched eyebrows shot up almost to her hairline. "No reason? I certainly think—"

"Justine, Megan will make the decision she feels is right," Winston cut in. Megan shot him a grateful smile, which he returned. "It's not our place to say what she should do."

"It is! Just the presence of a human here creates a problem for us. Her mind is weak."

"She's a psychic," Greyson said. He squeezed her thigh beneath the table. "Nobody's going to hypnotize or entrance her."

Justine frowned. "I think we should take a vote on it."

"Excuse me," Megan said. "I don't think it's up to any of you. I don't actually believe it's any of your business."

"Human vulnerability is our business when it affects us." Justine flicked her long hair, shining black in the candlelight, off her bare shoulder. "Look at that silliness going on in the hotel down the road, that flea-pit whatever-it's-called. That ridiculous man claiming to heal possessed people. And they believe him. They flock to him. They give him money—hmm. Maybe that's something we should look into."

A ripple of appreciative laughter flowed around the table at this. Megan didn't join in. "Wait, what? What man?"

"Some reverend man." Justine's shudder turned into a graceful undulation when the servants—not the hotel's, but demons handpicked by each House—brought the first platter, loaded with appetizers, and started parceling them out. Apparently being seen to react horribly to something was not on Justine's list of acceptable things. "He's holding some sort of weekend prayer meeting at that hotel over there."

"The Windbreaker?"

"That's the one." Justine picked up her fork and twirled it in her red-tipped fingers. "Why, are you planning on joining them?"

"No, I—no. No, I'm not." Damn it! She should have told Justine to go fuck herself, something she'd been dying to do for some time. She'd never forgotten her first glimpse of the woman, though they hadn't been officially introduced. It was the day Megan was forced to remember the Accuser, the demon who'd infected her with a piece of him almost seventeen years before. The day she'd been forced to watch Greyson tortured, chained, and whipped with an iron-tipped whip.

Justine had been there. She'd enjoyed the show.

Megan would never forget it. Would never forget that Justine had enjoyed the show despite the fact that she'd also enjoyed having Greyson in her bed at one time.

Or several times. He'd never really given Megan details, and she'd never asked. It was enough to know that it had happened, and that it wasn't happening anymore. Wouldn't happen again. When he was Templeton Black's second-in-command, Greyson had been called on to perform such acts, payback for favors, little treats to sweeten deals. As Gretneg he no longer had to.

She supposed that was Carter's job now. Although she preferred to think it wasn't anybody's.

Except . . . Greyson had asked his friend Nick to do something for him, back at Christmastime. Something he didn't want to do, something involving a woman. Could that have been . . .

But what favor would Greyson have been paying back then, when he'd been Gretneg for barely twenty-four hours?

Fuck Justine, and fuck all this stupid demon crap. The implication that Megan's silly human brain was so easily manipulated, that she would be just as likely to run off and join up with a fundamentalist exorcist as to do anything else, rankled. The implication that because she was human she didn't belong there, that simply hurt. As much as she didn't want it to, it did. She did want to belong there. She did want to fit in. She just didn't want to give up her humanity entirely, to lose things she considered valuable and important.

Allowing the demon to grow inside her, to become more of a part of her so she would be genetically demon, might not change that. But she couldn't be sure. And nobody could give her a truly compelling argument for doing it, so why should she? She'd thought it wasn't a problem.

And now with one little conversation all that had changed.

Food was put on her plate, and she picked up her fork without thinking, only to be stopped by Greyson's hand on hers. "Don't eat that one."

"Why?" Shit, she didn't want to sound bitter and pissed off, but she couldn't help it. She hated feeling like an outsider. "Is it made of human flesh or something?"

He looked at her strangely. "No. Bell peppers."

"Oh. Right. Thanks." Oops. She was allergic to those.

"Is everything all right, *bryaela*?"

She tried to smile. It didn't turn out too well. "I'm just—I'm fine."

His palm stroked her thigh now, gliding up and down over the silk of her skirt as he leaned over to whisper in her ear. "Watching you stand up to Justine was awfully sexy."

"I don't think I stood up very well."

"Oh, I do. Very few people ever even attempt it, so you get points just for that. I don't think I've ever seen her so surprised."

This time her smile did work. True or not, it was nice to hear. "Really? I would have thought you'd managed to surprise her a few times over the years yourself."

"No. She never got my best stuff."

"Well, didn't she miss out."

"I like to think so. But such is life. Unfair."

She looked up at him, into his eyes. The rest of the room turned into nothing but a discordant hum in the background, a blur of ivory and green, a set painting. "Sometimes it isn't too bad, though."

"No, sometimes it certainly isn't."

She didn't know how long they sat like that. Not long, she didn't think. Not in such a public place, in such a small group where everyone at the table could watch and probably were. But it was long enough to remind her exactly why she was still there, why she still wanted to be there. Long enough to know he wanted her there too.

"I was thinking," he said finally, giving her thigh another squeeze and taking a sip of wine with his other hand. The sound of the room rushed back, the others talking, the faint tinkle of silverware on plates. More servants moved in with larger trays, delivering what looked like pheasant. "We haven't been back to Italy. Want to go, week after next?"

"For your birthday? Oh . . . shit, I can't. I can't take more time off so soon, and the rest of my vacation time at the station is booked for Christmas. I'm sorry."

He shrugged. "No problem."

"I took your birthday off, though. And the day after."

"Oh? Planning something?"

"Maybe." Actually, she was; she'd found a nice hotel on an island off the coast, just a few hours' flight away, and had booked the night before and the night of, with a late checkout the day after. Malleus had helped her plan it; she'd needed him to check Greyson's appointments.

He started to reply but stopped when someone said his name. Winston's daughter, Leora, sat at his left side; Megan hadn't noticed before. The seating around the table was arranged boy-girl, with Win on Leora's other side and his girlfriend—Sarita, right?—on his other side. The assistants, exclusively male, sat at the end closest to the kitchen doors in a ring.

Gunnar Ryall from House Aquiast sat at her right. While Greyson turned to Leora, she spoke to him, making desultory conversation. No other kind could be made with Gunnar, at least not in her experience. He liked to talk about fish. A lot.

Her pheasant was placed in front of her. With gratitude she turned to it and accepted another cocktail as well, instead of wine. Her stomach practically screamed at the sight of the food; she'd hardly eaten all day, and while full-blood demons could subsist for long periods of time simply on energy like what she'd exchanged with Greyson earlier, she couldn't.

Not that demons *wanted* to subsist purely on energy—they wouldn't be such big eaters if they did—but they could. And they could eat enormous amounts without gaining weight, because of faster metabolisms. It was almost enough to persuade her to make the switch, but then, anorexics lost plenty of weight too, and that wasn't exactly healthy. Giving up her humanity in exchange for extra helpings of pie didn't seem like the greatest deal.

Although she could be tempted when the food was this good. The pheasant practically melted in her mouth, dark and rich and—what was that?

A shiver, almost like the one she'd felt the night before when the *litobora* was nearby. Tasting her.

This wasn't a demon, though. It was a human, nearby. A human where a human shouldn't be. Megan's responsibility. Her Yezer were guarding all of the entrances leading to this part of the building, making sure it felt so gloomy, creepy, and just plain scary that any person walking near it felt the sudden urge to be elsewhere.

If there'd been a problem, it would have been communicated to Roc. Should have been communicated to Roc.

So why the hell hadn't it been? And oh, shit, how long would it be before the others sensed an intruder as well and decided she'd had something to do with it?

# Chapter Seven

They all knew she'd been visited by the FBI the day before. Most of them knew of her friendship with Tera. Some of them knew about her friendship with Brian, and if they knew that, they might very well also know that Brian's girlfriend was a police officer.

She turned to look for Roc just as he appeared on her shoulder, and she jumped slightly. Expecting to find empty air over your shoulder and instead finding a small dark green demon floating there would make just about anyone jump.

"There's a human nearby," he murmured. "Ariago and Hefferus tried to stop it, but it would not be deterred, and they couldn't get its Yezer to talk to them."

"Its?"

"They didn't say."

"Shit." She stood up, trying and failing to keep her chair from scraping the marble floor, and set her napkin on the table. "Sorry, everyone. We're having a small issue in one of the hallways, I'm just going to go and have a look."

"Shall I come with you?" Greyson touched her hand.

"No, no. Stay and eat. I'll be right back."

Her heels clicked on the floor, too loud in the ensuing

silence. Everyone was watching her leave, with her dress swirling around her feet. The dress was a compromise; most Gretnegs wore their House's colors, but her House's colors, dark green and orangey gold, didn't particularly flatter her.

Besides, Greyson liked her in black. And so did she.

She loved the dress but couldn't help wishing instead for a pair of tennis shoes and jeans, as she let the servants close the doors behind her and reentered the ballroom in which they'd had cocktails. Her heels still made noise, and the last thing she wanted to do was announce her presence to anyone, so she slipped them off, cringing a little when her stocking-clad feet hit the cold floor.

Well, at least she wasn't barefoot.

The empty ballroom kicked the faint rustling sound of her skirts and her feet on the floor back at her. Unsettling. Almost as unsettling as her worries about what might be waiting for her.

A human, sure. No big deal; Megan was human. But how exactly was she supposed to deal with the situation? She hadn't really tried hypnotizing people demon-style yet. It felt unethical, like a step down the road to inhumanity. And if she was going to take one step, what would stop her from taking another? And another? And suddenly there she'd be, eating pie like there was no tomorrow.

When she hit the doors leading back to the hallway, she stopped, dropping her shields. Best to get an idea of what she was in for.

Trickles of curious energy flowed from her, feeling their way through the doors and along the hall. Even the walls here contained echoes of emotions and events; most hotels did. How could they not, really, with so many lives, so many events, taking place in them? Hotels were microcosms of life, and intense emotions could leave imprints that lasted decades.

The human who'd gotten past her demons felt triumph. Excitement. She was—oh, shit. She was the FBI agent, Elizabeth Reid.

For a moment Megan froze. She couldn't speak to the woman, couldn't even let the woman see her there, not after denying any knowledge of the meeting.

Then relief flooded through her. This was the Bellreive, and the private rooms had been rented for the week for an exorbitant price. She'd call the management and ask them to eject the intruder.

Yes, Elizabeth's ID would probably make a difference there. But it would delay her at least long enough for Megan to inform the others what was happening.

It wasn't a great plan, but it was a decent plan. Megan had just turned to head for the courtesy phone planted unobtrusively on the wall in an alcove when she felt the other presence.

Not human this time. Demon. Following Elizabeth Reid very closely. What the hell?

If something happened to Agent Reid, if she was attacked or even killed, they'd all be questioned. Their presence would be discovered. Agent Reid wasn't the only one who suspected their little group was more than the gourmet club they'd told hotel management they were. It would be an unholy mess.

She headed for the courtesy phone, keeping her

shields down, and reached into her black silk evening bag for her cell.

A bored receptionist answered the courtesy phone, her mind almost completely occupied by thoughts of the BDSM fun she'd get up to with her boyfriend later. Megan got a few very interesting images before she managed to shut the pictures down. Hey, it wasn't as if she was anyone to judge or had any interest in doing so. "I'm with the Gastrique party in the Moonlight Dining Room, and there's a woman screaming outside the main doors. Could you please send security immediately?"

The receptionist—her attention fully diverted by Megan's story—promised to do so. Megan hung up and scrolled through the numbers on her cell with her other hand until she found the one she wanted.

"'Ello, m'lady. Wot you need?" Malleus sounded, as always, alert and ready. She pictured him pacing the floor with the phone in his hand, just in case he was called.

In reality he was probably watching *Dancing with the Stars* or some such tripe with his brothers. It didn't matter. He'd be at her side as soon as he could get himself down the stairs.

"Hey. I need someone down here. There's a demon in the hall, and I don't know what it is."

"We're coming." The dial tone almost cut off the final syllable.

Okay. Security was on its way, and the brothers were too. She felt a little safer. Not much—she was acutely aware of the empty room behind her, of the demon getting closer—but a little.

She'd just turned to head back into the dining room and alert the others when the scream came through the double doors, loaded with terror so thick her own heart—both of them, actually—skipped a couple of beats. It was Agent Reid's voice. Agent Reid was in the hallway with a demon of indeterminate appearance and intent.

Megan's feet were moving before she thought of it. Whatever the consequences, they could be dealt with; if she couldn't hypnotize the agent, she'd get one of the others to do it. Security wasn't fast enough, the brothers weren't fast enough—they had fourteen floors to get down, damn the damn luxury top-floor suites—and if she crossed the room to get the others, the agent could be dead by the time they got there.

Of course, she could find herself dead, which was not a great thought. But she didn't have much choice, not when another scream rent the air, worse than the first.

A heavy thud came through the doors a second before she flung them open. Could she still feel Agent Reid? Yes, she could. She focused on her, and—wait. Reid was moving away from the doors; her thoughts were a bit jumbled, but she didn't seem particularly frightened. Had the demon, whatever kind of demon it was, altered her memories?

Too late to stop and think about that, to consider the implications. The doors were open, banging against the walls and bouncing back at her, the sound of them hitting the plaster loud in the heavy silence.

And it was silent. Dead silent. Empty, except for a

thin, horrible streak of red on the wall that she knew was blood, could smell was blood. Human blood.

A flicker of movement at the end, a figure disappearing around the corner. Agent Reid. What the hell had happened? Was she injured?

Injured or not, she was beyond the point where security would find her. Megan had two choices, neither of them right. To follow the agent and make sure she was okay would be the moral thing to do but would get her busted. To ignore the agent's possible injuries and head back to her dinner as if nothing was wrong wouldn't be the moral thing to do. It would be the negligent thing to do. But probably the correct thing.

She hesitated for a moment, then took a step forward. She'd follow, but she'd hang back. That way she wouldn't be spotted, but if Reid collapsed or something, she could—

Something slammed across the back of her legs, knocked her down before she even had time to feel the injury. Her shocked body moved of its own accord, scrambling to get away, already anticipating the next blow.

It didn't come. Instead a heavy hand tangled in her hair, yanked her up. The scent of—what the hell? Roses?—filled her nose, so strong and sharp her eyes watered even more than they were already from the pain.

Through them she barely made out the delineation between ivory wall and dark hallway carpet before the hand moved, closing tightly over her mouth and twisting her head further, up toward the ceiling. She tried to struggle, kicking back, jerking her torso, but an arm like iron closed around her waist, trapping her arms. Her bare feet, encumbered by heavy layers of taffeta, did no good at all.

Her ears rang. Dimly over the sound she heard something else, a low, thick voice like sandpaper. She couldn't make out the words but felt them. They vibrated over her bare skin, through it into her soul.

Magic. She'd been around Tera enough to recognize that feeling. Had even been able to do some energy manipulation herself, back before she'd attached herself to the Yezer. That connection made it difficult for her to do such things; their energy tended to color her experiments and send them in bizarre directions, so she'd given up trying.

But she still knew what it felt like. Wasn't likely to forget. And the person who held her—a man, she knew without thinking—was definitely doing magic.

She would have known that even if the wall behind them hadn't suddenly opened and swallowed them up.


Her head was still spinning when they stopped. Wind whipped her hair into her eyes, pressed her skirts to her body. She had one dizzying glimpse of stars whirling above her before she realized where she was, where they were.

On the roof of the Bellreive, fifteen stories above the ground, and her captor had her in what she was pretty sure was a literal death grip as he shoved her toward the low wall surrounding the gritty, rubbery tar beneath them.

He was going to push her off. Holy shit, he was going to throw her off the roof, this was it, she was going to die—

*No!* She struggled with all the strength she had, kicking, wriggling, trying to bite the hand over her mouth. He let go and moved his hand down to her throat. Shit, that was worse; he squeezed her throat so she could hardly breathe.

There had to be a way to get out of this. To save herself. The edge of the roof loomed before her, so bright and sharp against the city lights. She had to do something. Wind in her hair, so strong it was hard to think. If he would just wait a second and let her *think.*

He said something else, his voice slicing at her ears. The wind strengthened. Was he calling it? Controlling it? Witches were strong, they were powerful, they could manipulate elements as easily as she could read one of her radio callers. They manipulated energy. She read people. She couldn't read witches, generally, but she hadn't tried in a hell of a long time either, had she?

She went limp, dropping her head, letting her arms fall slack at her sides. She couldn't do anything about her pounding pulse, as much as she wished she could. Both of her hearts were beating furiously against her ribs, as if they knew what was coming and wanted to try to jump out and survive on their own. Which at least one of them could very well be capable of. She ignored that thought and focused on being heavy, limp, boneless like a heap of rags. Forced herself not to move even when he kicked the back of her leg. Her captor made a surprised, impatient sound and paused to readjust his grip on her.

She struck. Not with her body but with her energy, with all the power she possessed, forming it into a knife in her mind and driving it into his chest.

The shrieking triumph in her head drowned out his screams. He *filled* her; she couldn't think of any other way to put it, and it didn't matter anyway. He filled her with power, with light, with something that made her want to laugh and cry at the same time.

He let go of her and clutched at his chest; she felt him trying to expel her energy weapon, her psychic blade that was still embedded in him. Felt him grow weak. Watched him fall to his knees as she spun away from him on nimble feet. The height of the roof seemed to be nothing at all. The stars above shone down just for her, blessing her, as she filled herself with him and he crumpled closer to the edge of the roof—

He was going to fall. Because she was stealing his life.

Horrified, she tried to pull away, but the weapon was too bloated, too pure and full and strong to collapse. Her hands scrabbled at his shoulders, trying to yank him back away from the edge, but he struggled against her as if her touch burned him.

Which it might be doing; her skin glowed where it touched him, and energy pulsed up her arms from him. Feeding her. She was trapped in him, terrified but elated. Terrified *because* she was elated. It was beautiful and glorious and ecstatic and horrifying, and she gritted her teeth against it and threw everything she could into her shields, envisioning them snapping into place with a thick, heavy *clang*.

They did. The weapon broke. The man—the witch, whatever he was—gasped and struggled to stand, pushing himself away from her.

Wrong move. He stumbled, pitched forward. And fell over the ledge.

He didn't scream as he fell.

# Chapter Eight

"I have to call—Spud, cut it out, damn it!" She batted his eyeshadow-wielding hand away from her eye and glared at him. The glow from the lights behind him surrounded his cap like a bizarre halo. "It doesn't matter how I look, because nobody is going to see me but Tera, and even if they do, I was just attacked and almost killed, and I *think*—maybe I'm crazy—but I think perhaps that gives me license to have smudged mascara!"

"*Bryaela,* we can't—"

"No. No, don't you dare *bryaela* me. He almost threw me off the fucking roof, Greyson. And I—I—" *Shit.* She couldn't finish the sentence, because it hit her again, the way she'd fed off him, sucked out his energy. The way she'd gloried in it.

"You did what you had to do," he finished for her. He stood a foot or so away, his arms folded and his brows drawn down, with his hair moving in the breeze. After his initial clutching and holding he'd stepped away, and she was glad. If he'd touched her just then she would have broken down, and she did not want to do that. Not yet. The inner workings of the Vergadering—the witches' organization, a sort of magical law-enforcement agency, for which Tera worked—were pretty shadowy, but she was pretty sure that she'd need to hold on to as much of that grief and horror as she could for when they showed up.

Just in case it made a difference. She had no idea if it would.

When she didn't reply, he said it again. "You did what you had to do, Meg. It was you or him. You did the right thing."

*Shit.* "I didn't."

"You did. If you hadn't done whatever you did, you'd be dead right now, and I can assure you that would most definitely not be right."

Without meaning to, she glanced to her left again, at the spot where he'd fallen. She couldn't seem to stop looking at it; it pulsed in her vision, glowing. "I killed him."

"And that's why you're still here. Look, I don't mean to be insensitive, but we need to get back down to dinner immediately."

"I can't go back down to—Spud, if you come at me with that thing one more time I am going to stick it right up—"

"Spud, why don't you give us a minute?" Greyson cut in smoothly. "Go wait over there with Malleus."

Spud looked from him back to her, his heavy features sorrowful like a basset hound's, before nodding and lumbering away across the roof. Damn. Now she'd hurt his feelings.

"Meg. We have to get back to dinner now. Right away. Before the others start wondering what's going on."

"But—"

"No. We have to. One of two things has happened here. Either this witch attacked you of his own accord, in which case there's no point in freaking the others out, or one of them paid him to attack you, in which case—"

"The only way to make them sweat is to act as if nothing happened," she finished.

"Right."

"But what if he didn't act of his own accord? What if he was hired by someone else who wants to kill me, and it's not one of them at all?"

"Again. If you don't go back to dinner, you've shown them a vulnerability. A weakness. You may give them ideas, if they don't have them already. They will take advantage of any weakness they can find, darling. Anything. Please, come back to the table with me now."

She hesitated. He was right. She knew he was.

But how in the world could she go back down to that table and finish her meal as if nothing had happened? And what about— "What about the body?"

"I told Carter to take care of it." Seeing her look, he continued, "He'll stow it away until we decide what to do. He won't incinerate it yet."

She didn't really like the sound of that "yet," but there wasn't much she could do. "I still want to call Tera."

"And you can. As soon as we get through this meal, you can call anyone you wish. But we have to get through it. You have to get through it, Meg, and I know you can. Come on." He reached out and pulled her into the protective circle of his arm, tight at his side. His lips brushed the top of her head.

She wanted to call Tera, wanted to go back to the room and crawl under the covers and sob. She'd killed a man. And she'd liked it; well, no, she hadn't liked killing him, but she'd certainly liked what came before.

She'd gotten used to the occasional strange craving. Gotten used to—more than used to—trading energy with Greyson, as a way to keep from having to take energy from the negative emotions of humans. Well, she traded energy with Greyson for a few reasons, but one of them was that it meant she didn't have to feed off anyone or anything else. She didn't require a lot of energy anyway.

And she'd gotten used to the fact that taking that energy felt amazing. But taking it the way she had—she'd attacked him, stolen from him. It was a hideous thing she'd done.

She'd had to kill him. She hadn't had to like it.

She shuddered and circled her arms around his waist. For a long moment she just held on, feeling his body warm and solid beside hers and his grip on her tighten. Later. Later they would talk about it.

The ringing of his cell phone cut into her thoughts, sliced them apart like a pair of rough hands. He took a step away, held the phone to his ear. "Carter. What's—what? Are you—okay. Right. *Shit*. Yes, get back in there. We'll be there in a minute."

"What's wrong?" Malleus and Spud had descended on her with brushes and lipstick, but when Spud lowered one beefy arm, she saw Greyson staring at the phone as if he'd forgotten what it was.

He shook his head. "It doesn't make sense."

"Tell me anyway."

"There's no body."

"What? Ow!" She'd started forward without thinking, and Malleus had practically ripped a chunk of hair out of her head.

"Sorry, m'lady. But you know you oughter not move when we're—"

"There's no body," Greyson said again. He slipped the phone back into his pocket and crossed the remaining feet of roof between them. "Carter checked everywhere."

"So what does that mean?" Nothing good, she imagined. Although . . . "Did I not kill him?"

"You're sure he went over the edge?"

*Ugh.* "I watched him."

"All the way? Did you watch him hit the ground?"

"No. No, I . . . I couldn't. I didn't. I just saw him fall." Watched him tumble off the roof, his body disappearing over the wall . . . she shuddered.

Malleus's finger tapped her lips, magically setting her lipstick. She ignored it. If the man—the witch—was still alive, if she hadn't killed him . . . it was a relief. At least it was until she realized that if he wasn't dead, he'd be coming back for her.

Greyson must have thought the same thing. "No more going anywhere alone. Nowhere. We'll need someone . . . hmm." He checked his watch. "We need to get back down there. We'll discuss this later, okay? Meanwhile, nothing happened. We'll figure out a story in the elevator."

*          *          *

Dessert was some incredibly rich chocolate raspberry thing that Megan couldn't even come close to finishing. Even if her stomach hadn't been alive with nerves she wouldn't have been able to finish it.

She could finish her cocktails, though. Several of them. One good thing about the energy she'd taken from the witch, it allowed her to drink a hell of a lot more without feeling anything more than a pleasant buzz. She'd probably pay for it the next day, but at that point she didn't care. Everyone rose from the table and started milling around. Dinner was over. Thank God, dinner was over, and soon she'd be able to go back to their room and figure out what was going on. Or at least try to figure out what was going on.

The luxurious setting made everything even more unreal. What was she doing there? Yes, fine, she'd admit it. She'd gotten rather used to luxury over the last eleven months or so. How could she not, when she spent a few nights a week—okay, every weekend and several midweek nights—in a mansion? A real one, with servants. When her costume jewelry had slowly but surely gathered dust because she wore real diamonds now, real sapphires and rubies, all gifts from her very wealthy boyfriend?

But the dining room wasn't what she was used to. It wasn't simply a very fine restaurant or the Ieuranlier. It buzzed with energy, with demon voices and laughter. As if she was on a stage in a very bizarre play. She watched Greyson light Justine's cigarette with his fingertip.

Watched Winston and his daughter add a little blood to their wine from the flask in Winston's pocket. She stood in a room full of demons, nonhuman beings, and earlier that night another nonhuman being had tried to kill her, and she thought she'd killed him but his body had somehow disappeared.

Brian had once commented on how unfazed she'd seemed to be by the news that demons actually existed. And that had not disturbed her but concerned her, until she'd realized that a large part of the reason was that deep down she'd remembered. Remembered being possessed by the Accuser, remembered everything.

That didn't explain how she was still standing, still accepting the attempts to kill her or the fact that, upset as she was about taking a life, she was more worried about the disappearance of the body and the idea that she hadn't actually been successful in her murder.

That was where the unreality came from. It was the feeling that she was being watched, that eyes lurked behind those lovely ivy-covered walls or peeked at her from inside the air vents. Her skin tingled as if she were naked. Totally exposed.

Not comfortable, not at all. So she stood up and headed for Greyson, smiling when she saw Roc perched on his shoulder. The two were deep in conversation with Carter; she imagined they were discussing what had happened to her earlier, but that didn't dissuade her. Just being near them would give her strength.

Leora Lawden stepped into her path, a shy smile on her pretty face. Funny, Megan had never thought Winston's features would look right on a girl, but they did.

"Megan," Leora said, "I was hoping maybe we could talk."

Megan plastered on a smile and forced herself not to shoot a longing look at Greyson and Roc. Leora would see it, and the girl looked so . . . not out of place, but eager somehow. How old was she? She couldn't have been out of her early twenties at the very oldest. "Sure, of course. Is something wrong?"

"No, I just . . ." Leora sat down at the table. Megan did the same. "My father always speaks so highly of you, and he thought it would be a good idea. I guess he figures it will be easier on me, all of this, if I have someone to talk to. And if it's you, that's even better."

"I'm flattered," Megan said, because she didn't know what else to say. "I like your father."

Leora's face glowed. "He's wonderful. Everything he's done for me—"

"Attention, everyone!" Speak of the devil—er, demon. Winston Lawden had raised his full glass. "We've had a delicious meal, and I'm sure we all look forward to a productive week. But I think we must all pause now to remember one among us who is no longer here. I would like to propose a toast to Templeton Black. Long live his memory."

"*Alri neshden* Templeton Black," everyone said, and drank, their arms lifting in unison.

Everyone except Greyson.

# Chapter Nine

"Why didn't you drink to Templeton?" she asked him later, once they were back in their room.

"Hmm? Oh. It's not appropriate, since I took his place. It would be disrespectful."

"Really? Huh." Gently buzzed but more tired, she turned around so he could unzip her gown and waited for the little bra-strap tug. It always made her smile, but tonight she had something more serious on her mind too. "So . . . I still want to call Tera."

"I think that's a good idea."

She almost fell over. "What?"

"What?" He hung his tuxedo shirt up and reached for his belt. "If a witch came after you tonight, getting Tera involved is the smart thing to do. She may have information we don't. She may be able to track him somehow in a way we can't."

"But—"

"But nothing. I'm not playing around here, darling. Someone is trying to kill you. I don't care with whom we have to deal or what we have to do, we're going to find out who it is."

He'd turned away from her while he spoke, slipping off his pants and putting on a pair of plain black ones, but the emotion behind his words came through loud and clear just the same.

She stopped with her silk nightie above her head, trapped in her arms. "You . . . you really mean that."

"Of course I do. Did you think I wouldn't?"

"No . . . I just, I'm just surprised."

Maybe it wasn't fair of her, but she was. It wasn't that she didn't think she was important to him; she knew she was. But important enough for him to purposely involve witches in a demon situation, especially with all the other Gretnegs there? To purposely deal with witches at all?

Especially Tera. She may have been Megan's best friend—well, no "may" about it—but Tera also had a sister; actually, she had three sisters, but only one of them mattered. Lexie. And Lexie mattered because she'd dated Greyson briefly, and it had not ended well. Something about a spell on his car and a near-death experience. Megan didn't have all the details. All she knew was, talking about Lexie in front of Greyson amused Tera, who was not the most empathetic or socially adept person in the world.

So to encourage her to call Tera . . .

"You really are worried," she said. Her nightie swirled around her ankles, its black silk the only thing moving in the room.

He glanced up at her, then looked again. Standing still, his hands loose at his sides. "Yes."

"Me too."

His lips quirked. "I can imagine you would be. Now call Tera. I'm going to order some room service. Do you want anything?"

She did, actually. It didn't seem possible she could be hungry, especially with her notoriously weak stomach. But she was. Hungry for food. Hungry for all sorts of things. It occurred to her then that she really had been at death's door and had emerged unscathed—at least physically. That she had won and that there was joy to be had in that winning.

It may have been awful. It was also normal, as she would have counseled any one of her patients who'd come to her with the same sort of issue. Human nature was what it was.

In the morning, she had no doubt, she would feel awful again. But being there, alone in the room with him, looking over a menu full of hopefully delicious food—she'd had too much experience with room service to assume that it would be of the same quality as found in the dining room—and anticipating eating it with him in the big white bed . . . She was just glad to be alive.

Even with someone after her. Even with the FBI—*shit.*

"Greyson, I saw that FBI agent earlier, in the hall. She was the disturbance, you remember, the one I left for."

"She's here?"

She nodded.

"Shit." He sat down on the bed, still holding the thick leather menu he'd grabbed. "Okay, that's—actually, that might not be such a bad thing, come to think of it. If she's here alone—"

"No, hold on." She sat beside him. "She is here alone;

at least she was in the hall alone. But the witch, or whatever he was, attacked her too. I heard her scream. That's when I left the ballroom, but she seemed okay. Just kind of spacy, if you know what I mean. She was wandering down the hall. I started to follow her, and that's when he—that's when he grabbed me."

He squeezed her arm, hard and fast, like an involuntary muscle spasm. "She walked off on her own?"

"Yes, but that doesn't really make sense, does it? If I'd been attacked, I wouldn't just stroll away."

"No, you're right." He was silent for a moment, staring at the menu. "But a witch might very well have bespelled her. She might not have felt whatever injury he gave her—if he did injure her—or even remember what had happened or why she was there. Which could be good for us, if you think about it."

"Greyson."

"What? I can't help the fact that it would benefit us all if Little Miss G-Man would go away or the fact that if he did erase her memory, he simply saved us the trouble of doing it ourselves. But . . . damn."

He shook his head. Megan, used to his look of concentration, waited.

"If he did kill her," he said. "If he injured her badly enough to kill her, and she's found dead here, that could be a problem for us."

Megan sighed and stood up, stripping the nightie back off her head and reaching for the jeans she'd had on earlier. He was already opening the bedroom door, calling for the brothers in the suite's other bedroom.

\*       \*       \*

It only took a minute to get Agent Reid's room number from the highly susceptible desk clerk, and another minute to obtain her key as well. She was on the fourth floor, in one of the smaller single rooms.

"Figures," Greyson said, fitting the key into the door. "The FBI can't be bothered to pay for a decent room."

By Megan's standards the room was decent; better than decent, actually. It certainly beat anything she'd stayed in at one of the chain motels dotted along the highways. But then, she hadn't grown up in a Georgetown mansion watching her parents dress for inaugural balls either.

Malleus and Maleficarum entered the room first, with Spud staying outside to keep watch. Roc was still questioning the demons who'd allowed Agent Reid past them earlier to see if they'd seen anything, and would meet them when he was done. With something to report, Megan hoped, though she wasn't counting on it.

The room was empty. At least empty of humanity, empty of a body. It was far from empty in every other way. Fast-food containers littered the unmade bed; papers littered the floor. Clothes hung off the back of the chair and lay in limp clumps on the floor.

"Ugh." Megan wrinkled her nose and stepped over a greasy hamburger wrapper. "It smells funny in here. Like—"

Like blood. Not demon blood. It lacked the faint tangy, smoky scent of that, the whisper of power carried even in the fragrance. Megan had never sampled any demon's blood, although several times she'd allowed hers to be sampled, once under duress. But she knew the way it smelled. She was attracted to the scent of it; it was part of her demon powers, part of what the piece of demon in her chest gave her.

This was human blood. Old human blood too, in that it was drying.

Megan turned with the others to see the bathroom and grabbed Greyson's arm so hard she thought her fingers might break off.

Blood everywhere. It streaked the mirrors. It dotted the floor. A sodden towel hung over the edge of the counter, a blotch of violent crimson against the white tile.

"God." Her voice shook. "There's so much of it."

"Not that much, I don't think." Greyson's fingers covered hers. "A little blood spilled can look like a lot. And there's no body. No blood outside this room."

"How is that possible?"

He shrugged; she felt his muscles move through his shirt. "I guess she cleaned herself up."

He and the brothers moved through the room, picking up papers and stashing them in Malleus's big black bag. Greyson looked at her. "These are her files. Information on us."

"Right." Or wrong, rather, but it didn't matter. There wasn't much she could say about it, except that she thought they'd better hurry, but they were moving quickly enough.

"So where is she? If she's not dead, and she's not here . . ."

Greyson pulled one last sheet of paper from under the desk and handed it to Malleus. "I have no idea."

"Maybe them down at the front desk'd know," Malleus suggested. "Maybe she went by there."

That's when Megan saw the other thing, the thing they'd missed. She bent down and picked up the key ring, half hidden under the bed by the fallen sheet. "She left her room key, so unless she has another set . . ."

Her eyes met Greyson's. Faint circles etched the skin beneath his; she imagined hers looked even worse. He nodded. "Let's go back down to the desk."

# Chapter Ten

At least the breeze was cool, even if feeling it across her brow reminded her a little too forcibly of her ordeal on the roof earlier. The wind he'd kicked up, how could he—oh, right. Dumb question. Witches could do just about anything. She was so used to thinking of powers as specific skill sets that didn't translate; fire demons like Greyson could burn anything and had some basic mental powers but couldn't read people the way she could or the way any psyche demon could, for example.

But witches weren't bound by any of that. They dealt with energy, with the molecular structure of things, and could make almost anything bow to their will. It was one reason they kept such a rigid hierarchy.

Tera answered on the third ring. "Hey! I thought you were away." She sounded awfully chipper for one in the morning, but then she'd probably still been awake; Tera never seemed to need sleep.

"Yeah, I am." Megan bit her lip and, feeling a little guilty, turned her back on Spud, who had come out with her to keep watch. "I've, um, I've got a little bit of a problem here, and I was wondering . . . I was hoping you could come. Here. I'm at the Bellreive Hotel."

Pause. "What kind of trouble? Are you okay?"

"Yeah, yeah, I'm okay, but . . . it seems someone is trying to kill me. And I could really use your help."

"One of the demons? Do you need me to bring soldiers? How many? What—"

"No, no, don't do that." Megan wanted to roll her eyes at the idea of Tera showing up with an army of witches ready to blast holes in the Bellreive's stone walls, but she couldn't. The truth was, it warmed her heart. The truth was, Tera would do it in a second too. "It's . . . I hate to say this, Tera, but I think it's a witch. Or at least it was a witch earlier. He tried to throw me off the roof."

"No. Why would a witch try to kill you? Why throw you off the roof? One of us could kill you just like that, you know. There's so many easier ways to do it. We certainly don't need—"

Megan shuddered. "Yes, thank you for that reminder. But it wasn't a demon, and he did magic. He did a spell to get us on the roof and another one to control the wind. He made the wind blow harder."

"Shit." Tera paused, for so long Megan wondered if she was still there. "Weather magic is very difficult. He must be incredibly skilled. How did you manage to escape?"

She explained and added, "But there's no body. His body, it just isn't there. So if you—please, Tera. We really need you here. Can you come? For a few days?"

"We?"

"Greyson and I. He told me to call you and ask you to come. I mean, I said I wanted to, and he said he thought it was a good idea and that you should."

"*Greyson* wants me there?"

"Yes."

"To stay there, at the hotel?"

"Yes."

"Wow. I guess this really is serious."

Megan was prepared for what Tera said next, even allowed herself a small smile. It was exactly what Greyson said she would ask, and Megan answered the questions the way he'd told her to. "Yes, he'll pay for your room. Yes, a big room, at least a double, and he's trying to get you a view. Yes, he'll cover all your bills while you're here. Yes, all of them. Even pay-per-view. And the bar and the boutiques, sure. No, I don't need to double-check, he said all, and that means all."

Finally Tera asked, "You do know I would come anyway, right?"

"Yes, I know."

"But if he's offering to pay, I just want to be sure I know what's covered. I mean, demons are pretty well known for trying to get around their promises."

"Sure." Megan glanced back inside. The clerk was on the phone; Malleus saw her looking and gave her a thumbs-up. He was the only person she knew who still did that.

"Okay. I can be there in an hour or so. What room are you in?"

"Fourteen— Hold on." The glass lobby doors parted with a faint whir; the men stepped out onto the dark green carpet that lay just past it.

"The FBI agent's gone to the Windbreaker Hotel," Greyson said. He didn't look happy about it; she could sense his tension.

Not surprising that he would be tense, really. Of all the places for their wandering FBI agent to have wandered, that was the last place Megan would have expected. "Where the exorcism thing is happening?"

He nodded, his face grim. "She told the clerk she had to help Reverend What's-his-name rid the world of demons."

The contrast between the Bellreive and the Windbreaker couldn't have been sharper had it been etched with a razor blade. Where the Bellreive's lobby was a wide expanse of gleaming marble and shining wood, with suited bellhops and desk staff, the Windbreaker's lobby was muggy and loud with ancient air conditioning. The desk, a cheap slab of veneered pressboard, was empty; yellowish lights shone from the ceiling.

"We're going to need to roust a clerk," Greyson said. "I seriously doubt the good reverend is playing with his snakes this late at night. He'll be in his room."

"We should have waited for Tera." Megan hugged herself tighter; the buzzing at the base of her neck was growing. Something wasn't right there, not right at all. There was an . . . an *emptiness* in the building, somehow.

"Roc will get her here," he replied. His knuckles made a hollow sound on the desktop. "If our friendly G-girl is in mortal danger, it's best not to waste any time. We have enough to do this week without getting involved in some silly police business."

"Right." The goosebumps on her arms refused to be soothed away, no matter how hard she rubbed. There was really no reason for her to be so nervous, none that she could see. Whatever the odd emptiness was, that blank sort of pressure she felt, it didn't threaten. The brothers stood around her and Greyson, their poses confident and prepared; she didn't think a moth would be able to get past them, much less anything else.

Malleus caught her looking around. "Don't you fret none, m'lady. Nowt'll 'appen wiv us around."

"Yeh."

Greyson knocked on the desk again. "What a rat-hole."

She felt the clerk coming before she saw him, the stirring of thoughts and emotions in a back room.

Wait. How did she feel that? She wasn't open. Wasn't focusing. Usually in order to sense people in other rooms, she had to lower her shields a little. She'd had to earlier, when she felt Agent Reid and the wi—

No. That wasn't what she'd felt; at least it hadn't been what she thought she felt. She'd thought it was a demon. But why?

The clerk, a large man with dandruff dusting his cheap suit and the shiny look of someone who'd been sleeping rough, ambled out from behind a wall. "What do you need?"

"I believe you have a guest here by the name of Walther? Reverend Walther?"

"I can't give out that information, man. Our guests are—"

Greyson leaned forward. Megan felt his power slide through the air. "I think you can," he said softly. "Why not tell me his room number? That's all I need. It's not so much to ask, is it? No. Of course not. It's the right thing to do, really. So why not?"

A moment of silence, Greyson's power curling in the air. Megan shivered, and not just from the weight of it. That power was everything she felt in the hidden hours they spent together, alone, and her body responded. Couldn't help but respond.

His free hand reached for her, stroked her arm. The touch whispered through her body; she felt it spread through his as well, but he didn't look at her. He couldn't, she knew. To break eye contact with the clerk would break the hold on him as well.

"Room three thirty-three," the clerk said finally, in the slightly dreamy tone of someone asleep.

"Has he had any visitors this evening? Anyone ask for him?"

"A woman came, half an hour ago. The reverend came down and met her. They went back to his room."

"Has she left?"

"Didn't see her leave."

"Thank you. You can go back to sleep now."

The power snapped away as Greyson turned. They left the clerk, already shuffling off back behind his wall, and headed for the elevators.

Megan stopped halfway there. The emptiness was stronger there. She felt it like stepping into a cold draft. "Hold on."

They stood outside a nondescript brown door. The thin plaque on the wall beside it informed them that this was the entrance to the Flower Ballroom.

"What is it?" He'd taken her hand as they walked

away from the desk. Now he gave it a faint squeeze. "You look a little pale, *bryaela*. Are you okay?"

"Yeah, I'm just . . . it feels weird in here."

He examined her for a second, his gaze sweeping over her face and resting on her eyes. "Want to go in?"

She didn't, actually. But she didn't want to admit that. She wasn't scared, necessarily. It wasn't fear making her heart beat a little faster. It was that emptiness, that sensation of nothing. She hadn't felt that in a while. Or rather, she hadn't felt that outside Ieuranlier Sorithell, a houseful of demons she couldn't read.

She'd never felt it out in the real world, the human world.

So she nodded. Even as she did so, she was aware that they could be walking into a trap, but she did it anyway. "The room feels empty."

He glanced up, nodded at the brothers. The secret sound of knives being drawn from pockets and sheaths filled the air around them before Maleficarum opened the door.

The room wasn't empty.

What the hell?

How had she not been able to feel them? They were just people. Three hotel employees, two maids and what looked like a maintenance man, tidying the room. They glanced up when the door opened. Quick movements beside her were the brothers tucking their weapons behind their backs.

"C'n I help you?" The man plucked a screwdriver from his pocket. The brothers tensed around her, but he simply held it. Beside him were exposed wires and a wall sconce half dangling like an open seashell.

"We were looking for Reverend Walther," Greyson said smoothly, as if he'd expected to find people in the room. People she hadn't sensed. People she couldn't read.

"He's not here now." One of the maids picked up a chair, started carrying it to the stacks against the wall. The room was set up as for a seminar of some kind, with a table at the far end and rows and rows of chairs lined up to observe it. About half the chairs appeared to be gone, waiting against the wall for the next day. Or so she assumed.

"Bless him," the other maid said. "He must be just exhausted from what he did here earlier. You should have seen it. He was amazing."

"He's touched by the angels," the maintenance man agreed.

"I've never seen anything so amazing." The first maid turned around and headed back to the row of chairs. Her gold necklace caught the light and flashed at Megan before she bent again to grab another chair. "He truly has the power of Jesus behind him."

"We're lucky he's here," the maintenance man informed them.

"We're all blessed by his presence," said the second maid.

Megan and Greyson glanced at each other. His eyes were troubled; he cut them sideways, back at the chair-stacking maid, and raised his eyebrows.

Megan looked again but didn't see anything. He shrugged. "Well, thank you. What time does the show start tomorrow?"

The maintenance man frowned. "It's not a show. He's saving lives."

"Of course. What time does the life-saving start tomorrow?"

None of the room's occupants—none of the human occupants—seemed to like that comment, but finally the first maid spoke. "Eleven. Eleven in the morning, and he won't leave until everyone is clean."

"Until they're all free from the demon scourge," added the other maid.

Malleus snickered.

Greyson's lips twitched. "Thank you."

They barely got the door closed behind them before the demons started giggling. Megan understood their amusement but couldn't bring herself to share it. "Why couldn't I feel them?"

Greyson stopped smiling. "Did you try while we were in the room? While they were speaking?"

"No, I—no. I don't know why."

He reached for the doorknob. "Do you want to try again?"

"Careful now, Lord Dante." Malleus had not stopped smiling. He looked like the Joker. "There's a demon scourge about, there is."

Maleficarum slapped him on the back. "Aye, there is! Fink we oughter be scared? Nobody's safe wif demons about."

For once their humor didn't go completely over Megan's head, but for once she didn't feel at all like laughing. The only people she'd ever failed to read had not been people at all. They'd been demons. But the three inside the Flower Ballroom had most certainly been human. Since Christmas and the consolidation of her powers, she'd been more easily able to tell the difference. Demons had a certain feel to them, a power signature that humans simply didn't have.

Even as she thought it, though, something else occurred to her. No. There had been another human she couldn't read. Not a witch either; witches were also difficult to read but had a certain feel to them.

She'd had a radio caller just before Christmas, just before things with her demons and Ktana Leyak—a *leyak* demon, the one who'd created the Yezer—had gotten truly out of hand. The caller had called because of problems with her mother or something—Megan couldn't remember the details very well. She wouldn't have remembered the details at all if not for the fact that the woman had been unreadable.

Megan had suspected possession herself at the time. But perhaps . . . perhaps something else was going on?

Shit. The last thing she needed was for her powers to start going wonky again.

"That's enough," Greyson said, dragging her back to reality and dragging them all toward the elevator. "We need to find that FBI agent, and we need to figure out what exactly the reverend is up to. I don't like this one bit."

"Yes, what were you looking at, by the way? You raised your eyebrows at me."

"The maid's necklace," he said, and pressed the button. "Didn't you see it? There's clearly something off happening here."

"No, I didn't see it, why?"

The elevator doors opened. They all stepped inside. "She was wearing a Star of David."

# Chapter Eleven

"I don't—" she started, then stopped. *Oh, right.* "Most Jewish people aren't testifying about the power of Jesus."

"Correct. So unless she converted and forgot to remove her jewelry, we could have a problem here. You couldn't read them?"

She shook her head. "The room felt empty. And not even empty. More than empty, if you know what I mean. Like there was . . . an absence. A vacuum."

The elevator stopped, and the doors slid open, revealing a nondescript hallway empty of anything but doors. The patterned carpet made Megan think uneasily of *The Shining*.

They all stood for a second as if the opening of the elevator doors was an event they couldn't possibly have anticipated. Then the brothers exited, peering around the wall first, checking to make sure nothing and no one lurked in wait.

Greyson took her hand and led her into the hall, the dim light lost in the darkness of his hair. She hadn't noticed before how tired he looked, how the shadows under his eyes weren't just caused by the horrid plastic-covered fluorescents clinging to the ceiling, casting a greenish glow on everything.

But then she was sure she looked exhausted. She certainly felt exhausted, as if someone had attached heavy weights to her limbs. Being almost killed hadn't exactly pepped her up either; all the energy she'd taken from the witch on the roof had dissipated, worn away by fear and worry and the desperate search for answers.

Not that she really expected them to find any here. That would be too easy. The idea that Reverend Walther would open the door and announce, "There you are! I've been trying to kill you for days!" was a tad far-fetched.

But then the idea that he had anything at all to do with this was a tad far-fetched, even with the proof—circumstantial though it was—staring her right in the face.

"They were definitely human," Greyson said as they started walking down the hall.

"So maybe they were possessed?"

He shook his head. "I don't think so. They didn't feel like demon at all. Did you see their Yezer?"

"No, I—no, I didn't. But they're supposed to keep hidden, so I wouldn't."

"*Your* Yezer are supposed to keep hidden. If they belong to someone else, they might not."

True. She nodded. "I'll ask Roc."

They'd reached Walther's room at that point, an unassuming door like all the others, dark wood, with light showing in the slight gap beneath. The brothers stepped back, out of the way, and Greyson knocked.

After a moment a voice came through the door. "How can I help you?"

Shit. Megan hadn't even thought of what they might say, what sort of cover story they'd need.

Greyson apparently had. When he spoke, his voice had a hesitant twang. "Reverend, we're looking for our friend?"

He glanced at Megan; she whispered, "Elizabeth."

"We're looking for our friend Elizabeth? She left a note saying she was coming to see you, but that was a while ago, and we're getting—"

Shadows moved across the light on the floor. The door opened.

Megan wasn't sure what she'd expected. Some John Knox–esque character with raving eyes and a flowing beard, perhaps, or a slick Benny Hinn type with shellacked hair and an oily smile.

Reverend Walther was neither. Pale blue pajamas, frayed at the hems, covered his medium frame and gapped slightly at the front where his belly widened. Silver hair topped his head; his eyes were small and brown and full of what appeared to be honest concern.

"You're friends with that girl?"

Megan didn't listen to Greyson's reply. She was too busy lowering her shields, reaching out to see if she got anything from the man, unsure if she hoped she would.

She did. A church interior. Heads bowed over books. A wife and three daughters at home, dressed in exceedingly modest high-necked, ankle-length dresses. Roast beef and station wagons. Soup kitchens.

And beneath it all something that genuinely scared

her, a force that sent cold chills all the way to her toes. Not because it was demonic or otherworldly but because it wasn't. The reverend was a fanatic. He truly believed in what he was doing, honestly thought he had the power to expel demons and that God wanted him to do so, and he would do anything to obey that command.

Greyson had told her that the Christian God had very little to do with demons anymore, that there was no Hell, and that the concept of a good-versus-evil battle was outdated and silly. Or, rather, that the concept of a good-versus-evil battle being based on religion and the power of God was outdated and silly. Yes, demons did lead humans astray whenever they could, but that was for fun and profit. For power. Not because some devil told them to.

Walther believed the exact opposite, and just standing in the presence of someone with that much self-justified rage and self-exaltation made her twitch.

The other thing she got from him, the last thing, didn't help either. He didn't know who she was. Thought she looked familiar but didn't know her. Didn't know who or what Greyson and the brothers were.

"—but she left about fifteen minutes ago," Walther was saying when she snapped back to reality. "I'm afraid I can't tell you more than that."

Megan took a deep breath and reached for him with her mind again, focusing on Elizabeth Reid this time.

Yes. Okay. There was Elizabeth, her dark hair a little mussed, her eyes wide and hopeless. And she . . . Wait. She looked fine. Well, not fine; she looked upset, a little spacey. But she didn't look injured. Her bare arms and exposed throat were free of marks.

So where the hell had all that blood come from?

"I talked to her for a few minutes and told her to come back tomorrow."

"When you do your exorcisms," Greyson said.

"When God works through me to cast the demons out," Walther corrected.

"Of course. Thanks for your time."

"God bless you," said Walther, and closed the door.

They walked in silence back to the elevator. Megan didn't want to speak; too many thoughts circled in her head, too many unanswered questions. Plus, she was afraid Walther would hear. She pictured him with a cheap plastic hotel cup pressed to the door, spying on them. Probably a silly image but one she couldn't shake, and she didn't feel like trying to read him again to confirm or refute it.

But the others may have shared her discomfort or caution, because Greyson didn't speak until the elevator had started to descend. "Well. That was anticlimactic."

"She weren't even there," Malleus agreed. "'Ow'd she get out right past us?"

"Maybe she left out a different exit, or while we were in the ballroom." Megan leaned against Greyson, who wrapped his arm around her shoulders. "It doesn't really matter. She's alive and well anyway. She didn't even look injured."

"You saw her? So you could read him, then."

She nodded without opening her eyes. Exhaustion was starting to hit her hard; her head buzzed with it.

Without thinking, she reached out along the psychic line connecting the Yezer to her and gave it a little tug. The energy helped, but she still needed sleep. "He's kind of a kook. I mean, he's a fanatic. He really believes what he's doing. But he's not evil. Not in an Accuser sort of way, at least."

"But just as dangerous." Greyson's arm tightened around her. "Fanatics always are."

"That's so cheering."

"Hmm. What's even more cheering is that we have to come back here tomorrow and watch his little show."

"Right. She wanted his help." Megan stood up straight, her eyes opening. "She said she thought they could help each other. She didn't identify herself as FBI; he had no idea who she was. I mean, he figured she was just another wanderer—that's how he thinks of them, wanderers—looking for spiritual aid."

"She didn't say how she could help him?"

"No. But he told her to come back tomorrow morning, and she said she would."

He sighed as the elevator doors slid open again to reveal the shabby lobby. "And you're sure whatever attacked her is what came after you?"

"No." The clerk was sleeping again. The lobby felt too big, too cold; that spot of emptiness still hung around the ballroom door. Megan held Greyson's hand a little tighter and felt his answering squeeze. "But I feel like it was. What else could it have been? And—oh! I meant to tell you. When I sensed her and whatever attacked me, I thought it was a demon, because it didn't feel like anything. It felt empty, like the maids did in there."

Hot air blasted them when Malleus opened the lobby doors. The night waited outside, wrapped itself around them as they crossed the gritty sidewalk. "If she suspects she was attacked by something not human," Greyson said, "we have a much bigger problem. Why don't we head back to her room? We can erase the whole thing from her head. No, better yet, Tera can do it."

Megan hesitated. "I didn't see whoever it was who attacked me. Maybe she did."

"You can read her first, then. See if you get anything."

He was right. She knew he was. But she was so damn tired; her hands were cold despite the heat, her eyelids heavy, and the entire night had been reduced to nothing more than a confused jumble of images. Nothing more than a body falling off the roof, dark against the city lights, that moment of utter silence when she'd watched a man die.

At least when she'd thought she was watching a man die. And being fervently and purely grateful that it wasn't her.

"Can't we do it in the morning?"

He stopped walking, touched her cheek. "You're that tired?"

She nodded.

"I guess it— Actually, that might be better. We'll keep an eye on her. Maybe we can . . . hmm."

"What?"

They'd reached the car; not Greyson's Jaguar, which was back at the Bellreive, but the Mercedes SUV the brothers had driven to the hotel. Spud opened the door, then closed it behind them and climbed into the back.

Malleus and Maleficarum sat up front. Megan had gotten used to it, the feeling of always being under observation, but she'd also gotten used to saving some discussions for later, when the brothers weren't around. One of those popped into her head as she fastened her seat belt. She made a mental note not to forget again.

"I was just wondering," he said as they left their parking spot. The air conditioning kicked on, reviving her a little. At least, instead of feeling like her limbs were overcooked pasta, she felt fairly al dente. "Why a demon, or a witch, would want to get what's-her-name involved with some silly faith healer."

Megan had been wondering it too, but in an abstract kind of way. Now she realized it was the biggest question, the one she should have been asking all along. The answer she came up with sent cold chills down her spine and woke her up far more than she'd thought possible. Without much hope, she asked, "Because they thought it would be funny?"

He smiled. It was too dark in the car to see his eyes, but she could picture them just the same, that combination of pride and amusement that flooded her with heat every time. "I do wish that were the case. But I somehow doubt it is."

"So do you know why?"

His hand found hers on the seat, closed around it tightly, as if he was trying to keep it from escaping. "No. But I intend to find out."

# Chapter Twelve

By mutual consent, they didn't discuss the subject anymore, sticking to lighter topics such as which drive-through restaurant to go to, since Megan had effectively missed dinner and they didn't want to wait for room service. The food revived her a bit, as did the call from Tera informing them that she was all checked in and asking if they needed her to come down now, but Megan still felt half dead. She told Tera they'd see her in the morning and slipped between the sheets on the big, soft bed.

Perhaps "half dead" wasn't the best analogy. She shivered. Outside the wide picture window lights glowed yellow against the dark sky, like candles in a cave. Walling them in, watching them.

Greyson's arms closed around her, pulled her tight against his warm chest. They'd turned the thermostat down earlier; she didn't think it was necessary. It didn't feel as though anything could truly warm her. The entire night since those frantic minutes on the roof seemed to have taken forever and yet less than the space of an eyeblink at the same time.

She was too tired to sleep; her entire body hummed

with nervous tension. He wasn't sleeping either. His breath stirring her hair was too shallow and fast for it.

For a second she considered slipping off the little nightie, letting him take her mind off what happened. Probably make it easier to fall asleep too. But . . . shit. She didn't want to, she realized, because she was afraid of what might happen if they let their attention drift, if they weren't alert and aware, ready to go after anything that tried to slip through the walls and into their room.

They weren't safe there. They weren't safe anywhere. A being that could fall off a roof and somehow disappear before landing, that could get from the first floor to the roof in a thick tangle of words and magic, could get her anywhere. Her body tensed, ready to jump off the bed and hide if the room's energy changed, if the witch—if it was a witch—came after her.

"Spud is on the balcony." Greyson brushed her hair back from her face. "Malleus is in the hall. He won't get to us."

She relaxed a little. Not just from reassurance but because she didn't want him to feel her tension. She didn't like to think she'd been so obvious. Even after almost a year, she hated looking weak in front of him, even knowing he didn't see it that way. Didn't see her that way. It was oddly difficult to get used to, the way she couldn't quite adjust to calling a servant to bring her a snack instead of invading the Ieuranlier's big kitchen herself.

"But a witch could still beat one of them, right? Didn't you tell me once—"

"We're not sure it's a witch," he reminded her. "Unless you've remembered something."

"What else could it be? I mean, are there demons that can walk through walls?" She bit her lip, unsure what reply she was looking for. If it was a demon, she wouldn't worry so much. The hotel was full of demons; surely some of them would help out—although now that she thought of it, she doubted Greyson would approve of her asking them for help, and he'd be right. If looking weak in front of him made her uncomfortable, after eleven months of . . . well, of having a fantastic time and spending more and more time together . . . if that made her uncomfortable, the thought of looking weak in front of the other Gretnegs made her skin crawl. Greyson would never take advantage of her weakness. They would, the way a cat would take advantage of a mouse with its tail caught in a trap.

"No, not as far as I know," he said. "But I can't figure out why a witch would carry you onto the roof and attempt to throw you off. A witch could—"

"Yes, I know. A witch could kill me with just a few words, a snap of the fingers, or whatever. Tera told me."

"I imagine she did." The amusement in his voice slid over her bare skin, as intimate as a kiss. "That sounds like something Tera would say."

"You don't sound as irritated as I expected you to sound."

"Well, she's here. Of course, she didn't come for free—I shudder to think what that bill's going to be like."

"No, you don't."

"You're right, I don't give a shit. I hope she hits the damn jewelry store downstairs and buys herself a diamond tiara. It's worth it if she can help."

Megan shifted her position, lifted her head to kiss him. The hair at his nape was soft and smooth under her fingers; in the room's half-light his eyes glittered faintly when she pulled away, the barest tinge of red visible.

It wasn't that kind of kiss, though. Not that kind of moment. At least not yet.

"Thank you," she said, sitting up to face him.

He held her gaze; his hands slid up her arm, so lightly it was more like the suggestion of a touch. "I figured out some time ago that you and Tera were something of a package deal," he said. His smile made her heart give a little leap in her chest. "Since I don't plan to give you up, I'm stuck with her. Might as well make the best of it."

"You don't plan to give me up, huh?"

His eyes reddened a bit more. "No."

"And you think it's up to you?" She leaned forward, scraped his throat lightly with her teeth. "Don't I have a say in it?"

"Hmm? No. No, I don't think so." His hands moved with more purpose, over her shoulders and collarbone, down to caress her breasts through the silk. "I think it's best if you let me make those decisions, don't you? You just smile and look pretty, and I'll buy you more diamonds and a car."

She gasped, a sound halfway between laughter and

something else, as his hand moved farther down her body and found its way under the hem of her nightie. "A car? Aren't you afraid I'd leave?"

It was a flippant joke, nothing more. A joke in the middle of a joking conversation, like the ones they had often. She didn't expect him to stop, to place his hands firmly on her upper arms. The red light left his eyes as if she'd flipped a switch. "Yes," he said.

The change of mood was so abrupt it took her a second to catch it. She'd been so focused on forgetting, on moving back to a place she felt confident and safe, it didn't occur to her at first that he wasn't flirting anymore, wasn't joking. It didn't occur to her—and when it did, she was ashamed that it hadn't—that he'd just seen two attempts made on her life in as many days and that had their positions been reversed, she would have had a hard time speaking at all.

Her own smile disappeared. She sat back, resting her bottom on her feet. "I'm not going anywhere."

"I sincerely hope not."

"You're . . . you're kind of freaking me out now." The words came out hushed, expelled from a throat gone dry.

"Meg." A heavy cut-crystal glass of scotch sat on his bedside table; he took a deliberate sip, his serious gaze never leaving her face. "I know it's not a subject you enjoy discussing, but I think it's possible you'd be safer if you did the ritual."

"The—how? How in the world would that make a difference?"

"You heard Justine at dinner. They don't like that you

don't plan to do it. Any one of them could have decided that if you're going to remain human—"

"Not any one of them. Not Win, right? And I doubt Gunnar cares or—"

"Any one of them," he repeated. "Don't make the mistake of trusting them."

Had she thought the room was cold before? It felt like a meat locker; she rubbed her arms with her hands.

"I doubt Win's behind it," he continued. "But any one of them could have reasons we're not aware of. This is your life, darling, I don't want to take any—"

"If I do the ritual, it won't be my life anymore." She said it without thinking, but even if her education and training hadn't taught her that such moments usually brought the truth rushing to the fore, she would have recognized it. Since the night she'd done her first radio show, the night Greyson and the Yezer Ha-Ra had entered her life, she'd been desperately holding on to what little remained of her old life.

Doing the ritual would end it permanently. There would be no going back. There would be no leaving the Yezer behind, no moving forward simply as a woman with an interestingly different sort of lover—or boyfriend, for lack of a better term. The piece of demon in her body would grow, would spread its dark wings through her bloodstream, into her organs. Whatever she might gain or lose, whatever remained the same, she would be unalterably, permanently Different.

"It will be," he said. The urgency in his voice sent a nervous chill up her spine; she'd never heard that from him before, at least not when discussing a subject other than how quickly her clothing could come off. He'd never tried to talk her into doing the Haiken Kra before either. So why the hell was he so concerned about it now? "Very little will change, but you'll have that protection; they won't be able to see you as an outsider anymore. Your powers will strengthen again. Perhaps that thing wouldn't have been able to sneak up on you earlier if you'd—"

"Are you saying it's my fault?"

"Fuck, no, I'm just saying you might be safer, and right now your safety is—"

"More important than my happiness? Than what I want?"

"Maybe it should be. Are you seriously telling me you'd rather die than do it? Is becoming demon really a fate worse than *death* to you?"

She hesitated. Was it? She'd never thought of it in those terms before. Of course, she hadn't had any reason to. Her life hadn't been in danger, not like this.

And she'd never thought, either, of what effect her decision might have on him or, rather, of how he might feel about it. On the few occasions when the subject had come up, he'd told her it was up to her and he wouldn't get involved. She'd never doubted that he wanted her to do it but never dreamed it was that important to him.

"There's no guarantee it would make a difference," she reminded him. "You said yourself you don't know. We don't know who's behind this. It could have nothing to do with—with what I am. Right? And if I do this just because someone's after me, and it turns out to be totally unrelated . . . it just doesn't seem like the right way to make a decision, does it?"

His gaze slid away from her face, down to her hands resting on his flat, smooth stomach. "No," he said, his voice flat. "I suppose it doesn't."

"I know. I mean, I'm worried too. But you just told me we're safe in here. And really, it's not exactly the way I want to think, but if they're going to get me they're going to get me, aren't they? We'll find out what's going on. And Malleus, Maleficarum, and Spud will keep me safe. You'll keep me safe. I took a chance earlier. I shouldn't have gone into that hall by myself; I should have let you come with me. I won't do that again. Now that we know it's here, I'll be more careful, I promise. I just—I don't want to rush into anything."

"I didn't realize it was that important to you. Staying human." His hand covered hers, turned it palm up; he examined it with that same incurious stare. "I always assumed . . . I understand if you're scared, but I'd be there with you. It's not—"

"I'm not scared. I just don't want to. I don't see a good reason to."

He looked up at her, his eyes shadowed. "Isn't the— no. Never mind." His expression cleared, as if he'd wiped it clear with a cloth. "This is your decision, darling. If it's not something you want to do you'll never be happy with having done it, will you? I'm not going to try to talk you into it. If the possibility of death isn't enough, I don't see what I could offer."

The whole conversation felt wrong; her earlier exhaustion came roaring back, along with the odd certainty that something she didn't understand had just happened.

Something she didn't understand but should. She'd had that feeling before, hadn't she? Something lurking in the back of her mind, a memory she couldn't pin down. Hell, a memory she wasn't sure was there at all.

And she was exhausted, and she had survived a murder attempt and had spent fifteen or twenty minutes convinced she'd killed a man. So it was entirely possible she was reading something into it that didn't exist, spooking at shadows in her mind.

Not to mention the abrupt change of mood. And if she were honest, the fact that she didn't think he'd ever been that direct about his feelings in regard to her.

That she was important to him she didn't doubt, hadn't in months, in almost a year. That he wanted her, wanted her company, she didn't doubt. And although he'd never said it, she didn't doubt that he loved her.

It wasn't as odd as it might have seemed, the fact that he hadn't said it. She hadn't either. She'd never really felt the need. Actions worked better, said more; they both spent so much of their time talking, both at work and to each other, that it had simply never seemed necessary. Their Christmas together, when he'd given her the diamond necklace now sitting in her jewelry box on the dresser and told her he'd tried to find one as beautiful as she was but it had been an impossible task. The things she cooked for him and gave to one of the brothers to slip into his desk drawers or leave in his car when he wasn't looking, so he'd find them and know she was thinking of him. The day he'd told her it was silly of her not to keep things at his place. The day she'd found her radio show on his iPod, because if he couldn't listen to it live, he'd record it for later.

Those memories stood out, but there were hundreds of other, smaller moments that stood out just as much, that warmed her when she remembered them and made her feel secure. Words were lovely, but they were just words. They couldn't always be trusted; she of all people knew that.

She didn't always trust words. She hadn't always trusted Greyson. But since that Christmas, she had, and he trusted her. That trust between them had been something solid enough, strong enough, to support them both.

So the feeling that she had failed him somehow, that she'd misunderstood something, made her skin colder than it had been before. She ran her palms up his chest, leaned forward and rested her head on it, listening to the steady beat of his heart with her eyes closed; after a moment his hand came to rest on her hair, warm and reassuring.

"You should get some sleep," he said. "If I know Tera—and I do—she'll be banging on the door at some ungodly hour, wanting you to go out and play tennis and have a makeover or something."

"As if I'd let her talk me into that."

"And thank God. The last thing I want is for you to wander around looking like a Tera clone. I happen to think you're quite lovely the way you are, despite your crankiness and violent streak." He shifted position so she could stretch out more easily beside him and she did so, relieved. Whatever had changed in the air changed back; everything was normal again.

"Am I?"

"Cranky and violent? Yes. I hardly think that comes as a surprise."

She smiled. "No. I mean the other thing."

"Ah. Fishing for compliments is never an attractive behavior in a lady, you know."

"Humor me. It's been a rough night."

He was silent for a moment, absentmindedly stroking her thigh. Or perhaps not so absentmindedly, after all; his fingers kept inching higher and higher, urging the silky fabric out of the way.

"It has been rather rough." His other hand found her chin, lifted it to look in her eyes. "I think I know a way to salvage it, though."

"Really? That doesn't sound like humoring me, I have to say."

"Oh, I think you'll be very pleased when I'm done. In fact, I believe I can guarantee it." His hand moved with more deliberation, eliciting a sharp little gasp from her. "See?"

She managed to nod.

"And to answer your question, *sheshissma* . . ." His voice was none too steady itself; she'd managed to find a use for her own hands. "I think you know very well what you do to me, and how very much I hope you'll keep doing it."

"Show me," she said.

And he did.

# Chapter Thirteen

The knock on the door did indeed come bright and early; the clock by the bed informed Megan that it was quarter past eight. On a workday she would have already been up and moving, but then on a workday she wouldn't have been awake until almost three the night before.

Either way. All she wanted to do was go back to sleep, and despite her fondness for Tera and her utter gratitude that Tera had come, she wasn't in the mood.

Along with the sunlight slicing a path through her brain came the unwelcome memories of the night before. Yes, there were one or two very welcome memories in there as well, but for the most part . . . ugh.

Chief of all of them was the conversation she'd had with Greyson. She wanted to believe his sudden interest in getting her to do the ritual was related solely to her safety, but convincing herself of that was more difficult than she'd expected it to be in the hard sharp morning. Having the subject brought up twice in one night seemed a little much for coincidence.

It didn't matter. She grabbed her robe off the chair and slipped it on, while the pounding continued. Tera could sit and order some room service or something while she took a shower; judging from the closed door and the sound of water running, Greyson was already in there.

Of course, he could have simply leaped in when the knocking started in order to avoid Tera.

She tied the robe's belt around her waist and turned the knob. "Hi, Ter—Nick!"

Before she could even finish saying his name his arms were around her, squeezing her almost as tight as she squeezed him. Nick Xao-teng was one of Greyson's oldest friends and probably his closest, and had become one of hers as well. But Nick didn't have anything to do with the Meegras; he was, he'd once told her, "an independent contractor."

She hadn't asked him what exactly that meant.

"What are you doing here? I mean, I'm glad to see you, I just—"

He kissed her soundly on the cheek, gave her one last squeeze, and dipped into a flourished bow. "At your service, hon. Grey called me last night."

Right. "You're here to guard me."

Nick's eyebrow rose. He hadn't changed since she'd seen him last, two months before, but he never did. Descended from a Chinese half-succubus mother and a part-psyche-demon father of whom he never spoke, Nick was devastatingly handsome, with an aura of raw sexual energy that he used to full advantage.

Except around her. At least not after their first meeting, when she'd gotten a taste of what it felt like to be seduced by an incubus. He hadn't realized she was with Greyson, and Greyson had arrived before she'd been able to do much more than lose a little breath—along with dignity—but still. She didn't think she'd ever forget that feeling, or how angry she'd been.

She was glad she'd forgiven him, though.

"I am indeed here to guard you," he said. "Although 'escort' is really more the way Greyson put it. He said he has some meetings and stuff and asked if I would mind making sure you're never alone." He set down his suitcase and closed the door behind him. "Not that I'm complaining, of course."

"I should hope not." Greyson emerged from the bedroom, with his hair damp and his shirt untucked. "Not after what a last-minute ticket from Miami to here cost me."

"Like you can't afford it," Nick replied. "Have you traded in the Jag for a solid-gold Rolls yet?"

"You could have one yourself, you know, if you'd—"

"Don't even start."

Megan smiled as the men embraced. That was an old discussion, one they seemed to engage in out of habit. Greyson wanted Nick to move from Miami and work with him, to do Carter's job; Nick resisted. If she'd heard them talk about it once, she'd heard it a hundred times.

She slipped away while they conversed and hurried through a shower. Seeing Nick was a pleasure. Imagining the two of them sitting alone with Tera wasn't, and she had no doubt Tera would be there any minute.

Sure enough, the witch's voice floated through the closed bedroom door when she emerged fifteen minutes later. Megan tossed on a plain dark dress—if they were heading over to see Reverend Walther later, which they

were, she wanted to look as unobtrusive as possible—
and opened the door.

Tera was sitting in the dark leather armchair, a tray
over her lap loaded down with food. She barely looked
up from her plate when Megan entered. "Hey. Any new
information?"

"I was kind of hoping you might have had some
ideas."

Tera shook her head, making nodding wait-a-minute
motions while she forced down an enormous bite of
muffin. Witches never turned down free food. Or really anything free. Finally she swallowed. "I did a quick
check through the Vergadering mainframe last night,
but I couldn't find anything about you, or this hotel, or
any indication that someone on one of the watch lists
is in town."

Megan raised her eyebrows and settled on the couch
next to Greyson, who rested his hand on her thigh.
"Watch list?"

"Yeah, you know. Known assassins, criminals for
hire . . . There are a few mercenary witches out there,
and we keep tabs on them as best we can."

"As opposed to simply arresting them," Greyson said.

"We don't know exactly where they are," Tera said,
through another chunk of muffin. "We would if we did.
We just get rumors about them being in specific cities,
specific places. We do what we can."

"Funny. You always manage to know the exact location of any one of us who got a parking ticket at any
given time."

Tera made a sour face. Megan squeezed Greyson's

thigh hard and cut in before either of them could make it worse. "Thanks for checking, Tera. Is there any chance you just don't know whoever-it-was is in town?"

Tera glared at Greyson for another second or two before answering. "Of course it's possible. But if it makes you feel any better, I'm the only witch in the building at the moment. And I'm going to do a little something for you, so you'll be better able to tell if any of us are around you."

"You can do that?"

"Of course." Tera tossed her head. Her long, straight blond hair caught a ray of sunlight and glowed for a moment before falling obediently behind her right shoulder. She gave Greyson and Nick a significant look. "Actually, it's something we picked up from them."

"What do you—"

Greyson leaned forward. "You're going to do a *betchimal*?"

"You know what it is, then."

"Of course I know what it is. I don't know how to perform it, since you witches stole the knowledge, but—"

"Oh, will you give me a fucking break, Grey? It's not like you're so poor and downtrodden." Tera gave the walls around them, gleaming pale in the morning light, a significant look. "I didn't personally steal anything, okay? It's not my fault you guys lost."

"No, but you work for—"

"Okay." Megan stood up. "That's enough, you two. Can we get back to something that actually matters here? You know, someone trying to kill me? Someone who attacked an FBI agent and made her go seek out an exorcist, for whatever reason? I think we have bigger things to concern ourselves with than some centuries-old war. Don't you?"

Silence hung heavy in the air for a second. Neither Tera nor Greyson bothered to blush or look sheepish, but she knew them both well enough to know that had they been a little less self-contained, they would have.

Then Tera spoke, her expertly colored lips curving into a smile. "FBI agent? What's the FBI doing here, Greyson?"

Greyson smiled back. Megan could practically see the halo over his head. "How in the world would I know?"

"It doesn't matter," Megan said. She realized she was still standing, as if she was about to break into song, and plunked herself back down on the couch. "What does matter is that she's here, and I think the thing—the witch, if it is a witch, which I guess it is—attacked her, and then she ran to the hotel to talk to the exorcism guy. I have no idea why, or why he would be involved in all of this, but I'd like to find out."

Tera finished her muffin. "And where is this FBI agent now? Do you think she knows what attacked her?"

Megan shook her head. "She's probably in her room, and no, I don't think so. We went to see the reverend last night—"

"Reverend?"

"Reverend Walther, the exorcist. We went to see him last night, and I read him and saw his conversation with her. She wanted to join his crusade or whatever, but she didn't mention demons or witches or anything specifically."

Tera frowned and popped a piece of melon into her mouth. "Walther. That name sounds familiar. And don't you think it's possible that she wanted to join him because she knew what had come after her?"

"Yes, it's possible, but I don't think that's the case. She seemed . . . kind of dazed. And she said she could help him. I don't really see why she would offer to help him, if she knew she'd been attacked by something, well, not quite human. Or whatever."

"A superior being," Tera said.

"Hey! I'm human, remember."

"Oh, I remember. Okay. I think the best thing to do is head down to her room. I'll do a little spell so she'll forget the attack, and we can wipe our hands of her at least."

Greyson leaned forward. Had innocence been a tangible thing, like chocolate, he would have been brown from head to toe. "Perhaps it would be better to remove her memories of all of us and send her away. We wouldn't want her getting in the way and being hurt again, would we?"

Tera's eyes narrowed. For a long moment they all sat, silent, while she chewed her melon and thought whatever it was she was thinking. Megan suspected it had something to do with wishing desperately that Greyson's idea wasn't a good one and trying to think of a way to get out of doing what he wanted.

"I guess you're right," she said finally. "But I think you're going to owe me a favor."

"Done."

"Okay, then." Megan stood back up, this time for a reason. She wanted to get down to Agent Reid's room as quickly as possible, and not just because it was nearing nine o'clock. She could never be sure how things were going to go when she had Greyson and Tera both in the same room; sometimes they got along just fine, even managed to joke and at least put on a good enough show of enjoying each other's company. Other times they were like a couple of sharks fighting over the same tasty innocent victim. This was clearly one of the latter occasions.

Could she blame them? Perhaps they weren't as edgy as she was—they weren't the ones who'd almost been killed—but again, if either of them had been, she wouldn't exactly have been in a chipper mood. The thought of something happening to either of them, of the hole that would leave in her life . . . She shuddered as she slipped on her shoes.

Eleven months ago she hadn't known either of them existed and hadn't really had anyone in the world, except her patients, who would even have noticed if she'd disappeared. Perhaps Althea—one of her old partners in the group practice—would have worried. Althea had kept in touch, sort of, but Megan hadn't heard from her in a couple of months. Nobody else. She'd been alone, completely and totally, not even speaking to her family.

Now she had friends. A man she loved, who she knew loved her. A real family, even if they were a bunch of little demons who fed on human misery.

All that in less than a year. And the thought of something happening, of losing one of the people who'd enriched her life so much, sent a stab of fear straight to her heart. She shivered again, harder.

"Meg? You okay?" Greyson must have seen her shudder. When she turned around, he was watching her, his brows drawn together.

"Yeah, I'm fine." She gave him a bright smile. What the hell was her problem? Well, stupid question—someone was trying to kill her, after all—but where was this silliness about losing someone coming from? Tera had taken time off work—probably called in sick, but Megan had no idea what Vergadering's vacation policies might be like—and come to stay at the Bellreive just to help her. And yes, Greyson was paying for her room and everything else, but she would have come anyway.

And Greyson . . . was buying things for a witch, had actually requested Tera's presence. That's how much he cared, how much he wanted Megan to be safe. He'd flown Nick up here on a moment's notice, to protect her. And Nick had come—another person who cared about her.

So why, then, did she suddenly have the horrible feeling that it was all about to disappear, the way the body of her attacker disappeared over the edge of the roof, plummeting away from her so fast she couldn't stop it?

Greyson was still watching her. "Are you sure? You look a little pale."

"Yes, of course." The smile was starting to make her cheeks ache. "Goose walked over my grave, is all."

It was not the right cliché to use.

# Chapter Fourteen

"So," Tera said as they walked down the hall. "What's the deal with this FBI person?"

Megan hesitated. She glanced at Nick, walking beside them, but he just raised his eyebrows. No help there.

"I don't know," she said finally. This, more than the bickering, was the one thing she truly hated about being friends with Tera. Tera worked for Vergadering. If Tera had any proof that Greyson or any of the other Gretnegs were involved in criminal activities, she could haul them off to prison. And from what Megan understood, a regular human prison was Club Med compared to Vergadering prison.

She couldn't allow that to happen. Not simply because she couldn't but because if she did, her life wouldn't be worth a dime. Demons may have devoted a lot of their time to figuring out how to cheat people, but they took honor very seriously. A demon's word meant a lot; a demon's silence was something worth dying for.

So as much as Megan would have liked to have told Tera what Agent Reid had said to her and what the woman's suspicions were, she couldn't. Mentioning that the FBI was investigating Greyson and the others wasn't proof of a crime, of course, and wouldn't exactly surprise Tera, but Vergadering could get all sorts of information. As Tera had pointed out the night before, witches were powerful. Any one of them could dig into the FBI's files and find who-knew-what.

"She's just here as a guest, I guess. I only know she's FBI because we were behind her when we checked in."

"And she got attacked last night?"

Megan gave her a carefully edited version of the story. "There was blood all over," she finished. "Bloody towels . . . it didn't look like she'd just cut herself shaving or anything. But when I read Walther, she looked just fine, at least to him. So I don't know where all the blood came from."

"Huh. Weird. How are you feeling? Still woozy?"

"No." The *betchimal* Tera put on her had sent her running for the bathroom, certain she was going to be sick. She hadn't been, but it was a close call.

The nausea had only lasted a couple of minutes, though. And the spell certainly worked; Megan could *feel* Tera beside her, like a spot of heat seen through infrared goggles. "Just wishing we didn't have to do this."

"Yeah, I guess this isn't how you want to spend your birthday, huh? Maybe it will all be over by then."

Megan blinked. She'd forgotten about that.

"It's your birthday?" Nick asked. "I didn't know that."

"Not for another couple of days. It's no big deal."

"Why do you think someone is trying to kill you?" Tera asked, as if birthdays and murders were normally part of the same conversation. "I mean, have you thought about it?"

Megan shook her head. "I can't imagine. It's not like I'm particularly important or anything."

"Probably something to do with Greyson."

"Hey!" Nick said. Was it her imagination, or did he sound nervous? An edge seemed to lurk behind his voice that she'd never heard before. "You don't know that."

Tera shrugged. "What else could it be? You heard her. She's not important. Nobody seems to be after her little demons, but as far as I know, you guys are always trying to kill each other for one reason or another, and with Greyson being in charge now—"

"All the more reason why this probably has nothing to do with him. What could anyone possibly gain if Megan died?"

"I am still here," Megan said. "I'm walking right between you."

"Who knows what they might gain? But it's hardly possible someone wants to kill Megan just for herself. It's got to be connected to Greyson somehow."

"You act like he set this up or something. Don't you think—"

"What I think," Tera said, "is that being with him puts her in danger, and she should get out. Out of this whole thing. It's not like they're going to get married or anything. She—"

"Stop it!" Megan grabbed them both by the arms and forced them to halt. "Just stop it. Tera, what the hell is with you? Why do you keep picking fights?"

"I don't want to see you get hurt." Tera's cheeks were flushed; Megan had never seen her so emotional. "You're my friend, and I don't want to lose you. And you wouldn't be in this situation if you hadn't gotten so mixed up with them."

"*Them?*" Nick's expression was close to a snarl. "Mixed up with *them*? Jesus. You witches are all the fucking same, aren't you? Thinking you can just order us around, telling Megan she should leave—"

"I'm not going anywhere," Megan said, loudly and slowly. "Except on to this woman's room. And you two are coming with me, and you will keep your mouths shut, or I'll— I don't know what I'll do, but you won't like it. Okay?"

Pause. Then they both nodded. Megan would have laughed if she hadn't been so angry. "Good. Now, let's go."

She'd taken about two steps down the hall when it occurred to her to wonder why Tera had sounded so certain that she and Greyson weren't going to get married. Not that she expected to—well, no, that was a lie. She did expect to. Hoped to. At some point, not yet; they hadn't even been seeing each other a year, but then she was going to be thirty-two in a few days, and he'd be thirty-eight a few weeks after, they weren't getting any younger . . .

Whatever. If it happened, it would happen. She wasn't getting younger, no, but neither was she in a hurry, and she refused to start worrying about a subject she could honestly say she rarely thought about. They were happy the way things were, and she looked forward to the future but wasn't in a rush. Period. So she was not going to start wondering why her best friend seemed so damn confident that she was going to be single forever.

Besides, what did Tera know? Her longest relationship had lasted a month.

Perhaps it was a little mean of her to think that way, but Tera was the one who started it. And after the way they'd behaved, both Tera and Nick deserved to have some mean thoughts being thought about them. So she kept doing just that, focusing on Tera's pickiness and Nick's buffet approach to women, until they reached Agent Reid's door.

The woman who opened it looked like Agent Reid. Sounded like Agent Reid. But Megan had the unsettling sense that Agent Reid had in fact left the building; emptiness haunted the woman's eyes. "Yes? Dr. Chase, can I help you?"

Okay. For a second Megan had considered the possibility that Agent Reid was possessed. It didn't happen a lot, but it certainly did happen, as she knew for a fact, having been possessed herself at the age of sixteen. But she didn't feel like a demon to Megan; since the consolidation of her powers, she'd been better able to—wait. No, she could feel demons.

She'd thought the thing outside in the hall, the thing that had attacked the agent, was a demon. It had *felt* like a demon. And yet it had been able to perform witch magic.

Fuck, that could not possibly be good.

"I wondered if I could come in and talk to you." Megan kept a bright, vacant smile on her face.

Elizabeth's face didn't even change. If Megan hadn't already known in every cell in her body that something was wrong, that would have told her. The Elizabeth Reid who'd come to her office had been bright and driven, so much so that she'd taken an enormous risk like tipping off the subjects of an investigation. Now here Megan was, and for all Elizabeth knew she was ready to spill her guts or snitch or blab or whatever the terminology was these days, and Elizabeth looked as if she'd unwrapped a Christmas gift and found a pair of old sweat socks inside the box.

But at least she was still herself enough to shrug and step back, admitting them to the room. "If you like."

Megan lowered her shields and reached out as she passed Elizabeth, steeling herself for whatever darkness she might receive.

Nothing.

No, worse than nothing. Tera's damned spell, which was supposed to be so helpful, interfered with what Megan actually felt, the kind of emptiness she usually associated with demons but something stronger, more sinister. Something that didn't feel like demon but didn't not feel like demon either, and it certainly didn't feel like witch. Tera practically vibrated in Megan's mind. Elizabeth did not.

She felt human. Just unreadable. Just with something extra around her, something soft and solid that resisted Megan's attempts to see it. She tried using her power as a weapon, tried pulling whatever it was back to herself. It stung where she touched it, but she felt humanity behind it, hiding there. If she could somehow push through whatever it was, past it, she could find out what was really going on.

Something screamed in her head when Tera bumped

into her, hard enough to make it obvious she'd done it deliberately. "Are you okay?"

"What?" Megan looked around. Nick was sitting in one of the small bucket chairs by the room's little desk, with Elizabeth on the bed. They looked settled, as though they'd been there for a few minutes already.

The door was closed behind her. How long had she been standing there, trying to fight her way through that thick dull veil surrounding Elizabeth?

Tera inspected her from head to foot, which made Megan want to slap her more than she had before from the stupid bickering in the hall. "Did you get anything?"

Megan glanced at Elizabeth, then realized it didn't matter. Tera was going to remove the entire incident anyway. They could speak as freely as they wanted.

"No. It's like there's some kind of cloth or barrier wrapped around her. Maybe it's a spell or something. Could he have cast a spell that deadened people? Hid them behind a psychic or magical shield?"

Tera shrugged. "Of course. If it was a witch. I don't think a demon could do something like that."

"What in the world are you people talking about?" Elizabeth wasn't completely gone after all. She'd half risen from her perch on the sage-green patterned bedspread and assumed a defensive stance, ready to fight.

Tera waved her hand. Elizabeth subsided.

Nick glanced at her. "A psyche demon might be able to do something like that, but not that strong."

"Can you feel it, Nick?"

He nodded, with his eyes on the floor. Nick's father had been part psyche demon, she knew, but only because Nick had used the bit of power his heredity had given him to help her back at Christmas. Aside from that she knew nothing about his family, except that both of his parents were dead. He never spoke of them.

She knew there was a reason for his reticence. She didn't know what it was, but every once in a while something would happen, she'd feel his energy just a little too strongly, and it would blow her away with the injury of it, the anger and pain and fear lurking beneath everything else. It didn't scare her. But she was aware of it, always.

So she didn't press him. "I don't know, Tera. I've never felt or seen anything like it before. I can't get anything from her at all."

"So you can't see what she saw, what attacked her."

Megan shook her head.

Tera sighed. "Okay, well, look. I'll see if I can get anything from her, but the longer we let these memories sit around in her head the stronger they get, as you know. And the longer she holds on to a false memory the more she'll come to believe it. So every minute that goes by . . ."

Megan nodded. It was pretty basic knowledge, how memories were created and the difference between short-term and long-term. Someone who'd suffered a head injury and been knocked unconscious wouldn't remember how it happened; the brain wouldn't be able to "set" those memories.

Tera took a deep breath, shooting a glance at Nick. Megan caught his eye and jerked her head to the right; he got up.

That was the last thing that seemed clear in what happened next: the image of Nick, his body strong and graceful, lifting from the chair and moving silently to the left. A shaft of light caught his black hair and gleamed like the wing of a raven. Tera said something under her breath at the same time, and a cool wave of energy hit Megan, rocked her gently.

Then it exploded.

Megan fell, down to the carpet, through the carpet. The air left her lungs as if a giant hand had wrapped around her chest and squeezed, an iron band that refused to yield. Pain, pain so sharp and fierce it blinded her, tore into her chest, into her head, bright white and terrifying.

She tried to scream but nothing came out; she had no air to scream with. She was going to die. She was going to die here, on the floor of a nice hotel room, and she would never even know why or what killed her.

The thought sent a wave of rage all the way to her toes. That was bullshit, utter bullshit. It was almost her goddamn birthday, for fuck's sake, and— She reached for her demons, needing their strength, knowing that if she had it she might be able to fight back, to push at whatever it was that squeezed the life out of her on the carpet.

The Yezer were attached to her by an invisible thread, one she saw in her mind's eye but not with her physical ones. She grabbed the thread with every bit of strength and will she had left, sent her panic and fear along it.

A second to send it out. A second of waiting. And back it came, thick, strong power, filling her up. She was air; she was lighter than that. She'd never taken this much from them, not even the awful day of her father's funeral when she hadn't realized they were feeding her. She'd been high then. Now she was somewhere in the stratosphere.

Without her consciously doing anything about it, the band around her chest eased, then disappeared completely. She was left alone on the floor, with energy still coursing through her body and her hair sticking to her forehead and cheeks in sweaty, itchy tendrils. She wanted to scratch them but didn't dare move, afraid that if she did, she would either fly off the floor and into the sky or collapse in a sobbing heap.

It took a second for the spinning room to stop. When it did, she saw Tera leaning against the wall, her face pale but composed. Nick hunched on the floor a few feet away, eyes wide, but also alive, which was Megan's chief concern.

It wasn't until Tera took a step toward her that Megan realized how shaken she was; the hand she wiped her forehead with trembled. "Are you okay?"

"Yeah, I— What the hell was that? Nick, are you okay?"

His face shone with sweat. "Okay," he said, but Megan didn't like the weakness in his voice. He sounded as if he was very far away, rather than a few feet across the pale green carpet.

"Whatever it is that's got her, it resisted me." Tera jerked her head toward Elizabeth Reid, who still sat on the bed as if nothing at all had happened.

Okay, that was weird. Well, obviously, it was all weird—

it had been some months since life had been as bizarre and full of attempted murder as this, and Megan could honestly say she hadn't missed it a bit—but it seemed especially weird, particularly weird, that any person, much less an FBI agent, would watch someone else have a fit on the floor and still be sitting there, smiling faintly. Which was exactly what Elizabeth Reid was doing.

"How? I mean, how did it resist you?" Her legs felt rubbery. She forced them to move, pushing herself off the floor.

"I don't know. It was stronger than me. Or whatever the spell is around her, or the aura or whatever, I didn't have the right way to break through it."

"So she remembers everything. She knows we were here, she heard you, everything."

Tera raised her eyebrows. "Does she look like she cares?"

"Good point." Okay, her legs really would support her. They didn't want to, but they would. If she couldn't control her own legs, things were at a pretty sad pass. She used them to cross the room to Nick, then let them collapse beneath her again to join him against the wall.

She reached out to touch his arm. He looked so dazed. "Nick. Hey, are you sure you're all right?"

"Whatever it was . . ." he said, and she realized it wasn't the physical attack, or whatever it was, that had so shaken him. "Whatever it was, it affected us because of what we are."

"It's really bad for psyche demons, you mean."

He nodded. "It felt . . . I could feel it. It didn't man-age to do exactly what it wanted to because I'm not entirely psyche. It didn't manage to do it to you because you're human still. And Tera's not demon at all, which is why she's still standing."

"I felt it, though." Tera joined them on the floor. They sat there like a trio of early-morning drunks with their legs stretched out before them, Elizabeth Reid in her simpering catatonia essentially forgotten. "It got me; I mean, that really stung."

Silence fell heavily. Megan knew what they were thinking, what they didn't want to ask or even think about. But she couldn't help but think about it. She asked, "So what the hell *was* it?"

"I don't know," the other two replied in unison, followed by equally weak smiles.

"It was beautiful," Elizabeth said.

Megan didn't know which surprised her more, what Elizabeth said or that she so obviously meant it. Her entire demeanor had changed. Where she had been affectless, she was animated. It sent cold chills creeping up Megan's spine.

"What was it, Elizabeth?" No point bothering with "Agent Reid"; the woman obviously didn't care.

"It touched me."

"Yes, but do you remember what it looked like? What it is?"

Elizabeth looked at her watch. "I have to go."

The three on the floor exchanged looks, basically all variations on what-the-fuck. Then Megan caught on.

Her own watch told her it was almost ten. Reverend Walther's little psychological freak show—maybe she shouldn't think of it that way, but she did—started at eleven, he'd said. So if Elizabeth planned to be there, she'd want to start getting ready.

Which meant they needed to get ready. Megan's entire body felt sticky; her hair was drying against her cheeks. She wanted another shower and a change of clothes. She wanted a stiff drink—who gave a damn how early it was—and she wanted to tell Greyson what had happened. He was bound to know something or have some idea how to proceed beyond following Elizabeth over to the Windbreaker and simply watching what happened.

They'd have to watch either way. But she'd feel a hell of a lot better if he was there too, and she knew he'd want to go.

She stood up, noticing with some pleasure that her legs felt almost normal again. "Come on. We have to go see this."

# Chapter Fifteen

Unlike the previous night, the lobby of the Windbreaker teemed with people, hiding the generic wallpaper and grubby carpet. The crowd overwhelmed Megan; she still didn't quite have her equilibrium back, psychically speaking, and she clung to Greyson's hand a little harder than normal.

He glanced at her. "They are a bit much, aren't they?"

She rolled her eyes in response, not quite trusting her voice while she locked her shields as tightly as she could. The despair in this crowd, the anger and misery and fervor that could only be described as bloodthirsty . . . It wasn't that she was afraid of their emotions touching her. It was that her body, still worn and woozy and a little buzzed from what her demons had given her and the gin she'd downed in the room, instinctively wanted to keep going. To keep feeding. She hadn't felt her demon this strongly in months; for a moment all she saw were negative emotions coloring the air and making it taste like wine. All she felt was the desire to open up and take it all in.

Greyson returned the pressure on her hand. He didn't look at her, too busy scanning the crowd, but she knew he knew, that he was simply there waiting until she had won her battle and was ready.

It only took a minute; she'd gotten much better at controlling it. And now that she faced it without the crippling fear and shame of months before, it was much easier to handle. Sort of like getting her first period as a teenager, several years after all the other girls did. A completely alien thing the first few times, gradually becoming just a nuisance.

Beside her Malleus, Maleficarum, and Spud giggled and elbowed each other, with Roc's little head bowing and dipping as he joined in from Spud's shoulder. She didn't think she wanted to know what they found so amusing.

The ballroom doors opened; the crowd pushed forward. "It's like a wave of stupid," Tera said behind her. In her hand was a Coke can frosted with cold.

Megan jumped. "You got a drink already?"

Tera shrugged. "I can get through crowds pretty easily if I need to."

She still looked a tad pale, troubled. Megan didn't know how powerful Tera really was. She'd always figured Tera was pretty damn powerful, considering her job. But she'd never known her to use that power among humans. Keeping the existence of the supernatural secret was one of Tera's highest priorities.

Well, hell, if Megan had been able to mutter a few words and get herself a cold Coke faster, she probably would have too. The last thing she wanted to be doing at that moment was getting ready to join the throng of humanity spreading like an oil slick into the ballroom.

She started to anyway, but Greyson held her back. "Let's let the others get themselves settled first. We'll stand in the back in case we have to leave."

"Do you think we're going to have to leave?"

He shrugged. "I'd rather be able to escape this ghastly horde as quickly as we can, wouldn't you? We'll probably catch ringworm or something if we spend too much time with them."

But the joke wasn't quite working. Shadows lurked beneath his eyes, the kind she rarely saw, and his smile didn't reach them; he wasn't the type to walk around wringing his hands but the signs of worry were there for anyone who knew where to look. She squeezed his hand a little harder, leaned into his side. "I'm more worried we'll miss lunch."

"Think the reverend will mind if we order pizza on his time?"

"Well, if we're there, *and* he's there, that makes it *our*—"

"Grey," Carter cut in, "I just got a text from Win. He said he has an opening around three, you guys can meet then?"

"No. Tell him I'll call him when I have an opening."

They were alone in the lobby, except for a few stragglers messing about with tissues and hard candies just outside the door. The brothers shoved themselves forward, peering into the ballroom as though it were a top-secret nuclear base under fire from aliens, and motioned the others forward. Great. That didn't attract any attention at all.

And the brothers were so unobtrusive to begin with, in their black caps and clothing, gold glinting on their wrists and fingers. They looked like extras from *On the Waterfront*.

Of course, she'd forgotten for a moment what the rest of the crowd looked like. Sure, it was a mix. She'd seen enough with her own patients to know that just because a person was religious, that didn't mean that person was stupid; she would never make such an assumption or generalization, not when faith had so many positive aspects and was so valuable to so many people. And she of all people couldn't judge those who believed demons existed.

But the desperation of these people, the sadness in the air, set her teeth on edge at the same time as it made her demon heart skip a little beat. These people needed help; they had real problems. And yes, while it was true that some of their problems may very well have been—okay, absolutely were—caused by demons, not all of their problems were. Who knew what kinds of issues they were dealing with?

And instead of something that would really help them, would give them the tools to cope with their lives and feel good about themselves, they were being given gobbledegook about being possessed. As if all of their problems stemmed from that and once they exorcised whatever was living inside them, they'd be perfectly happy, and everything would be fine.

Life didn't work that way. One of the ways she was able to reconcile what she did for a living with what she did as Gretneg of House Io Adflicta was that without the negative emotions, people couldn't appreciate the positive. Someone who never made a mistake, never put a foot wrong or did something he or she was ashamed of or regretted later, wasn't emotionally healthy so much as sociopathic or a chronic shut-in.

People made mistakes; they erred in their judgment or acted rashly or whatever. Coping with and learning from those mistakes was what made them stronger and healthier. Blaming all of those mistakes on circumstances beyond one's control . . . well, it might be all the rage, but Megan found it very difficult to approve.

Not to mention that she had no idea how much Walther was charging these people. And quite a few of them looked as if they had to sell plasma in order to eat. Painfully thin arms stuck out from beneath threadbare thrift-store shirts with missing buttons. Too-short pants rode up to expose pale ankles, incongruous against arms so deeply tanned they looked as if they'd been imported from other bodies. Vinyl shoes covered feet, cheap polyester covered legs, sunburned skin covered shoulders.

Not all of them, of course. Scattered through the crowd were a fair number of people who looked as if they could buy and sell the others. No, there was really no way to stereotype the crowd, only a way to pity them.

She and the others found a place against the back wall, not far from the door, to settle. A chair would have been nice, but she couldn't have everything, and she didn't dare mention it. One of the brothers would have attempted to make her sit on his back; it had happened before. Being in the room with a gang of demons was bad enough. Having one of them drop to all fours so she could use him as a bench would be unthinkable.

To take her mind off both the anger building in her stomach at the crowd being taken advantage of and the absurd desire to start giggling from the memory of the demon-bench incident, she settled herself against Greyson and said, "Is everything okay? Did something happen with you and Win? Something I should know about, I mean."

He shrugged, his gaze still wandering restlessly over the crowd of obedient heads before them. "He wants me to do something for him, and I don't particularly want to, and he's being rather adamant. Not a problem, simply an irritation."

"Anything I can do?"

He smiled and looked at her, the worry gone from his face. "I can think of a few things, yes, but nothing that would be appropriate here."

Her reply was lost in the general uproar as Reverend Walther entered.

The meek, pajama-clad man she'd seen the night before had disappeared. Instead Megan stared at a man who looked like a cross between Liberace and Wyatt Earp. He wore a black broadcloth suit, and his hair swooped up in a pompadour to rival the highest horn-hiding demon hairdo. It gleamed with oil or shellac or whatever the hell he used to keep it in place. Instead of a white shirt he wore a hot pink one, with a black string tie in an enormous bow at his throat; it was tied so tightly his collar wrinkled. His head appeared to erupt from the bright fabric like a mushroom from the mud.

Most different of all was his aura, his energy. It waved around him, so thick Megan felt it whisper over her skin and so strong she shivered. It wasn't drugs or alcohol or anything like that, turning him from a man into something like a high-powered light. It was his fervor, his fanaticism.

The crowd, perhaps too awed to continue speaking after their first enthusiastic burst of welcome, hushed almost immediately. The atmosphere in the room changed. It was as if Walther's energy filled it, and the audience's answered, as if he'd pulled something vital out of them to flavor the air.

But along with that flavor was fear and sadness. Emotions Megan recognized and forced herself not to want to absorb. Roc, of course, had no such compunction; she saw his beady little eyes darken.

Did Walther's do the same? Did he somehow—no. No, he didn't. The man was nothing if not human.

Greyson must have been thinking the same thing. "He's certainly an energetic little cur, isn't he?"

"I didn't think he'd feel anywhere near that powerful," she agreed. "He certainly didn't last night."

"Hmm. He apparently wasn't as powerful as this, even a few months ago. Basically came out of nowhere back in June. He'd been doing the exorcisms and dabbling in some faith healing, if you can believe the ridiculousness of that, but in June he started to catch on. Attendance at his bizarre little church rose, donations jumped up, that sort of thing. Makes you wonder, doesn't it?"

"How do you know that?"

He shrugged and settled himself more comfortably against the wall. "I looked him up online after you fell asleep last night. And made a few phone calls."

"You didn't sleep?"

He shook his head.

"Did you sleep at all?"

"Eventually. Don't worry about me, darling. The point is, he was a quiet, dull little nobody until recently. Now he's filling the ballrooms of horrible budget motels. Why do you suppose that is?"

"Did he make a deal with the devil?" she asked, only half joking.

He smiled, squeezed her hand. "Not with any I know. But . . . hmm."

"What?"

"No, nothing. I just wonder . . . no. There has to be some other explanation."

"But what were you thinking?"

"I'll tell you later. I think he's about to start banishing demons to Hell or whatever silliness. As if he could do anything of the kind."

Megan looked back toward the front of the room. Greyson was right. Walther was preparing to begin; at the same moment she looked up, the rest of the room bowed their heads, and Walther began intoning a long, wordy prayer so histrionic it made Megan nervous. He was a true believer, she knew he was, but the speech was so devout it felt fake.

She let her mind drift and the words turn into nothing more than a rush of sound in the background, rising and lowering in volume and pitch like a song on a far-away radio. She'd been so busy trying to settle herself to wonder if anyone in the room was readable, or if they all had that horrible emptiness the hotel employees had had the night before. She hadn't thought to check if any of her demons were in attendance either.

Roc still sat on Maleficarum's shoulder, having a whispered and, Megan imagined, highly amusing conversation. Certainly the two of them looked as if they were about to burst into hysterics. She'd never seen Maleficarum's eyes so bright.

"Roc," she said, "ask them to show themselves. I want to keep an eye on them and make sure everything is okay."

Actually, she wanted to see if perhaps some of the people in the room were without Yezer. As far as she knew, every human being in the world had one; she'd killed hers at sixteen and had thus been without one for fifteen years, but although Roc didn't attempt to lead her astray, he was technically hers.

But being without one had made her an anomaly. She wondered if somehow Walther really was banishing Yezer, and the hotel employees the night before had been without them, and that's why they'd felt so bizarre.

If her Yezer—those in her Meegra—had been banished somehow, she would know about it. But they weren't all hers.

Those who were began appearing, exploding into existence like bizarre and incredibly unattractive popcorn popping. Okay. Most of the people in the room appeared to be local, and their Yezer were hers.

"Good idea," Greyson murmured. "Gives us a better idea what's happening."

She smiled again, pleased, but the smile faded when Walther finished his prayer and, without warning, yanked a man out of his chair and dragged him to the front of the room.

"You! I can see the demon at work in you! What is your name, and what has been done to you?"

The Yezer on the man's shoulder gave Megan a cheery wave. Beside her Maleficarum snorted.

"I—I'm Matt. I've been gambling. I can't stop." Tears thickened the man's voice; his pain reached out to lick at Megan's hands. She'd been torn between laughter and calling the police herself. Now the first emotion disappeared, washed away by a red tidal wave of fury. How dare this man take advantage of these people, how dare he damage them—

"You haven't been gambling. The demon has been gambling. What did he make you do, Matt?"

"I bet on horses. On sports. On how many seconds before a light turns green, on which elevator will come first, I play cards . . ."

"That's not you doing it, Matt. It's that beast inside you. It is the evil being which has attached itself to you and wants to send your soul straight to Hell!"

Several audience members gasped; Walther had, as he shouted the last few words, made a sweeping motion with his arm, his finger pointed as if he was condemning the entire room along with poor Matt. Which maybe he was, for all she knew.

Probably not, though. The Yezer on Matt's shoulder

and the one at his feet appeared totally unconcerned. One of them was picking at his toes, the other scratching behind his ear.

Matt began crying in earnest. "Help me. Please help me."

This was appalling. This wasn't healthy. Megan itched to run over to Matt and pick him up off the floor, to give him her card and the number of the local Gamblers Anonymous chapter.

"I can't help you. You can't help you." Walther was really warming up now; sweat ran down his cheeks. "Only Jesus can save you. Only God can cast out that gambling demon and give you back your soul."

"I lost everything. I took out a second mortgage on my house and gambled all the money away. I can't do this anymore . . ."

Walther placed his hand on Matt's head. "I'm speaking now to the demon trying to steal Matt's body. It's Reverend Bill Walther, you unclean beast. Show yourself! In the name of God, identify yourself! I command it!"

Beside Megan, Maleficarum's big body shook with laughter. Roc had completely given up attempting to be silent; nobody but herself and the demons could hear him anyway. Same with the rest of her Yezer. Those bothering to pay attention were rolling on the floor, or lying flat on the pads of air above their humans' shoulders, their shrieks of shrill laughter forming a background like demonic church bells pealing over the shouting of the reverend.

Even Matt's scream didn't drown them out. Sweat

beaded Megan's own head too. The screaming and Walther's yelling and the demons' laughing made her a little dizzy; the realization that Walther had essentially put Matt into some kind of trance, watching Matt's face transform as his already battered psyche struggled to give Walther what he wanted, to create a demon for him, nauseated her. She swallowed hard.

"I am Azazael," Matt shrieked, in the manner of a Monty Python character. "You can't have this man back!"

Maleficarum hooted. Megan glanced over and found Spud and Malleus hanging on each other, their blunt-featured faces red with suppressed laughter. On her other side Greyson and Nick were biting their lips and staring at the ceiling; Carter just looked bored and annoyed.

Greyson caught her looking. His lips brushed her ear. "Azazael was a major player in Hell. The chances of him hanging around in this moron's body in order to put twenty bucks on USC are pretty slim, don't you think?"

"I never know what a man will do in order to bet on football," she responded automatically.

Greyson's hand slid down to her behind and stayed there. "Some of us have other interests as well."

"Really? I never would have guessed." But she let him keep his hand there—they were against the wall, and nobody could see anyway—and flashed him a quick smile.

"Be gone, demon! In the name of Jesus, be gone! I command you to leave this man alone!" Walther's right hand flew into the air, pointing at the ceiling. For a moment he looked terrifyingly like John Travolta in *Saturday Night Fever.* Megan wondered if the Bee Gees were going to start playing in the background.

Yes, perhaps she was being flippant. She couldn't help it. At least she wasn't behaving like the brothers. Fat tears rolled down their cheeks; they looked on the verge of stroking out.

Matt screamed again. Megan caught a glimpse of his face—talk about someone having a stroke—and wanted to slap herself for forgetting, even for a second, what was actually happening and why they were there. That man's already fragile emotional health was being further compromised; who knew where this could lead, what kind of trauma he was experiencing, whether this demon persona his fevered and desperate subconscious was creating would stick around after the so-called exorcism?

"You are gone! Be gone, foul thing!"

Matt collapsed.

Unfortunately, so did Maleficarum. He huddled on the floor next to Megan, shaking with laughter. That was bad enough. What was even worse was that the movement caught Walther's attention. He stormed up the aisle—he reeked of Hai Karate, sweat, and psychotic—grabbed Maleficarum by the hand, and tugged.

# Chapter Sixteen

"No, you can't—" she started, but Maleficarum was already pulling away from Walther's hand.

"This man needs my help," Walther informed her. "God has ordered me to help him."

"Don't be scared, brother!" someone shouted. "You can be saved!"

Maleficarum gave Greyson a helpless look. Megan knew exactly what Greyson was thinking, at least. To leave at this point, before they'd seen anything un-usual—or, rather, anything that went beyond the spe-cial superdeluxe crazy and into the sort of supernatural crazy that had characterized the night before—would mean this had been a wasted visit, and they couldn't afford to waste any time. She was acutely aware that somewhere out there someone was scheming to kill her, and she knew Greyson was too.

On the other hand, the thought of Maleficarum being subjected to such a thing mortified her. How the hell would he fake his way through that?

Of course, she, Greyson, and their friends seemed to be the only ones in the room who failed to see what a fantastic idea it was to let Maleficarum be exorcised. Malleus and Spud made incoherent mewling noises, they were laughing so hard. Roc had fallen to the floor with Maleficarum and stayed there. The laughter of the Yezer had increased to the point where Megan started fantasizing about the quiet and peace found in textile mills.

"What is your name? Why have you come to me today?"

Maleficarum shot Greyson a terrified glance. "I . . . I dunno."

"Don't be shy, brother! God knows everything. He sees into your heart."

Maleficarum looked down at his chest, then back up. Megan's lips twitched. No, this wasn't funny. It was not funny. She had a duty not to laugh; she was a psychiatric counselor, for fuck's sake, she could not start finding this horror show funny.

"Think maybe I oughter go." Maleficarum tried to turn away, but Walther grabbed him.

"That's the demon, the evil beast possessing you, speaking. It wants you to leave, it wants you to—"

"Aieeeeee!"

Megan jumped. She'd had no idea Maleficarum was capable of such a scream. Apparently he'd decided the best way to get out of being exorcised was to imitate Matt; his panicked glances at her and Greyson, the trapped look in his beady eyes, spoke of the kind of desperation that led animals to chew off their own legs.

Walther looked almost as shocked as the others, but then Megan saw his eyes. The flash of confusion left them, replaced by calculation, replaced by fervor.

He was a true believer, all right; she knew that. But in that second she saw the showman, saw him realize that Maleficarum was faking and decide to continue anyway.

The sleazy scumbag.

"Tell me your name, you foul thing! You do not belong in this man, you do not belong in this world! Name yourself, demon!"

Maleficarum's expression changed from panic to agony. Megan held her breath. What name would he come up with? Oh, please let him catch what he was supposed to do, oh—

Maleficarum glanced at her, at Greyson. He squeezed his eyes shut, threw his head back, and howled, "Joseph!"

The moment of confused silence that fell over the room was one of the longest seconds ever in Megan's life. Reverend Walther looked completely taken aback; he opened his mouth, but whatever he said was drowned out as the demons in the room began their hysterics again.

The humans, the audience, didn't find it so amusing. They seemed not to understand quite what had happened and waited patiently for Walther to continue. They reminded Megan suddenly of people who in medieval times would have gathered in hordes to watch executions, who would have attended Elizabethan bear baitings. People who wanted to see others suffer, who thought that through that suffering they could themselves feel cleansed.

It wasn't fair of her, she knew. The audience was there

because they wanted help. They were desperate for it. They weren't simply gawking; if anyone was doing that, she was. But they seemed so cold, so inhuman . . .

Her breath caught; her fingers closed around Greyson's arm. Apparently they closed pretty damn hard too, because he winced and tried to pry her hand off. "Ow, shit, that—what? What's wrong?"

She didn't answer. She was too busy looking, tuning out whatever bullshit Walther had started spouting again, while Malleus moaned like a bad actor doing a death scene. That empty feeling, that sick absence of feeling and warmth and . . . vibration, the absence of energy, had caught her again.

At the far end of the room was another entrance to the ballroom, a single door rather than the double ones they'd come through. It had been closed. Now it was open, and Elizabeth Reid stood just inside it, with her hands at her sides and a blank expression on her face.

Behind her . . . behind her was a man, one of the most nondescript men Megan had ever seen. Her gaze seemed to slide off his features; there was nothing to catch her eyes, just the vague impression of features and dark hair.

That emptiness loomed around him. The hairs on Megan's arms stood on end. What the fuck was wrong with him? What was he?

"That man," she managed to say. She didn't look away from him, afraid that if she did so he would disappear. "The one behind Elizabeth."

"Where?"

How did Greyson not see Elizabeth? Oh, right. He

wouldn't know what she looked like, would he? Remembering that brought her back to earth a bit. "She's just inside the other door, the dark-haired—"

"Oh, fuck. We have to go." His hand closed around her arm, tugging her to the side. "We have to go now. Malleus, Spud, get your brother, we have to go right—"

White light flashed in Megan's head, searing pain like she'd never felt before. It blinded her, it burned, she couldn't see or think or do anything, and somewhere she vaguely knew Greyson was dragging her across the floor.

The light eased up enough for her to see Maleficarum leap up from his position on the floor. Through the spots in her vision she saw him coming toward her, evading Walther's grasping hands, heedless of the audience's confused sounds, which seemed to come from miles away.

Elizabeth Reid's smile taunted her, followed her, as Greyson pushed Megan out of the room and across the lobby, with the others grouped like pallbearers around them.

The sun hurt her eyes, still sensitive and blurred from whatever the hell had happened inside the ballroom. Greyson appeared haloed in white spots. She wanted to ask him what was wrong, but his expression, seen between floating balls of light, did not invite questions; it was the face of a man who'd seen a ghost. So she kept her mouth shut until they'd piled into the back of the truck and Spud had peeled out of the parking spot at Greyson's urgent command.

She glanced back in time to see Elizabeth Reid

exiting the lobby. Somehow she didn't think that boded well.

Greyson sighed and leaned back with his eyes closed. His hand found hers, held it tight. A shiver of fear danced up her spine. What could be so bad that he didn't want to tell her? The last time he'd been this reluctant to give her information, she'd been up against an actual Legion of Hell. She could only hope that whatever the problem was this time wouldn't be as dangerous, but somehow she suspected her hope was in vain.

"Just tell me," she managed. "Whatever it is."

His lips tightened, as if they wanted to smile but couldn't summon the strength; his voice was barely audible. "I never thought I'd actually see one. I didn't even think they still existed."

"One what?"

"Lord Dante, I'm sorry. I never meant for him to grab me, I din't. I just couldn't 'elp but laugh, seein' as 'ow they was being so silly and all, an' then he—"

"Never mind, Maleficarum. It doesn't matter." Greyson cleared his throat, lifted his head. "We have a bigger problem."

He hadn't let go of Megan's hand. She pulled both into her lap and turned to face him. "What?"

He hesitated. For a second she thought he wasn't going to tell her, that he wanted to think about it first to be certain. He didn't like to say anything until he was absolutely sure he was right, she knew; she would have believed it was something he'd learned in law school if she didn't suspect he'd been that way all his life. He didn't like to be wrong.

Finally he spoke. "It's an angel."

"Don't be silly, Grey," Tera started, from the seat behind them. "Angels don't—"

"They do exist, Tera. We were just in the presence of one. Although why . . . well, who the hell knows why they do the things they do."

Megan licked her lips. "Seeing as how it tried to kill me last night, I'm guessing this isn't the angels-bless-and-guide-you type of angel."

"No angel is that type of angel. They're all complete bastards. Dangerous ones. Fuck!"

Tera's hand pulled at the seat as she leaned forward. "There's no evidence in Vergardering's files that angels actually exist. None. Our records go back to ancient Rome, and in all that time there hasn't been a single confirmed angel sighting."

"Of course there hasn't." He glared at her. "They don't generally announce themelves. And they *are* rare."

"It felt like a demon," Megan said.

"Angels is real, all right." Malleus looked pale beneath the black brim of his hat. "Seen one before. Musta been a hundred years back at least. Yeh, it were, 'cause Victoria were on the throne. Seen it at a party, a gathering like our one now. Scared the life out of me, it did."

"So you should be able to see them," Tera said. "But you didn't see this one."

"Weren't lookin'. If Lord Dante says it's an angel, it's an angel, Miss Tera."

They'd pulled into the long drive of the Bellreive; trees lined the edges and cut the bright sun. It made the SUV's interior feel icy, or perhaps it was simply what the men were saying. Megan shivered. It didn't seem possible. Not that angels existed but that they were the bad guys. She supposed it made sense that demons would see angels that way, but she wasn't a demon.

Greyson had told her once that God had nothing to do with demons, that he had very little to do with anything, in fact. The afterlife was the afterlife, and people went where they thought they were going, and there were hundreds, if not thousands, of gods. He wouldn't lie about such a thing.

But even if he had, which she didn't believe, she wasn't a demon. If angels and demons were locked in some sort of battle—again, which she didn't believe, and she was pretty sure she would have seen evidence of it by now if it were true—why would an angel be after her, when she was human? What possible reason would an angel have to want to kill her?

It was the most important question and the one she most didn't want to ask. The one she feared asking.

But she feared a lot of things. And part of her job was encouraging her patients to face their fears. She didn't always succeed at it, and she didn't always do it herself; being a psychological counselor didn't make her any less susceptible to normal foibles and fears, just more aware of when she was succumbing to them.

But she tried. It was all she could do. So she took a deep breath. "Why would an angel want to kill me?"

"It's possible someone paid him to," Greyson said. "That when the *litobora* attack didn't work, they hired an angel to finish the job."

She digested that while Spud braked just beyond the

valet stand, waiting for the okay to pull up and sur-render the vehicle. She appreciated him not interrupt-ing the conversation but found herself wishing that just once he wouldn't be so polite; she could have used a few minutes' distraction. Pretending everything was okay often led to feeling as though everything was okay, and while it would be fleeting and illusory, it would have been nice to feel okay. As opposed to terrified, hunted, and sick.

Then Nick spoke, and everything got so much worse. "You're assuming the angel attack is related to the *lito-bora*. It might not be."

"Jesus, Nick, thanks for the cheer." She turned to look at him. "How many people do you think have rea-sons to kill me?"

"I'm not saying it's definitely more than one, just that we can't assume anything."

He was right, and she knew it. She hated it when that happened.

"I still think you guys are crazy to say it's an angel," Tera said.

"And I say I'm not," Greyson replied. "Do you have a better theory? Any theory at all? Or do you just enjoy contradicting mine?"

Tera folded her arms over her chest and glared at him. "No."

"Good." Greyson nodded toward the windshield; through it Megan saw one of the valets coming for them. A car had just swerved around them as they idled like a barnacle in the drive. "Go on, Spud. We'll talk more upstairs."

# Chapter Seventeen

Lots of things did not appeal to Megan. Skydiving, for example. Root canals. Lamb chops. Things she simply avoided.

Way up at the top of that list she would have to put "Making a list of people who might want me dead and why."

It wasn't the making of the list that was so awful, although—actually, yes, making the list was really fucking awful. Watching the list grow longer and, worse, realizing that she could provide legitimate reasons why any one of the people on it might want to see her dead . . . it felt as if she'd swallowed an anvil.

Oh, no, wait. The best part of all was getting to see how fucking enthusiastic her supposed friends were.

"Don't forget any of the patients of that Fearbuddies group or whatever it was called." Tera popped a tortilla chip into her mouth. "They might be pissed that you killed their therapist."

Roc plucked a chip from the bag too. "Wouldn't they have come after Megan sooner?"

"Not necessarily. Maybe they've been saving up the money, just plotting and planning all these months, obsessing over her—"

"Hey, do you think whoever it is has pictures of her all over his house?" Roc's beady little eyes lit up. "Like, they've drawn big black X's over her face and written 'Die Megan Die' on their walls, or—"

"That's enough, Roc," Greyson said.

"I'm just wondering, I mean, someone who's been planning and waiting that long must really hate Megan, right, so—"

"Cut it out, Roc," Megan said, and not a moment too soon; she thought Greyson was going to leap off the couch and throw Roc out the window. Not that she would mind. And not that it would hurt Roc. Because of what he was, he could simply dematerialize before he hit the ground. But—

"Hey!" She sat up, Roc forgotten. "The angel. He could fly. I mean, he could materialize and dematerialize. Just like Yezer. Right?"

"Apparently," Greyson said.

"So can the Yezer follow him wherever it is he's going? If we tell them all to look for him, maybe they can find out where he's staying."

Roc nodded. "We're already on it. But don't forget, he can hide himself from us too, so I don't know how effective that will be."

She slumped. "Shit, I had forgotten."

Roc had reported to her in the morning the results of his conversations with the Yezer who'd been guarding the door the night before. Unfortunately, none of them had seen anyone except Elizabeth Reid, so there wasn't anything to go on with that.

"It's something to start with, though." Greyson patted

her thigh, a second's touch that made her feel a little better, while he spoke to Roc. "It's very possible you guys will be able to see him if he dematerializes. Certainly if he wanders into the psychic plane, you might be able to feel him, if you're paying attention."

"He'll feel like a demon, right?"

"Yes."

"Why?" Tera and Megan asked at the same time.

Greyson smiled, a thin smile that bore only a touch of humor. "They're related to us. Not exactly the same but close enough."

"I guess that makes sense," Tera said.

"Yes. The only good thing Vergadering ever did was to wipe those psychos off the planet. Of course, they didn't entirely succeed, obviously, but then you witches do tend to be overconfident."

"Whatever." Again with the tortilla chips. Tera's eating habits never ceased to amaze Megan; she had a demon's metabolism and a cast-iron stomach. "I told you, there is nothing in the files. No proof. No evidence. So I'm not sure how you think we warred with angels when as far as we're concerned they don't exist."

"Yes, I know. But trust me, you did."

Tera's eyes narrowed. Her hand, full of tortilla, stopped halfway to her mouth. "Wait a minute. You said they're related to you. Did we think they were you? Did you—you guys used us to beat them, didn't you."

Greyson shrugged. "Don't look at *me*. I wasn't even alive then."

"And even if he was," Nick cut in, "we would have done whatever we had to do. Just like you did. Do I need to remind you of Columbia? How about Oakton? Do you remember the demon children your soldiers murdered? The camps you sent innocent demons, demons who didn't fight, into?"

"Okay, what the hell is your problem?" Tera actually dropped her chips. "You've been sniping at me all day. What did I ever do to you?"

"It's what you witches did to me," Nick snapped. "It's your—"

"Nick." Greyson's head was turned away from Megan; she couldn't see his face. But Nick could. He stopped, paled a little, and nodded.

The silence following was as awkward as any Megan had ever experienced, and her work certainly lent itself to uncomfortable moments. Her instincts at work led her to remain quiet herself while her patients worked through whatever they needed to, or at the very most to ask a quiet, unobtrusive question if the conversation seemed to have stalled completely.

But this wasn't work. These were her friends, and somehow they'd hit a wall again, a wall that had something to do with Nick and whatever horrors his past contained. They'd brushed up against the subject before, but Megan had never actually spoken to him about it. It was private, and one thing she didn't find at all disorienting about demon culture was how much they all valued their privacy.

So she reached for a chip herself and forced it down her throat. It tasted a bit like sawdust, but that wasn't the chip's fault, and she needed the delay more than she cared about how she took it. "So do you think the angel's really after me, or does it just like hanging around Reverend Walther? Maybe it's not what attacked me at all."

"It had attached itself to that FBI agent," Greyson said. "It attacked her before you, remember?"

"It was there last night." The chip fell from her hands. "Right before it showed up today, it felt like everyone suddenly became unreadable. Just like those employees felt last night."

Greyson nodded. "Doesn't surprise me. I wouldn't have seen him if he hadn't been so absorbed in watching Maleficarum that he forgot to keep himself hidden. At least so I assume. I doubt he was deliberately unmasking himself."

"Maybe he was." Nick seemed to have regained his composure. "Maybe he was picking a fight. Taunting us."

"Anything's possible. I guess we—"

"Grey?" Carter appeared at the bedroom door; he'd been in there doing some work or whatever it was he did. Megan was never quite clear on the details, but she knew he was always available and always busy, just as Greyson had been for his boss Templeton Black.

Greyson had overthrown Templeton—protecting her, not to mention furthering his own interests—and had him sent to a Vergadering prison, where Templeton had died just before Christmas. An apparent suicide; they'd never discovered exactly how he'd done it, but he'd left a note.

Greyson was already up, walking across the room. "I'll be right back."

The others sat there, with Nick and Tera exchanging cautious looks and Roc cheerfully snacking. "So," he said, after swallowing another enormous mouthful. "Do you think whoever it is who hates Megan had to pay a lot of money to have her killed?"

Three hours later Megan was sick of TV. Sick of the suite. Sick of the Bellreive.

It wasn't that she was having a bad time. Once Tera and Nick had decided to bury the hatchet—figuratively—they'd actually gotten along okay, and if conversation occasionally suffered an abrupt pause when one of them, usually Nick, bit their tongue, it flowed easily enough the rest of the time.

But she was sick of this. Sick of Roc's gentle snores on the couch beside her. Sick of Malleus's ceaseless wanderings through the rooms, checking all the closets on every pass. "Lord Dante said make sure you're safe, m'lady, and I'll keep you safe, you c'n Adam 'n' Eve that."

"I do," she said, for what felt like the dozenth time and probably was. "You know I do. But you're getting on my nerves."

Malleus looked wounded. "You oughter have more care for yerself, you ought. Think what it might do to Lord Dante if something 'appened to you. Me an' Lif an' Spud, we fink you take too many risks, an' it's time you quit and settle down. No offense, m'lady, but Lord Dante needs—"

Nick leaped up. "What's that, out the window?"

"What?" Malleus hurled himself across the room

with the kind of speed that constantly surprised Megan; one didn't expect to see a tank move that fast, but the brothers all did when they wanted to.

She caught Nick's eye and smiled her thanks. Was it her imagination, or did his return smile look rather uneasy?

Well, so what if it did? There was plenty to be uneasy about. Attacks on her life and angels and the whole witch-demon thing and whatever it was Nick was carrying around with him.

"Nuffink 'ere," Malleus called over his shoulder. "I'll stay, though, an' keep watch for a few minutes to make sure."

"Thanks, Malleus."

Someone knocked at the door, and Malleus once again zipped over before the knocks resolved themselves into the complex little passcode the brothers had devised. For a second Megan's heart jumped in her chest, hoping it was Greyson back from whatever business had called him away, but he wouldn't have knocked, and it wasn't him. It was Carter returning just ahead of him.

He settled himself on the couch beside Nick. "You guys having fun?"

Megan rolled her eyes. "An absolute blast. I wish someone was trying to kill me every day."

"Thanks a lot," Tera said. "Here I'm sitting watching dumb TV instead of shopping, just to keep you company. The least you could do is appreciate it."

"If you guys are talking about shopping, I'm going into the bedroom." Nick smiled, but Megan couldn't shake the feeling that something was bothering him.

She couldn't ask, though. Not then, in front of everyone. So instead she just smiled. "We're going to talk about shoes for the next hour, Nick. Escape while you can."

"If you put it that way."

They all watched him go. That day he wore black jeans and a black T-shirt; Tera raised her eyebrows when he closed the bedroom door behind him. "He's kind of a touchy asshole, but he's awfully sexy."

"Tell me about it," Carter said.

Megan blinked; she had the horrifying suspicion her mouth had fallen open. It didn't matter, not one damn bit; it was simply the fact that she'd known him for months now, and it had never even—it made her ashamed of herself. Why should she assume he was straight? What was the matter with her?

He caught her look. "You didn't know?"

"I—no. I'm sorry. I don't mean to—"

"Of course I'm gay." He looked at her as if she had just grown an extra head. "Grey isn't stupid."

"Well, no, but I don't—"

"Maybe we oughter check and see if Lord Dante's coming back now." Malleus rushed across the room again; watching him was like watching a very large black tennis ball in play. "I'll just get th' door open 'ere—"

"I won't be having any children," Carter explained. "At least not the kind I'd need to have. Right? You know this. So I can't possibly overthrow him. Once he has a son, it won't matter so much, and he'll be more secure, but with how vulnerable he is already because you're human, he really needs to get moving—"

"That's enough, Carter." Greyson stood in the doorway. Icy cold energy danced over Megan's skin; his anger, the only emotion she could always feel from demons, translating as a frigid blast.

For a second she just sat there, totally confused. Why would he be so angry just because Carter was telling her something about demon tradition or culture or whatever? Lots of people grew up with cultural traditions; the whole "sons" thing was a bit sexist but wasn't such a big deal, really. Demons were pretty paternalistic—not to mention sexist, judgmental, egotistical, superficial, and a whole host of other social evils—so how this was—

Then it hit her, with the force of a semi slamming into her head-on. He was vulnerable because she was human. He was vulnerable because he didn't have sons to take over once he was gone, to strengthen his position. She remembered he'd mentioned it to her, all those months ago: *"Half the Meegra was ready to overthrow Temp and put me in his place anyway—he never had any sons to take over."*

He was vulnerable because they couldn't have children together. She was human. He wasn't. It was physically impossible for them to—unless she did the ritual. The one he'd tried to talk her into just the night before, without ever *once* mentioning how important it might be for their future. Not his, not hers, theirs. The future that apparently didn't matter to him anywhere near as much as it mattered to her.

All of this went through her mind in just a few seconds, a series of feelings like the images she got when reading people rather than coherent thoughts. Greyson must have seen them in her eyes or on her face; his went blank, the careful mask he presented to hide his emotions.

"Fuck." The word was so quiet she wasn't sure she'd actually heard it; for a dizzy moment she wondered if she'd somehow at this late date developed the ability to communicate telepathically.

Greyson closed the door very slowly behind him and stood perfectly still with his head bowed for a long moment. "Tera, Carter, Malleus, would you mind leaving us please? I think Megan would like to talk to me alone."

# Chapter Eighteen

She sat on the couch, unable to move. Unable even to look at the others as they retrieved Nick from the bedroom and left; she felt their eyes on her but refused to give them hers back. They'd all known this too, hadn't they? This was why Tera didn't seem to think she had any kind of future with Greyson, why Nick had interrupted Malleus and Malleus had interrupted Carter. They'd all known it, and they'd all kept it hidden from her. While she'd swanned along, tra-la-la, thinking—fuck. Just, fuck.

Ice cubes clinked into glasses, then cracked when liquor hit them. She didn't particularly want to be grateful to him for a damn thing at that moment but she certainly hoped he was pouring for both of them.

He was. She grabbed the glass he set in front of her as if it was a jug of water in the middle of a desert and knocked it back, not stopping until the ice hit her nose. Good but not good enough. She held the glass up and listened to him refill it.

"So," she said, picking up the refill. It was harder than she'd thought not to look at him. Part of her insisted she was wrong, that she was reading things into this, imagining a situation that didn't actually exist. Any second now he was going to ask her what was wrong, kiss her head or pull her into his arms on the couch . . . it wouldn't be the first time he'd sent others out of the room so he could be alone with her.

But not this time. She knew it, and every stupid hope, every silly fantasy she had, faded with each passing second.

And the bastard wasn't even going to speak first. He was going to let her do it, he was going to take that tactical advantage from her. Jesus, was everything a fucking game to him? Had he ever even cared about her at all?

Those questions choked her, fought to jump out of her throat and fling themselves at him in suicidal leaps. She refused to let them. Instead she said, "So who are you marrying, then?"

"Jesus, Meg. You don't pull any fucking punches, do you."

"Me? *Me?* I'm not the one who's been lying all this time, I'm not the one who's been planning behind your back and leading you on—"

"Not—damn it, do you think this is what I want?" The frustration and pain in his voice sounded genuine enough, but she couldn't trust that, and she couldn't look at him.

"Why wouldn't you? You'd—oh, right. Of course. I'm supposed to be your mistress, right? Or do I not even get to do that?"

Long pause. She stole a glance at him, quickly so he wouldn't see her looking. At least that's what she tried to do. Her head didn't seem to be in her control. None of her body did; she had to squeeze her glass hard as she lifted it to her lips, because she couldn't seem to feel the cold against her fingers.

Finally he spoke. "When was I supposed to tell you? Right at the beginning, when neither of us had any idea where this was going? You'd just been attacked and betrayed by demons. You'd just found yourself attached to them. Would that have been a good time to inform you that if you wanted to marry me one day, you'd need to become a demon? Assuming I did end up in a position where it became necessary?"

"You had plenty of other chances," she snapped. Arguing with a demon was bad; arguing with a lawyer was bad. Arguing with a demon lawyer was infuriating.

"Oh, sure I did. I could have mentioned it right away, when Roc told you about the ritual and you insisted you didn't want to do it. Or any other time since, when you insisted you didn't want to do it. What the fuck was I supposed to do?"

"You should have told me. You should have let me know this was—"

"Meg, darling, last night you refused to do the ritual even to save your own life. Was I really supposed to assume being with me was more important than that?"

Shit. He had her there. Mostly. "Don't you think I was entitled to all the facts? Don't you think I had a right to know all the reasons to do it, all the implications?"

He took a step toward her, then stopped when she glared at him. His face was pale, a little drawn; he looked extremely tired. She fought her instinct to get up and put her arms around him, cursed the fact that even in the middle of this conversation, that was her instinct. That no matter how hurt and angry she was—and both boiled in her stomach like a bowl of acid full of nails—she still loved him.

He leaned back against the wall. One hand clutched a glass full almost to the rim with straight scotch; while she watched he drank half of it off. "What if I had?"

"What?"

"What if I had told you?" His tone echoed oddly in her ears. Either she was on her way to drunk—she realized her second drink was almost gone—or he was simply speaking very quietly, in a subdued way she'd never heard. "What if I'd picked a moment—I don't know, three months ago or six months ago, or when the subject first came up—and we'd discussed it? What would you have done?"

"I don't know. That's not the point, the point is—"

"No, that is the point. That is *exactly* the point. When was I supposed to put that kind of pressure on you? On us? Would you have appreciated that? Some guy you've been seeing for a couple of months suddenly telling you about the ways you have to change your life if you want things to go farther? What if you'd decided it was too much for you to deal with and you'd left? Or what if you *had* done it?"

Her mouth went dry, as if she'd been drinking cotton balls instead of gin. "So you don't even want me to do it, that's what you're saying." She stood up. "You—fuck you, Greyson. I'm out of—"

"Sit down."

"Don't tell me—"

"Sit *down*." Pause. "Please."

It wasn't the most gracious request she'd ever heard, but he generally didn't say please unless it was something important. Something he really wanted—no, she was not going to start thinking about that.

She sat down, though. "What."

"What if you had done it, just for me," he said, as if the interruption hadn't taken place at all. "What if I'd somehow found just the right moment to bring it up—not too early, not too late—and you'd been understanding of why I hadn't mentioned it before, of course, since as time went on it became more and more glaringly obvious that I was leaving it too late. What if all that had gone perfectly, and you'd done it, and you regretted it? And blamed me? Would you like to spend the rest of your life resenting me because of everything you gave up for me?"

"That's not fair," she replied, but she couldn't put a lot of strength behind it. He did have a point there. It didn't make hers any less valid, but he did have a point. "You didn't give me a chance to make a decision."

"Life isn't fair, darling. That may be banal, but it is unfortunately true. I didn't think it was very fair of me to ask you to give up everything, not when neither of us knew where we'd end up and you didn't seem particularly interested in finding out. And then I didn't think it was fair of me to ask you to give up everything when you were so adamant about not wanting to. And let's be clear on this, since we're laying our cards on the table, so to speak. When I say give up everything, I mean everything. You wouldn't be able to keep doing your job, not the way you do now. Certainly the radio show would have to go. It makes you too vulnerable. And yes, there would have to be children as soon as possible. You've never even really mentioned wanting them."

Of course she wanted them. But when was she supposed to bring that up? How far into a relationship did one start talking about having children and not be seen as some grasping, desperate female with an iron biological clock attached to her ankle? Especially when she knew they couldn't have them naturally. Just as there were—well. She guessed she understood what he was saying, after all.

But the rest of it . . . Yes, she loved him. She wanted to be with him. Wanted to marry him. None of that was a surprise. But her work? Her radio show?

"What do you mean, I wouldn't be able to work? Too vulnerable how?"

"Oh, come on, Meg. It can't have escaped your notice that someone is trying to kill you."

"But that's not—"

"No, we don't know who it is or why. It may be you, it may be me. And in the years to come it probably will be me. You're not stupid. You know not all of my business is legal and that it sometimes involves disagreements that can't be settled with a friendly meeting. Sometimes problems have to be eliminated. Sometimes warnings have to be given. To have you out there, working a job that requires you to be alone with strangers, one that puts you in the public eye? Bad enough you do it now. If we're married? Impossible."

Her glass was empty, and she didn't feel as if she'd

managed to swallow a drop of it. "Why do I have to give up my job? Why can't you give up yours?"

"What?"

"No, really. Why can't you give up your job if it's so dangerous? Why do I have to be the one who loses everything? I mean, if we're really talking about this here, and not just as some kind of abstract concept. Why do I have to stop working, stop being human, stop being anything at all, and you give up nothing? Hell, Greyson, you don't even have to quit dating, apparently, you could just get yourself a series of girlfriends on the side and—"

"Jesus, is that what you think? Do you really trust me that little?"

"It's not a matter of not trusting you. I don't even know what you want! You haven't even said, this whole time, what you want. You've never said how you feel about me, where you want this to go. How am I supposed to even consider all of this when I don't even know how you feel, you won't even tell me?"

"What? You don't know how I—for fuck's sake, what do you think we've been doing for the last year? Do you even know me at all? Do you think I've just been playing with you this whole time? Do you have any idea how vulnerable being with you makes me, how dangerous it is for me—"

"Oh, sorry, I don't mean to inconvenience you."

"God *damn* it, that's not what I mean and you fucking know it. Or shit, maybe you don't. I thought you did. I thought we didn't need some fucking words—which you've never said either, may I remind you—to know where we stood." He shrugged and stared at his empty glass as though he'd never seen anything like it before. "I thought we meant more to each other than that, frankly."

Shit. He had to go and say that, didn't he? This time she couldn't stop the tears; they rolled down her cheeks, almost faster than she could wipe them away. They were talking about marriage and children, they were saying all the things she'd hoped they'd say someday, had assumed they would say—he was right. She had known where she stood. She had thought the words weren't important.

But this didn't feel the way she'd thought it would. Didn't feel like a beginning. It felt like the end.

Because it was. She couldn't do it. She couldn't give up her humanity, her job, and her radio show to become a sequestered housewife. There was nothing in the world wrong with being a stay-at-home mother or stay-at-home wife; she'd always assumed that she'd give up work for a few years if—when—she had a baby, that she'd arrange her schedule to be home after school once her child reached that age. It was one of the benefits of doing her kind of work.

But she'd never planned to give up her career entirely, for good. Not for five years but forever. And she'd always assumed—damn it, she'd always assumed it because it was the way it was supposed to be—that it would be a decision she made, one they made together. Not an edict. Not a condition. But a choice.

"If you really loved me," she managed finally, "you'd want to be with me anyway. You'd figure something else out. But the way you want it, I give up everything, and you get everything. You won't give up your life, I have to give up mine. You won't give up your work, I have to give up mine."

"Be reasonable, Meg." The pleading look on his face would have broken her heart if it hadn't already been shattered. "I make seventy or eighty times what you make. You wouldn't have to work. You could spend your days doing anything you wanted—"

"But what I want to do is work!" Fuck. For someone who was supposed to be good at resolving conflicts, she was not doing a great job. But then it was always so much harder when it wasn't simply advice given to others; the path wasn't so clear when you were walking on it yourself. "I worked hard to get where I am, Greyson, it's important to me."

"And my work is important to me. And far more lucrative."

"I didn't get a PhD so I could become your fucking concubine."

He winced. "It wouldn't be—forget it. You've obviously made up your mind. I'm a scumbag who wants to use you and lock you in a basement."

"That's what it feels like." The words came out hoarse, forced through her aching throat. "Greyson, can't you see, making me give up my job and everything—I don't think I can do it."

He poured himself another drink, glanced back at her glass. She nodded, and he took it and filled it. For a moment the only sound in the room was him draining his glass and filling it again.

"There is another option," he said. "I can't believe I'm saying this, but there is, if it's what you want. You—"

"If you suggest I be your girlfriend on the side, I will slap you."

"What the hell do you want, then, Meg? You don't want to marry me because of everything you'll have to give up. You don't want me to marry somebody else because—I don't know why. Do—"

"You don't know why? You can't even imagine why I might not want to be your other woman?"

"I told you yesterday, it's not like that. An arranged marriage is only—"

"An arranged—oh." The penny dropped then; she couldn't figure out how or why it took so long, but it did. "Win's daughter, right? Leora. That's why she's here, isn't it?"

He sighed. "Yes. Yes, Win wants me to marry her."

"And what did you tell him?"

She waited for his answer, waited through one of the longest and loudest conversational pauses she'd ever experienced in her life. She'd started to wonder again if this was simply a terrible nightmare, and he wasn't speaking because she was about to wake up, when he said, "I told him I'd think about it."

"You told him you'd—you're thinking about it? You're fucking *thinking about it*?"

"I was trying to put him off until I had a chance to talk to you, to really explain. I wanted you to go to Florence with me, remember, I thought we could—"

"No. I can't fucking believe you would do that to me. Now Win thinks you're considering making me your mistress? Who else knows that? Did you even think how that makes me look?"

"Did you even think how it makes *me* look, to have you refusing to do the ritual for me?"

"You never asked me to do it for you!"

"Fine." In a flash he was across the room, hauling her to her feet by the shoulders and looming over her, his dark eyes flaring red, his body throwing off heat like a furnace. "I'm asking you now, Meg. Will you do it for me? Do the ritual and be with me. Give up your job and be with me. Marry me, damn it."

His lips cut off any answer she could have made.

# Chapter Nineteen

Harder, and harder still. It wasn't just a kiss, it was a demand; it was him taking charge of her, taking control. And in the blink of an eye she was controlled, helpless in his arms, her own twining around his neck, tasting salt from her tears as their lips devoured each other's and the flaring bright energy in her, his energy pouring into her, threatened to send her over the edge before anything even happened.

His lips left hers to travel down her throat, kissing, biting. His fingers squeezed her ribs almost hard enough to hurt. "Please, *bryaela*. Please."

She wanted to say yes. Would have wanted to say yes even if his hand hadn't slid up under her shirt and found her breast, even if his mouth hadn't found her earlobe and was sucking on it the way he knew she loved.

But she couldn't. She couldn't because he'd lied to her; no matter what his reasons or how sensible they were, he'd kept something that important from her. She couldn't because asking her to give up her job and her show would have been different if he hadn't presented it as a requirement.

But those were incidentals. She could have gotten over them. What she couldn't get over was the idea that he'd actually considered marrying someone else. He'd actually thought, even for a moment, about taking another woman into his bed, making another woman the mother of his children. She couldn't get over the way he'd spoken of her giving up her job as if it was nothing but refused even to consider giving up his.

Of course it made more sense financially for him to keep his. He wasn't lying about how much more money he made than she did; she had a box full of diamond jewelry and several stamps in her passport that attested to that, not to mention the other things, things he bought because he was thinking of her, or he thought she'd like them, or whatever other reason he'd come up with.

But he hadn't even considered it. Hadn't even paid her the respect of pretending to consider it. Hadn't even attempted to work out some kind of compromise, to discuss it. As if her work meant nothing, was just play-acting she did while waiting for some man to sweep her off her feet.

Too bad that was exactly what had happened. And too bad she couldn't let him do it again.

All of this passed through her mind in a flash, while his lips found hers again, searingly hot, almost driving her few coherent thoughts away. Without her realizing it, her hands had found his bare skin under his shirt, the smooth, strong expanse of his back, the row of *sgaegas*—little spikes—down his spine.

Those *sgaegas* were what he'd shown her to convince her that he was really a demon. And she'd touched them, and her body had gone hot and shivery, and suddenly she wasn't kissing him anymore because she was crying too hard.

"You lied to me." The words choked her; she pushed him away, and it felt as if she'd ripped something out of her chest. "All this time you kept this from me, you didn't tell me. How can I trust you? How can you act like my job is nothing?"

"I don't think it's nothing." She could feel his eyes on her, pleading with her, but she refused to meet them. "But it's too dangerous, it's—"

"If it's too dangerous," she said, her voice shaking, "then it's been dangerous all along. You said yourself, whoever's after me now might be after me because of you. And you never mentioned it. You let me be in danger all this—"

"No! God, no, it's—"

"Can you promise me that? Can you swear that just being with you, just seeing you, didn't put me in any danger? That someone isn't trying to kill me right now because of you, and it has nothing to do with my job or anything else?"

The room was so cold. His chest was warm, she knew, the way he always was, the kind of warmth she could curl into, the kind that would never fade.

But she couldn't do it. All she could think of were lies and betrayals and the idea that everyone had known but her, that they'd all been conspiring to keep it hidden, that she'd looked like a fool to everyone.

The idea that he'd known she might be in danger and had still not told her.

"No." He took another step back. "No, I suppose I can't."

The pale green carpet had a subtle pattern to it; she hadn't noticed it before. Now it swirled at her feet, blurred with her tears, became nothing more than a fuzzy wash of color as her eyes lost focus. They stood there, a few feet apart, so close she could have reached him in a few steps.

She'd never felt so alone in her life.

He cleared his throat. Paused. Did it again. "So what are we doing, Meg. I don't . . . What do you want to do?"

It wasn't a matter of what she *wanted* to do. She wanted to take his hand and go to bed. She wanted him to sit down so she could curl up in his lap and feel, just one more time, totally cared for. Totally understood and approved of.

But she wanted more than that out of life too. So she said, in a voice that didn't sound at all like her own, "I think I should get my own room. I don't think I can do this. I can't trust you anymore."

He made a small sound. She couldn't look at him to determine if it was a laugh or . . . something else. She didn't think she could stand knowing. "No, you stay here. I'll have one of the boys come later for my clothes. Unless you want me to pack now."

"No. I'll get my own room. I can get my own, you know. I have my own money, I don't need yours." It was a low blow, and she knew it; she saw him twitch out of the corner of her eye. "I'm going to go now."

This couldn't be real. It couldn't be actually happening. She glanced at the clock; half an hour had passed.

Half an hour, and her life had fallen apart into sharp, horrible little pieces.

"Okay. Okay, then. I'll . . . I'll have them bring your things."

She walked toward the door, every cell in her body screaming to stop. To turn around, to run back to him. She loved him. Surely they could work this out. Couldn't they work it out? How could this be happening?

How could he have considered marrying someone else? How could he have even *considered* it?

She paused in the doorway for a second. He stood where she'd left him; his eyes looked damp. She quickly skipped over them. The late-afternoon light streaming through the windows caught his dark, shiny hair, the sharp bones of his face, and the almost hawklike nose. She loved those bones. Loved that face. Loved *him,* fuck, what—

But he'd lied. Not about unimportant things but about their future. And she couldn't accept that, couldn't forgive him, at least not yet, if ever.

She closed the door.

She stood for a second staring at it, listening to the sound of it closing over and over again in her head. Then she made her way down the hall on legs she couldn't feel and called the elevator for the lobby.

"Megan?"

The gentle tapping on the door was like a hammer bludgeoning her skull.

"Megan? Can I come in?"

Tera. Megan lifted her aching head and tried to find the door; her eyes, emptied of tears, were so dry her lids felt sticky when she blinked, and her vision was blurry.

"Yes, come in." Her throat was sore; no big surprise, considering she'd barely managed to get through the endless paperwork of getting herself a room and made it up there—a nondescript hole on the seventh floor— before being messily, horribly sick. Her wonderful stomach struck again.

Her fumbling fingers finally grasped the lock. Turning it felt like lifting a thousand-pound weight, but she managed it and stepped back.

Tera held up a white paper bag. "I brought you some fries."

*Ugh.* "Thanks, but I'm not really hungry."

The room wasn't a suite, just a typical hotel room like Elizabeth Reid's—bed jutting out from one wall, small desk, TV. It was still the Bellreive, so still larger and nicer than a budget hotel, but the difference . . . She didn't want to think about that. Or about that suite. Or especially about who was in it.

Tera sat on the bed. "Nice room."

"You should have seen the desk clerk. He looked at me like he thought I was going to leap over the counter and try to eat his brains."

"I'm not surprised. You look like you died three days ago."

Normally Tera's casual bluntness didn't bother Megan, even amused her. Not today. "Yeah, thanks, Tera. I feel just great, so—"

"No, Megan, listen." Tera took her hand. The touch

of her skin felt odd, too cold somehow; it had to fight to reach her through the numbness. "I know I'm not the most sensitive person in the world, okay? I know that. But . . . you look bad, like you *feel* bad, and I don't want you to feel that way. It bugs me. I want you to feel better. So you should talk about it if you want. And I won't say anything mean about him, I promise."

Megan shrugged. This wasn't helping her fight the hard ball of pain in her chest. "Say anything you want about him. I don't care."

"Yes, you do."

"I don't."

"I don't believe you."

"He lied to me, he . . ." She'd thought she was out of tears. She was wrong. "He lied to me, Tera. I never thought he would do that. Not like that. Not about us. And then he . . . he asked me to marry him, like that was supposed to fix everything, and I said no . . ."

She couldn't finish. Couldn't say anything more. And lucky for her, she didn't need to, because Tera reached out and held her while she cried.

It may have been five minutes or half an hour, she didn't know, but when she pulled away, she felt better. Just telling someone what happened felt better. Well, of course it did. What the hell did she do for a living, if talking to someone about problems didn't help?

It was her job. And it was important. And she was good at it. She still had that; she was still who she was. She still wasn't alone. Somehow that gave her the strength to wipe her eyes, to lift her head and straighten her back. "What time is it?"

"Almost six."

"Shit, I have to get ready. Dinner's earlier tonight, there's going to be business discussions, and . . ." He would be there. God damn it, why did this have to happen now? When she'd have to see him that night and every night for the next week? When she was—oh, shit, she was trapped in a hotel with a bunch of demons who would be absolutely fascinated to know what had happened.

She wasn't just going to have to see him and pretend everything was fine. She was going to have to see all of them and pretend *she* was fine. Wasn't that just fucking great?


She made it to the reception room by seven, luckily. Late was not a good thing to be when one was attempting to behave as though nothing at all was the matter, but it was a close call. She'd spent almost twenty minutes with cold wet teabags over her eyes, and Tera promised she looked fine, so she guessed she did, even if she felt like a bombed-out building. One thing about Tera, her judgment was believable.

Tera had also gone back up to the suite to get her a few things, her suitcase and makeup bag. That was when Megan realized Nick had been sitting on the floor outside her door the entire time.

He stood beside her now, his arm reassuring under her hand. Roc sat on her opposite shoulder; she felt bracketed by the two of them, encased in what little protection was available.

"I assume you'd like a drink," Nick said.

She nodded. The room was fairly full, with the Gretnegs and their assistants . . .

"He's not here yet. He told me he'd come late, so it wouldn't look so odd you two arriving separately."

She forced a smile and hoped it hid her embarrassment. "Was I that obvious?"

"No. But I can imagine what I would do in your situation. I mean, if I ever actually sustained any kind of relationship."

"Honestly? Right now I think you're better off."

They'd reached the bar. The demon behind it—one of Gunnar's, she thought—poured her a gin and tonic, but before she could get it to her lips, someone touched her shoulder.

Leora. *Shit.*

The girl's wide blue eyes met hers without guile. She was wearing a dress almost the exact same color; the effect was to make her look like innocent youth on legs, and Megan feel like a crone in her own black sheath. All of her dresses were black, damn it. She hadn't brought anything else. If she hadn't been so busy being miserable and sick, she would have tried to run out and buy something, but as it was, she was just hoping desperately to make it through the evening without bursting into tears.

Her entire body hurt. Her chest felt as if a bomb had gone off inside it.

"Megan, I was hoping I could talk to you for a few minutes?"

Megan shot a desperate glance at Nick, but his lifted

eyebrows indicated the same sort of helplessness she felt. To deny the girl would be rude, and demons were fairly obsessive about manners. On the other hand, though . . . the thought of actually speaking to Leora made her palms sweat.

No real choice, though. So she nodded. "Sure."

Leora led her off to the side, to the pole where she'd had her discussion with Greyson what felt like hundreds of years before. A new wound opened in her chest.

"My dad wanted me to talk to you," Leora said. "He thought maybe if we got to know each other better, it would help."

Oh, no. Oh no no nonononono. "I don't think we have any issues that need helping."

"Well, you know, he thought maybe if I talked to you, you could talk to Greyson. I mean, I'm not supposed to tell you that, I don't think—I'm not very good at all of this stuff." The blush on her cheeks was very becoming. Megan wanted to slap them. Not so much because she was angry but because it was the only way she could think of to make Leora stop talking.

"I think Greyson can make up his own mind about things."

"Well, yeah, but my dad says it's because of you that he hasn't said yes yet, and . . . I'd really like him to. I think you and I could be really good friends. I don't want to get in the way of what you two have, but I want to—"

Greyson walked in.

Leora hadn't finished talking, but Megan heard her voice only as a dull buzz in the background. She was too busy staring, not sure if she was proud or furious that he looked perfectly elegant and well rested, as if not a thing had happened.

Leora followed her gaze. "Oh! There he is."

He saw them. The faint down-twist of his mouth and wrinkle of his brow gave Megan some satisfaction but not much. She was just miserable, and things did not improve when he approached them.

"Ladies," he said, with a fluid bow that raised her suspicions. "How lovely to see you both. I hope you're not talking about me."

Leora giggled. "Of course we are."

He cocked his right eyebrow. "I assume you want me to ask what you're saying? I won't, you know."

Megan's suspicions were confirmed. He was drunk. He never behaved like some Regency ballroom rake unless he was completely plastered. She'd only seen him like this twice; it took a shitload of liquor to make a demon drunk, and he didn't tend to drink that heavily. He must have spent the entire afternoon guzzling scotch.

Of course, she'd spent hers puking and sobbing. So she couldn't help feeling he'd had the better idea.

Leora didn't seem to realize anything was wrong. "You know we'll tell you anyway."

"Oh, *you* might," he replied. Carter brought him another drink; he tossed it down his throat with an efficiency that made Megan wince. "But Megan? She'd never tell. And I'd certainly never ask her. Her responses to my questions are horrible."

Megan choked out what she hoped was a close

approximation of a lighthearted laugh. "Maybe you just don't ask them correctly."

"Maybe I don't, at that. I always thought women found begging undignified. Looks like my suspicions were confirmed."

"Maybe begging doesn't mean anything when it feels like all the decisions are being made *for* us instead of *with* us."

He scowled. "Seems to me the decision was entirely yours."

"Oh, does it? Here I was thinking—"

Leora gave a delicate cough, more suggestion of a sound than an actual one. Megan practically jumped. She'd forgotten the girl was there.

"I think we're ready to go in to dinner." Leora pointed at the open double doors, at the others filing through them.

"Of course." Greyson hesitated for such a brief time that Megan felt certain Leora hadn't noticed it; then he offered Leora his arm. "Shall we?"

She giggled and took it, blushing again, while Megan wished desperately that an entire herd of angels or FBI agents or exorcists would burst into the room and end her misery right there.

No such luck. Instead she stood alone and watched the two of them sail off to the doors until Nick and Roc came to get her.

It wasn't until she settled herself in her chair—blessedly they'd been shifted around for this meal, and Greyson was across from her rather than right beside her—that she realized the implications of her discussion with Leora.

Did Win truly believe she was the reason Greyson hadn't agreed to marry his daughter? And did he want that marriage badly enough to kill for it?

# Chapter Twenty

It was the longest meal of her life. The food was probably delicious. She didn't taste a single bite of it, but she forced it down anyway for appearances. The others seemed to be enjoying it, so she figured she should too.

She'd thought having Greyson opposite her would be easier than having him beside her. She was wrong. If he'd been next to her, she wouldn't have had to see him every time she looked up from her plate. Looking to his right didn't help, because Leora was there. Looking to his left was worse; Justine eyed her like a cat watching a broken-legged mouse.

In all it was an absolutely shitty evening, made only slightly worse by how vulnerable she felt—any one of these people could be plotting to kill her—and worse again by watching Greyson swallow scotch like water.

They'd just had their desserts placed in front of them—some sort of gooey cake covered with berries and whipped cream, which Megan couldn't even think about attempting—when Winston cleared his throat.

"Last year we agreed that control of the lake-perimeter nightclubs would be shared equally by myself and Gunnar. I think he'll agree it's working well so far. But there's a problem in the Boarwell area. We've had a few *rubendas*—employees in the clubs—disappear, and a chef at Galloway's. Which has made the police nose around, as the chef was human."

"You had a human employee?" Justine directed her question at Winston but didn't stop staring at Megan. "Why on earth would you do such a thing?"

"He was an incredible chef," Gunnar cut in. "You must have seen the review in the *Hot Spot*. Business doubled after we lured him away from—"

"There had to be one of us who could do just as well. Humans can't be trusted. They shouldn't be anywhere near us."

Megan wasn't sure who the rest of the table was staring at harder, herself or Greyson. The latter was inspecting the bottom of his empty glass with the sort of concentration most people reserved for lottery tickets or subpoenas, but he must have felt their gazes.

He sighed and looked up. "Now, Justine, let Winston finish speaking before you rush off on one of your little tirades, won't you?"

Damn it. She should have spoken up, not him. She was letting herself get distracted. Not a good idea, especially not in this gathering.

Especially since that distraction—well, all of the distractions—had kept her from asking him the night before whether he thought Justine's hatred of humans had led her to try to eliminate Megan not just from the demon world but from the land of the living entirely.

Okay, so now she had motives for two at the table. Who wanted to step up next?

Justine opened her mouth, her beautiful face

darkening, but Winston stepped in quickly, shooting Greyson a surprised glance as he did. "The point is, we have reason to believe they're being attacked by another demon. So we'd like to nip this in the bud here. Have any of our rubendas been stepping on toes? Or is our arrangement causing problems with any of you? You all agreed last year to let us control the area."

His voice stayed perfectly calm, almost affable, but his anger tickled cold on Megan's skin.

The others were silent. Winston sighed. "Do we have a rogue demon in the area? Are any of you aware of any problems in other cities that may have been carried into ours?"

Greyson's voice cut through the general demurrals of the others. "Why are you so sure it's a demon?"

"What else could it be?" Gunnar pushed his empty plate away—the smear of fruit juice on it looked like blood—and leaned forward. "What else could attack us without our sensing it or being able to overpower it? Seven missing now. We've been on alert for weeks. Are you suggesting a human might have been able to sneak up on them and injure them?"

"It could be a witch," Baylor Regis said. His gray eyes shifted toward Megan. "Has your witch friend been asking questions?"

"It's not a witch," Winston said dismissively. "We've performed a *betchimal* on all of them. They would have been aware—"

"Well, well," Greyson drawled. "Been holding out on us, Win? You never mentioned you know how to do the *betchimal*."

"Nobody asked me." Winston seemed to realize this answer didn't exactly satisfy the others; Baylor looked as if he wanted to slit Win's and Gunnar's throats. "I'll be happy to teach you all, of course."

"No need." Greyson accepted yet another drink from an unobtrusive servant. "I can do it myself."

What? He'd said—oh, of course. Tera had performed it on her that morning; he must have been listening. She wished she could add it to the long list of reasons to be angry at him, but she couldn't; she wouldn't have expected anything less, really.

"I'd certainly like to learn it," Justine snapped. "Don't speak for the rest of us, Grey."

"I wouldn't dream of speaking for you, Justine. I have far too much intelligence even to be capable of it."

The entire table held its breath. Justine looked mollified for a second, then realized she'd been insulted; her face flushed, and her icy blast of rage almost knocked Megan out of her chair.

Shit, he really was wasted. She'd never seen him be so rude, at least not without an excellent reason.

"Good thing it wasn't my intelligence you needed just before Christmas." Justine's eyes had gone so narrow they'd almost disappeared; for a second the beautiful woman disappeared, and something much less attractive sat in her place. "It's—"

He yawned and turned away from her. "Win, you were saying nobody sensed their attacker? If they've disappeared, how would you know? Do you have a witness?"

"We did have one," Gunnar said, after a pause. "He

didn't see anything but was close enough that the *betchimal* would have alerted him, had it been a witch. So a magical attacker, gone unsensed . . . it has to be another demon."

"Not necessarily." Greyson looked at her; their eyes met. Something flared in his, just for a second, and it was gone. "It could be an angel."

It took a moment for his words to register in her head. She was too busy trying to keep the spasm of sharp pain his gaze had summoned from showing on her face and too busy trying to keep her mind from worrying at Justine's last sentence like a pit bull with a rodent. Which was just what it felt like: something dirty and riddled with sickness being tugged, a bit at a time, from the depths of her memory.

"What the hell would an angel be doing here?" Gunnar said. "I thought Vergadering had wiped most of them out, and they'd gone into hiding."

"Oh, there's one here. I saw it this morning." Greyson lifted his glass, nodded at a servant. Megan wondered if he would be able to stand when this hellish meal finally reached a conclusion.

Of course, if he wasn't, little Leora would probably be perfectly happy to help him back to his suite. Now, there was a cheerful thought.

What the hell had Justine done for him? Just before Christmas . . . he wouldn't be where he was . . .

Templeton Black had died just before Christmas.

But that was a suicide. He'd left a note and everything. Tera said Vergadering didn't suspect any foul play. Surely if there had been reason to suspect any, they would have suspected it. They suspected just about everyone, of everything.

What difference did it make? It was over between them. Done. He wasn't her concern anymore.

She wondered if any sentence she'd ever uttered to herself had hurt more. No, it didn't seem so. That was a personal best in the pain and misery department.

"You saw it?" Winston's face—always susceptible to coloring, the way all blood demons seemed to be—went bright red. If he'd had a beard, he would have looked like a very angry Santa Claus. "And you didn't tell us?"

"I believe I just did."

"Yes, but—yes. I would have thought you would tell us sooner."

Greyson shrugged. "I would have thought you'd have mentioned your *rubendas* going missing sooner, Win. Want to explain why you didn't?"

"That's different. That's private business."

"You thought there was a rogue demon in the city, and you didn't warn the rest of us." Baylor glared at Winston and Gunnar each in turn, like a teacher trying to figure out who threw the spitball when her back was turned. "Grey is right. You should have told us before this."

"We weren't sure what it was," Gunnar said. His black hair was slipping from its Gordon Gekko sweepback; he reached up to try to push it out of his eyes but only succeeded in making it worse. Gunnar didn't handle stress well. "We didn't want to alarm anyone."

Justine licked whipped cream off her fingers. "That was totally irresponsible."

"And totally our business," Winston replied. "Have any of the rest of you had issues? No? Then it doesn't matter."

"It does to me. You let the rest of us take a risk." Justine's impressive bosom heaved.

"We take risks every day. We're taking a risk even bringing this up. What if it's one of you, trying to start a war?"

"If it is one of us," Justine said nastily, "it's probably Greyson. He's the one giving us all some bullshit story about an angel."

"He's not." Here, at last, was something Megan felt qualified to comment on. "I saw it too. And I—I felt it last night. It attacked me."

She wanted to look at him, to see if she'd done the right thing. She refused to let herself. What she said and did wasn't his business anymore either. Which was the way he wanted it, as he'd proven the minute he'd said "I'll think about it" to Winston.

Winston, who looked at her with his eyebrows raised. "You felt it? You can feel it?"

Of course. Not "It attacked you?" Not "Are you okay?" But "You can feel it?" The others leaned forward—all except Greyson, of course, who was fiddling with his cell phone—making her feel as if she was in an interrogation room from an old TV cop show, with a bright naked lightbulb in her face.

"It feels like an absence," she said finally. "Like an empty space. I think the Yezer can feel it too, if they focus."

"Particularly if it travels on the psychic plane," Greyson added. "But I don't think it's doing much of that."

Gunnar pushed his hair back again. "Oh? Why not?"

"I think it's found several people to use as shields."

"Like who?"

He hesitated. "It seemed particularly interested in that reverend person over at the Windbreaker. That's where we saw it. Megan seemed to think it was feeding on the gullible little crowd, which makes sense, if you think about it. Zealots like that, desperate to believe . . . ripe for the picking, really."

"Perhaps I'm in the wrong business," Baylor said.

Greyson raised an eyebrow. "Perhaps you are."

Another uneasy hush around the table. Megan waited for someone to call him on his rudeness, but no one did. Funny, that.

Win cleared his throat. "The point is, I suppose, that this angel is here. And it may be after us. Is that correct?"

There were general nods around the table.

"I have my Yezer on the alert," Megan said.

"But we don't just want to sit and wait for it to attack us. We want to find a way to solve the problem," Win said. "Since you and Greyson saw it, why don't you two see what you can come up with? We'll all think tonight, and we'll meet in the afternoon to go over plans. You two will have something for us then, I hope?"

Okay. Maybe nobody else felt awkward—she was fairly certain Greyson was incapable of feeling anything at that point—but she certainly did.

But she was pretending nothing was wrong. Vulnerability was not her friend in this situation, and she wouldn't show any. So she smiled, as if that was a great idea, and nodded, and very carefully avoided looking at Greyson.

But she felt him watching her just the same.

# Chapter Twenty-one

The view out her window wasn't anywhere near as lovely as the one from the fourteenth-floor balcony she'd been on the night before, but she didn't give a shit. She looked out the window but didn't really see; through the glass more buildings sat silent, watching her right back, their edges blurred.

Everything was blurred. After that hideous meal had finally ended, she'd grabbed Nick and two bottles of bourbon from the bar and hauled all three back to her room. Her puny, lonely little room.

Greyson had left with Leora. She'd put her hand on his arm, and they'd left together. The fact tore at her like a flesh-eating virus.

She could have called Tera. Maybe she should have. But somehow thinking of Tera's sympathy—damn, Megan had always known there were genuine feelings under there somewhere—combined with her bluntness and . . . whatever. No, if she were honest, the way she was always trying to get her patients to be, she'd admit she didn't want Tera because she wanted someone more connected to Greyson. She wanted a man who wouldn't try to make her talk.

And hell, she had to be with Nick anyway, because he

apparently still wanted to guard her. So why bring Tera in, so they could snipe at each other and flirt while she watched? If there was a worse way to spend an evening than nursing a broken heart while two very attractive people threatened to have angry sex in front of her at any moment, she had no idea what it could be.

"So what do you think?" he asked. "Think the Yezer will be able to track down the angel?"

"I imagine so." She looked out the window again. This time the view seemed colder; she pictured the angel out there, watching her. Saw it again falling over the edge of the roof, relived the moment when she'd thought she killed it and couldn't remember how it felt. It was all overshadowed now; she had much darker memories taking up space. It didn't seem right that Greyson loomed so much larger, so much higher, but she couldn't change it; she'd thought she killed a man, yes, but she'd done it to save her own life. And, as much as she tried not to think of it, he hadn't been the first person—or whatever—she'd killed, had he? She'd killed the Accuser. She'd killed Ktana Leyak.

Had Greyson killed Templeton Black? Or ordered him killed? He'd been ready to ask Winston for the death of Orion Maldon, because Maldon had threatened them—had conspired against them and tried to end their lives.

But why would he openly discuss having Maldon killed with her and not tell her about Templeton?

She hadn't asked either. Well, why would she? The man was found dead in a Vergadering prison cell with a suicide note. Was she supposed to guess that was murder?

Nick sighed. "I don't know what to say, Megan."

Not a topic she wanted to get into. "Don't say anything. Just pour me another, okay?"

He did, topping up both their glasses. "I never thought this would happen. I always thought you—"

"I don't want to talk about it."

"Okay. Sorry. I just thought you might want—"

"I don't."

He smiled. "Okay, so you don't. What do you want to talk about?"

His straight dark hair fell over his brow; below his strong chin the top couple of buttons of his tuxedo shirt hung open, the bowtie long discarded and the pants exchanged for jeans.

Megan hadn't bothered to change. They both sat in the middle of the bed, with the bottles between them. She'd tugged the skirt up so she could sit cross-legged. It felt like a naughty picnic.

She smiled back. "Read any good books lately?"

"Tons. Let's discuss them all, in detail."

So they did. They talked about books for an hour or so, while the level of bourbon in the bottles steadily dropped and her mood grew giddier and giddier, the kind of manic joy that signaled a huge crash waiting in the wings. They moved around on the bed, finally ending up shoulder-to-shoulder against the headboard, giggling at the TV and everything else.

Nick emptied another glass. "So have you heard anything from your family? Since the funeral and everything, I mean."

"No. I didn't expect to, and they didn't disappoint me."

"Sorry."

"It's okay," she said, and she meant it. Would have meant it even if she hadn't been drunk enough not to care. Greyson, the lying bastard, really had had the right idea; this was much better than trying to sit through that hideous meal feeling as if she'd swallowed a paperweight.

He'd left with Leora. *Shit.* "Really. I mean, maybe it would have been different if all this demon stuff hadn't happened to me. But I have people now, I mean, I have . . . I have the Yezer. And Tera and Brian. You know?"

He nodded. "It really makes a difference. I didn't have anybody for a long time after—after my parents died. Then I met Grey, and he didn't care what had happened or what I was."

"What do you mean?"

He hesitated, and her question, which she'd asked in genuine curiosity and nothing more, took on new meaning. "You don't have to tell me. I mean, if there's something you're not comfortable—"

"No, it's okay." He poured another glass, downed it. She wondered if he was as drunk as she was. Probably not, but she figured he was close; he'd finished his bottle and was sharing hers. "Well. You know I'm half incubus."

She smiled, raised her eyebrows a little. "Yeah, I kind of remember that about you."

"Oh, right. Of course."

He was so close to her; she reached out and stroked his knee. "It's okay. Really. Go on."

"Well. My mom was a succubus. She was . . . she was

great. I mean, she was strict, but she was great. And my dad was part psyche demon—a *vershet,* you don't really find a lot of them in America—and part water demon. He'd really wanted me to take after his side more than hers, but I'm pretty balanced. Anyway. His family didn't really approve of her, and they didn't want them to get married, and that didn't change after I was born."

"That sucks."

"Yeah. So things seemed okay, he found work finally—the family business wouldn't hire him, and they talked him down all over so nobody else would either— and I remember things being okay. I mean, I remember being pretty happy. And then . . . I came home one day, I was six, and Vergadering was there, and they wouldn't let me go inside."

"They were dead?" Megan asked softly.

He nodded. "They'd had a fight, I guess. I mean, I assume; nobody ever told me or let me see the files or anything. And he killed her, and then he killed himself."

"Oh my God." Her right hand tightened on his knee; her left flew to her throat. "Nick . . . I'm so sorry."

"Yeah. Yeah, it pretty much sucks." He gave her a rueful smile, sad around the edges. "And then her family wouldn't take me because they, um, they thought it was my fault. And his family wouldn't take me because I was part incubus and they thought she'd corrupted him and I was unclean or something. I don't know. So I went into a Vergadering school, a boarding school for orphan demons or those of us whose parents were threats or just . . . whatever."

She thought about his energy, so angry and so hurt.

And about his comments to Tera. "I guess it wasn't a very good place to be."

He gave a short, bitter laugh. "Yeah. You could say that. You could definitely say that."

"Weren't there demon schools? Places for the orphan demons?"

"Things were pretty different then, Meg. I mean, it was only thirty years or so ago, but a lot has changed in that time. Back then, because of what my father did, it wasn't just my mother's family who considered me tainted. It was demon society as a whole. My father's dishonor reflected on me. It wasn't until I turned sixteen and won a scholarship that things changed, really, at least for me. I met Greyson, and . . . well, like I said, he didn't care."

Tears stung her eyes. She blinked them back, ducking her head in hopes he wouldn't see. "Yeah. I guess he wouldn't, would he?"

"Megan . . . what happened?"

Shit. She didn't want to do this. "You'd have to ask him."

"I did."

"So you know what happened."

"I know his side of it."

"What did—no. Never mind. I don't want to know. Tell me something else. Tell me what exactly it is you do in Miami. You never would tell me before."

"I'm a male stripper."

Her mouth fell open. "Really?"

"No. But it sure would be interesting if I was, wouldn't it?"

It wasn't that funny, but Megan found herself laughing anyway, laughing way too hard. The room blurred around the edges and tilted gently like a rowboat on a breezy lake, not enough to make her sick but enough to remind her that she was sitting on a hell of a lot of alcohol.

"How come you don't have a girlfriend, Nick, when you're so funny?" It came out "sho funny." She hoped he hadn't noticed.

"Do they have anything to do with each other?"

"They do to me. And to any woman with a brain."

"Maybe I just haven't met any women with brains, then. Or maybe they don't think I'm funny. Or they just don't like me."

"How can they not like you?" Shit, that came out a little loud. "I like you."

"I think you're drunk."

She giggled again. "I think so too. Are you drunk?"

He considered it. "I think so, yeah."

"Good. I don't want you to be sober when I'm drunk."

"Right. That would be rude. Of me. I would be rude, if I were sober."

"Yes, you would."

This struck them both as funny, and they laughed until Megan started to feel a little sick from it and shook her head slowly. "But seriously. Why no, no girlfriend? The whole time I've known you, you never dated anyone, did you?"

"No. Don't date much. I just—"

"But you're . . . you're an incubus. How does that

work? Don't you need—oops. I shouldn't ask that, should I?"

She wanted to know, though. And she was drunk enough to ask. Drunk enough to sit up and face him, with her palm on his chest. Beneath it his heart pumped steadily, vibrations rising into her hand.

"I don't mind," he said. He patted her hand, paused, patted again, with great solemnity. "Yes, I do need, as you put it. But long-term . . . I couldn't date a human, could I, and keep everything secret? And demon women don't really want much to do with me. They think— let's just say I have a reputation."

"What kind of reputation?"

His raised his eyebrows. "Not a good one. That whole thing with my father? Passes down to me, remember?"

"Ohhh, right. So you date humans, then. For a short period of time."

"You could say that. One night is a short period of time, isn't it?"

"So you sleep with a lot of women," she said, and saying it shocked her. What was she doing? Her hand was still on his chest; her legs were bare, her long skirt pushed up almost to her hips. She was alone in a hotel room, drunk, nursing one hell of a broken heart, with a very sexy man. Whom she genuinely liked. Genuinely cared about.

Which was why she shouldn't even be considering what she was pretending not to be considering.

Greyson had left with Leora. What were they doing now? Talking? Laughing? Other things? Was he looking at her the way he'd always looked at Megan?

Nick either hadn't caught on to her drunken calculations or was ignoring the way the air had just stilled around them. Or he was too drunk; her voice wasn't the only one beginning to slur a little.

"I do, yeah. I'm not really proud of it."

"Oh, yes, you are."

He burst out laughing. "Okay, yeah, maybe I am. Some. But seriously, Megan. I'm too old for that shit now. It's kinda pitiful. Pitiful and . . ." Their eyes met. "Lonely. It's lonely."

"You shouldn't be lonely. You're so great, why should you be lonely?"

"Nobody else thinks so. Thinks I'm great, I mean." He blinked, as if he was having trouble focusing. "They think I'm scum. And maybe they're right."

"No. No, they're not."

He shook his head slowly, more of a sway than a shake. "I think they are. Otherwise, why'd I still be alone? Must be something wrong with me, you know? Makes me nervous when I really like somebody, and then I just feel all weird about 'em. And they all seem so silly, the ones I meet. They're not like you, all smart and stuff. They—"

"You think I'm smart?"

He blinked. So did she. It was a little hard to keep him in focus. "Well, yeah, 'course. Grey said so all the time, and how intre—inster—inneresting you are, and he wanted me to meet you—"

Even with the random and shameful thoughts she'd been having before, she wasn't sure why she did it. It might have been the thought of his lonely life and an attempt to make him feel better. It might have been that he was complimenting her and she desperately needed those compliments, when she felt lower than plankton on the intelligence-and-happiness food chain.

It might have been that in that deep dark place in her mind, the one that was all her own—she'd never had a personal demon, until Roc, and had still done things she shouldn't have done, things that other people did because their demons persuaded them to—she was still thinking of Greyson leaving dinner with Leora and wondering what they were doing. Wondering if he had any idea how much it had hurt her to see them walk out together. And that deep dark place wanted revenge.

Or it could have simply been that the alcohol wasn't erasing that pain as effectively as she'd hoped, and she thought she'd try something else.

Whatever the reason, she leaned over and kissed him. Hard, right on the mouth, with her hand still on his chest trapped between his ribs and her own.

His surprise jumped through her; her shields were down, and apparently so were his. She hadn't expected to be able to read him so easily; well, she couldn't *really* read him, but she definitely felt his shock. Felt his short, sharp burst of desire shoot straight to her ego and stay there.

"Megan," he started, but she didn't let him continue. She rested her hand on the back of his neck, where his short black hair tickled her fingers, and kissed him a little harder.

Her heart pounded. This was wrong, this wasn't right, she should pull away now. Now, before things went any farther. A kiss could be forgotten, shrugged off, and never visited again, leaving not a trace of awkwardness in its wake; it was no big deal, especially not between very drunk friends. She should stop, apologize, and start thinking of passing out.

But she didn't. After a second his hesitation turned into something else; his hand found her cheek, his lips moved against hers, and—*holy shit*—she found out what kissing a sex demon really meant.

It meant a blast of pure sexual energy, sharp and strong enough to make her entire body go stiff. It meant feeling herself melt over him; when his tongue found hers, she cried out, overstimulated already. It meant feeling herself go liquid, filled with a hot wave of desire that made her want to yank up her dress and shove down her panties and let him have her, however he wanted.

She'd experienced something like it when they'd met at Mitchell's restaurant the year before, when he hadn't known who she was. That had just been through his eyes, through the touch of their hands. This . . . this was that pulsing need times ten.

Still not the way it felt with Greyson. Nothing could touch that. But this was awfully damn good, she had to admit.

"We can't," he mumbled. "Shit, we can't do this."

"Yes, we can." She slid her hand over his chest, curled herself down to kiss his throat. So odd, so different from Greyson. Nick's skin was musky and spicy, cooler to the touch. His chin moved, giving her better access even as his hands rested on her upper arms, as if he was going to push her away.

But he didn't. She pulled his earlobe between her teeth, sucked on it, felt another sharp burst of desire, stronger this time. "We can't, Grey's my best friend, I can't—"

"Shut up." She closed his mouth for him, took the energy he'd given her and sent some of it back; he gasped. He was right about how wrong this was, she knew he was right, but she couldn't seem to remember it. Couldn't seem to stop herself.

Couldn't seem to stop wondering if Greyson and Leora were doing the exact same thing seven floors above them. If they'd already finished and were sleeping, snuggled together in that big four-poster bed. If he'd put a ring on her finger—

Nick pushed more power into her, thick with lust, red-tinged with anger the way his energy always was, and she stopped thinking. Instead she let him drive his fingers into her hair and shift her so she lay beside him. Let him take charge, deepening the kiss, her lips parted beneath his. Power flowed into her, so strong it made her shake.

"We can't," he whispered. His hand slid up her ribcage, stopped just beneath her breast, radiating warmth. "We shouldn't be doing this."

"I don't care." Her hand found the hem of his shirt and snaked up beneath it, across his smooth bare skin. No *sgaegas* there; this was a different back. A different man.

And she knew it. Knew she wasn't kissing Greyson. Knew the power coursing through her wasn't Greyson's. It was warm, and it made her entire body tingle, but it wasn't his.

Which was just what she wanted, despite the twinge of pain, the feeling in the back of her mind that this was even more wrong than she'd thought at first.

But Jesus, he was a good kisser. Without her mind's consent, her body ached and throbbed; her right leg wrapped itself around him and pulled him closer, close enough that she could feel him hard against her, so close he made a small sound in the back of his throat, and his hand finished its journey. She arched her back into it. He touched her so lightly, rubbing his palm in slow circles over her hard nipple through her dress. She felt it through her entire body, gave him a gasp of her own, and captured his mouth with hers, let her teeth close gently over his tongue. More power, more lust, surged into her.

She took that feeling and sent it back to him. In a second it came back to her again, a tidal wave of passion she couldn't escape. Couldn't do anything with but let it wash through her and chase away the last vestiges of her sanity. The last vestiges of doubt.

She let her hands play, slid them around to feel his chest, his heart pounding beneath. Ran them down his sides, then around again to his front, finding him through his jeans and rubbing hard enough to make his breath catch. "Shit, Megan."

Her dress bunched at her waist, pushed by his impatient hands as his mouth traveled down her throat into her open neckline. Her heart pounded. Her body went loose and liquid everywhere, dark lust pumping through her veins, her fingers scrabbling at his zipper. He caressed the top of her thigh, his fingers just brushing the edge of her panties and dancing away, brushing the edge, then dancing away, until she realized she was shifting her hips, trying to get those fingers where she wanted them, frustrated that they weren't there—

At first she thought the knock at the door was just her imagination, the voice calling her name even more so. Until it came again, more insistent. So loud she couldn't ignore it.

Greyson was outside her door.

# Chapter Twenty-two

Nick realized it only a second after she did. They sprang apart as if they'd just found a dead cat in the bed between them.

"Megan, please open the door. I need to talk to you."

The mirror above the dresser showed her a wild woman, hair bunched up in the back and falling in tendrils down the side of her face, the straps of her gown falling off her shoulders. Her lips looked bruised, her mascara smeared. She looked as if she'd just been doing exactly what she'd been doing.

Nick turned shame-filled eyes toward her. "Shit, I knew he'd do this, fuck, I—"

"Just calm down, okay?" She tucked her hair back behind her ears, yanked out the pins holding it up, and tried to fluff it out. "We didn't do anything."

Greyson's voice through the door again. "Meg, please. I know you probably don't want to talk to me but . . . shit, please."

"We didn't not do anything." Nick seemed to be fighting some sort of minor war with his shirt; he tucked it in, then apparently decided that didn't look right and tugged it back out, then repeated the process. "I mean— shit, I'm drunk—we did do something. We did."

"No, actually, we didn't. A little kissing is nothing."

"It won't be nothing to him," Nick muttered.

Megan was inclined to agree and furious about it. Why the hell was she worried he might find out? They'd broken up, hadn't they? What fucking business was it of his whom she kissed? Or let feel her up, a little bit. She refused to feel that guilty about it; they hadn't gone any farther than a couple of high school kids might have while their parents went out to pick up pizza. What was it, first base? Possibly second? She had no idea, but she was pretty sure third was bare skin, so—oh, whatever. It hadn't gone very far, was the point.

"*Bryaela,* I know you're awake, I can see the lights on. Please don't make me say this through the door."

One more glance in the mirror, a quick swipe under her eyes and over her mouth in an effort to normalize. The doorknob pressed cold into her hand while butterflies jumped in her stomach. It was not really the most comfortable sensation, on top of the nerves, fear, and misery. Not to mention the sex energy still simmering in her blood.

"I'm begging you, please—"

He was leaning against the door frame, looking every bit as drunk as he had earlier but considerably less elegant. Dark circles edged his eyes; his shirt hung open, and a splotch of what she was pretty sure was spilled scotch decorated his chest. The smell of scotch and cigarette smoke blew through the doorway in waves. Not unpleasant but worrisome; fire demons, especially, smoked sometimes. It gave them energy.

But he didn't do it often, and never in such quantities as to reek of it.

Seeing him was like hitting herself in the chest with a hammer.

They stood there, staring at each other, for what might have been a minute or maybe an hour. She didn't know. Her head still spun; she didn't know if she should yank him into the room and hold him or tell him to fuck off and leave her alone. He'd lied, yes, and she was still pissed off about it. Still incredibly hurt by everything else.

But she loved him so much. And he looked so sad, and she missed him, God how she missed him.

"Thank you," he said. "May I come in? Please?"

She nodded; given half a chance, she was pretty sure her voice would squeak or croak or something else both embarrassing and unflattering. Voices had a way of being sneaky like that. So she just nodded and stepped back, closing the door behind him.

"Meg." He started to reach for her, then stopped. His gaze stayed fixed on her face. "Meg, I'm so . . . fuck. I'm, I'm sorry. I'm sorry. I should have told you sooner, I fucked up. I fucked everything up, and I'm so fucking sorry."

Her mouth fell open.

He'd never said that before. Never. Not to her, not to anyone; she'd never heard the word "sorry" cross his lips about anything. Her eyes stung. Of all the things he could have said, he probably couldn't have picked one that would have meant more to her.

Maybe he knew that. Maybe he didn't. Ordinarily she would have thought for sure he did, but he didn't indicate it, didn't pause to see if his words had any effect. "But I know we can . . . I've been thinking about this. About us. We can work this out, can't we? Figure something out. I can't . . ."

His fingers touched her cheek. Her eyes fluttered shut. Now she was crying, damn it. "I know I never said—oh. Hey, Nick."

Megan turned her head to see Nick standing just outside the bathroom door with his hands deep in his pockets and his gaze cast down. "Hey."

"Listen, would you mind giving Megan and me a minute? I just need to talk—"

He stopped so short Megan didn't realize at first what was happening; for one wild second she thought he'd finished his sentence and she'd simply misunderstood the words.

Then she realized he was glancing around the room, an expression of pure horror spreading across his face. His fingers pressed tighter against her cheek, dropped to her hand and squeezed. His energy breezed over her hand, up her arm, a weak imitation of what it would be had they been closer but still enough that she felt it slip over her, felt it recede. "No."

What? No what? What had he—

She looked again. Saw Nick, his hair mussed. Saw the faint smear of lipstick on his throat, the rumpled cover on the bed, the two glasses cuddled together on one of the small bedside tables. *Oh fuck, oh no, oh shit*—

Greyson shook his head. "No. No, tell me—I'm,

shit, I must be crazy, right? Drunker than I thought?" His forced laugh echoed in the dead air. "Please, please tell me—"

Megan opened her mouth, ready to say something— she wasn't sure exactly what. Probably something along the lines of "What are you talking about?"

She never got the chance. She didn't know what did it—the look on Nick's face, maybe, shameful and distraught. Or possibly it was that when he touched her— when he slid his power over her—he felt Nick's energy, felt the last vestiges of that screaming, desperate lust that had engulfed her before. It could have been either, or any combination of the two, or anything else. He wasn't a stupid man; he hadn't gotten where he was without being quick on the uptake, without *noticing* things.

And it didn't matter what tipped him off. What mattered was that one second he was looking around the room as if the bodies of his nearest and dearest hung on the walls dripping blood, and the next he was gone. Halfway across the room before she realized what was happening.

His fist slammed into Nick's face with a sound unlike anything she'd ever heard before. Nick fell against the wall, his hands up. Not fighting back.

"I'm sorry," he managed, but that was all before his head snapped back from another punch.

"Greyson, stop!" She ran over there, then hesitated, feeling like some goddamn weak girl in an action film but genuinely unsure what to do next. Nick was on the floor, blood running from his nose and smearing down his cheek. Still not fighting back as Greyson hit him again, yelling something in the demon tongue. Should she try to pull him off, should she—

Fuck this. She reached out, grabbed his arm, then yanked back when his fist burst into flame.

It spread up his arm and across his back, eating his shirt, leaving his bare skin covered with blue-white fire. Heat so intense sweat broke out on her forehead, and made her step back, but she didn't stop speaking.

"Greyson, please stop, we didn't really do anything, it was my fault, please stop hitting him, please—"

He jumped back. She caught one glimpse of his stricken face, his glowing-coal eyes, before he buried them in his hands and fell forward.

His flaming skin touched the carpet. Megan started to scream, ready to leap over him to fill tiny hotel glasses with water, but the flames died, both on the carpet and on his skin.

"Oh fuck, oh God, no, tell me you didn't. Not with Meg, Nick, tell me not with her."

"Wait a minute." This was probably one of the dumbest things she'd ever said, but at that point she didn't care. Not when Nick was still on the floor, his nose and eyes already starting to swell, staring at the ceiling.

And it was her fault.

"Don't I have some responsibility here? This was my fault, Greyson, I made him—"

"*What?* You—what?"

Oh, shit. She was supposed to be an intelligent woman. How the hell had she managed to fuck everything up with such brutal efficiency?

"I kissed him," she said, as calmly as she could. "I started it. But that's all it was, a couple of kisses, it didn't go—and what the fuck are you so mad about anyway? We broke up, remember? You went off with Leora tonight. What were you doing with *her*?"

"With—what the hell do you mean, what was I doing with her?"

"I mean exactly what I said. You certainly made a big enough show of leaving with her tonight. What was I supposed to think? You think I didn't—"

He sprang to a stand. Those burning eyes focused on her; she had to look away. She couldn't stand to see the pain in their depths, the anger and disbelief. The shattered pieces of his trust in her lay in those eyes like mirror shards. "Are you—is that why you did this? Some kind of revenge? You dragged Nick into—because I left with Leora?"

"You hurt me," she said, and it sounded so lame she wanted to smack herself. "You left with her, and you made sure I saw you do it, and you—you—"

"So you *used* Nick?"

"Didn't you use Leora?"

"That's different. I don't give a fuck about Leora!"

"So you did use her."

"Maybe I did," he snapped, "but I didn't run off and leap into bed with her. I didn't even touch her."

"We didn't do anything," she said again. She wanted to say it loudly, to sound strong and confident, but she just couldn't manage it. "Nothing really happened. I kissed him—we kissed a few times. That's all. Greyson,

I'm sorry, and I'm drunk, and I feel sick, and I was so mad . . . Can't we just forget it? Can't we just move past it?"

His head jerked back, as if she'd waved ammonia under his nose. "I can't believe—I can't do this right now. I can't be here. Not now."

"I—"

"I never thought you would do something like this."

"And I never thought you would lie to me like you did."

"Right. This is my fault. Because I'm such a fucking beast, how dare I try to wait until the right time—"

"If that's the way you feel about it, why come here to apologize? If you were right all along, why do that?"

"You're right. I shouldn't have fucking bothered."

He glanced down at Nick, who was struggling to sit up. "Sorry, Nick," he muttered, and turned and sped out of the room.


The pounding of her head woke her up. For one dizzied, horrified moment, her nightmare followed her into waking, and she thought the pain came from the angel, perched on the head of her bed, squeezing her temples in vise-tight palms.

No such luck. With full consciousness, memory flooded back, and all the bright morning sunlight in the world couldn't chase Greyson's horrified black gaze from her mind. Her groan sounded more like a sob; she rolled over and buried her face in the pillow.

"That's not a happy morning face," Tera said.

Tera? What the hell— Megan looked up to see Tera perched on the edge of the bed, holding in each hand a mug of what Megan could only hope was coffee. Or hemlock. She'd be happy with either at that moment.

"Hear you had some excitement last night," Tera continued.

"Oh God." Megan slumped back to the pillow. "Does everyone know?"

"Um, yeah. It's all over the hotel. Are you surprised? It's not like people wouldn't hear about something like that. The demons are all in an uproar."

"Because I kissed Nick? How—"

Tera almost spluttered her coffee. Almost but not quite. "You kissed Nick? What in the world?"

"Isn't that what you're talking about?"

"What the hell happened? You kissed Nick? You mean like a real kiss, with tongue? Was it good? He looks like he'd be a good kisser. Look at you, all racy gadabout. Didn't take you long."

"Racy gada—what century do you live in?" Megan reached for the coffee and took the biggest gulp she could manage. It burned her tongue. She didn't care.

"Hey, I'm not the one running around kissing people. Does Greyson know?"

She cringed. "Yeah. He knows."

"Ooh. That good, huh."

The bathroom door opened; Nick emerged in a cloud of listless steam. His chest was bare above jeans. "Oh. Hi, Tera."

"Wow. I guess it didn't go well."

Demons healed very quickly as a rule; only the faintest shadows of bruises remained on Nick's face. But it was enough, the tinge of darkness around the slight swelling of his nose.

He cleared his throat. "Morning, Megan."

The words made her want to cry. How could he still be speaking to her? Still be willing to greet her in the morning after what she'd done to him? Every tiny discoloration on his face, every bit of swelling, every second of pain he'd suffered since the moment Greyson saw the smear of lipstick on his throat . . . her fault, all of it. Entirely her fault.

Something told her this wasn't the time, though, not with Tera there. Instead she forced herself to say "Good morning," in what she hoped was a tone cheerful enough to let him know she appreciated him acknowledging her but subdued enough to let him know she was sorry.

Tera turned back to her. "So how much sleep did you get, then? I thought you might want to go shopping with me, but if you're too tired, that's okay. I don't suppose you slept much, what with the kissing and I guess Greyson beating Nick up or whatever he did *and* the murder—"

"Murder?"

"What?"

She and Nick both spoke at once. They glanced at each other, a glance that gave her a bit more reassurance, then he nodded for her to continue.

"Murder? Tera, what are you talking about?"

"You don't know?"

Nick sighed. "She's a genius, Megan. I can see why you're friends."

Tera gave him a sour look. "I'm just surprised. It never occurred to me that you wouldn't know. I thought it was a huge deal when a Gretneg died."

Megan's heart stuttered in her chest. It couldn't be Greyson. Couldn't be. Even Tera wouldn't be so blasé if it was Greyson dead, Greyson murdered. Would she?

"Tera, who was it? It wasn't—was it? Who?"

"Oh. Um, what's-her-name, the bitch. What's her name?"

Megan swallowed. "Justine."

# Chapter Twenty-three

Tera nodded. "Yes, that's her. Justine."

Her first thought was, Thank God it wasn't Greyson. Her second was to be a little ashamed that she couldn't bring herself to be too upset. "What happened to her? Murdered how?"

"Oh, man. How did you miss all this?" Tera glanced at Nick, sitting very still in the chair at the desk. "Oh, right. You were sexing up the love god here or whatever. She was slaughtered, apparently. I don't know much about it, really—it's not like any of them are going to talk to me—but Roc told me what he could find out from Malleus."

"Where is Roc?"

"Eating breakfast. Charged to my room. Hey, is Greyson still going to pay for all that?"

"I assume so. He said he would." Megan closed her eyes. Apparently Tera's moment of concern and sympathy from the night before was over. She supposed she couldn't complain. She hadn't even expected as much as she got. And really, the question about the room was a legitimate one. It was just bad timing. But since when had Tera been alert to social niceties?

She reached out to Roc with her mind, giving the

invisible strand that connected herself to her demons a little tug, and waited for him to tug back. "I've called Roc. He should be here in a minute."

She slumped back on the pillow. Now all she needed was a shower—and a new stomach and head—and for the last twenty-four hours or so not to have happened.

"Well, I guess he'll tell you, then. But I think that FBI woman was involved."

"What?" Megan sat up too fast. Spots swam in front of her eyes. She clasped her hand to her forehead in a vain effort to stop her brain from exploding and lay back down.

"Yeah. I got there in time to see them take her out of the building. She was all bloody. Apparently it was some mess in there. Hey, are you okay? You look a little green."

"Yeah, I'm . . . I drank too much last night."

"Ah. Here, sit up. I'll help you."

"Tera, this is—what do you mean?"

"Trust me. Come here."

Megan obeyed, over the furious protests of her stomach. She was still in her evening gown, having barely managed to tumble into the bed and pass out after Greyson left the night before. It would need to be cleaned; no amount of hanging in a steamy bathroom would take care of those wrinkles.

Then again, maybe she'd just burn it. She didn't think she'd ever be able to look at it again.

Tera raised her arms and muttered something; cool energy flowed through Megan, from her head down. The pain disappeared. Her stomach settled. She even felt more awake, although that might have been the coffee kicking in.

"Better?"

"Yeah. Thanks, that's great."

"Better" was relative, wasn't it? Physically she felt fine. Mentally, emotionally, without the dubious distraction of the hangover, she felt as if she'd just dipped herself in liquid doom.

Tera looked over at Nick. "How are you feeling?"

He hesitated.

"Oh, come on. I promise I won't play any evil witch tricks on you. Looks like you've been through enough."

Tera got up and stood behind him, with her hands over his head. The look he gave Megan might have been comical any other time or had she not known what she knew about his childhood.

But he sat there, and after a few seconds the last of the swelling and bruising disappeared; another few seconds, and he no longer slumped under what Megan knew was the dreadful weight of a throbbing head. At least if he felt anything like she did, which come to think of it, he probably didn't. He probably felt much worse.

"Thanks," he said.

"You're welcome. Now—"

Another knock at the door. Roc; Megan felt him. "Come in."

He materialized in the room. Obeying their compromise even though it really wasn't necessary anymore. After a hideously embarrassing incident one rainy afternoon early on, she'd forbidden him ever to appear unannounced in bedrooms, no matter what time of day or night. So now he knocked first.

His little eyes immediately went dark. "What happened? You feel awful."

"Greyson caught her making out with Nick," Tera said.

Megan glared at her. "Thank you, Tera."

Sarcasm was a waste of time with Tera. "You're welcome."

"Wow, really?" Roc looked impressed. "What'd he do?"

Nick glanced at her. She couldn't tell if the look was accusatory or beseeching and didn't wait to decipher it. "Never mind. What happened to Justine?"

"Oh, gosh. It was a mess. I mean, I only saw it after, but Malleus was one of the first there, and he told me about it. He said—"

"Wait, what was Malleus doing there?"

Roc's beady eyes shifted a little, in a way Megan didn't like.

"Roc, what was he—"

"He was walking past, he said. He heard a scream. When he busted the door, he found, and I quote, 'Lady Riverside were all covered in blood, dead as I ever seen a dead woman, an' that FBI agent were screaming wif blood all down 'er front an' 'ands an' all. Looked like she'd taken herself a baf in it, she did.' "

His impression actually wasn't bad. Megan might have laughed if what he described wasn't so horrible.

"But how did Justine die? Shot? Stabbed?"

"He'll tell you himself, I guess." Roc glanced at the door. "He'll be here in a minute."

"Here? Why?"

Roc looked uncomfortable. As uncomfortable as a small green demon could look anyway.

"Roc, what's going on?"

Another knock at the door. Why did Roc look so unhappy? What was—well, only one way to find out, right?

She managed to get off the bed, almost falling when her long skirt tangled in her legs. It did feel ridiculous to be greeting visitors at nine in the morning wearing an evening gown. Her jeans and shirt from the day before were on the floor by the bed. Malleus was at the door, but what the hell. She scooped them up. "Let him in, okay? I'll be right out."

Tera had been being tactful, surprise surprise. The mirror showed Megan a woman who looked as if she'd been in a bar brawl with a vat of mascara and lost badly. Her hair stood straight up on one side; her skin had the shiny, pasty look of a dead pig under plastic wrap.

"Hideous," she muttered, and set to work.

It only took a few minutes—she was aiming for presentable, not attractive, as she doubted that was possible—and she emerged with clean teeth and skin, her hair twisted up at the back and held with the long silver barrette she used when washing her face at night. She hadn't wanted to use it. It was a gift from Greyson. But it was either that or let it hang limp and dead, and at least this looked tidy.

She thought it did anyway. But having three large

demons look at her as though she had just lain down in her coffin made her wonder.

"What?" She looked down. Her feet were bare, but it wasn't as if—

Oh. Maleficarum shifted his weight; she saw the box behind him, and her heart fell right down into those bare feet of hers. Peeking over the top edge of the cardboard was one of her books, one she'd left on the bedside table at Ieuranlier Sorithell.

"M'lady." Malleus rubbed his right eye with his fist. "We brung—Lord Dante, he tole us to bring—"

"Why'd you do it?" Maleficarum interrupted. "Why'd you leave us? Lord Dante, 'e's a wreck, 'e is. We thought, when 'e bought the—"

"What're we s'posed to do now?" Malleus raised his red-rimmed eyes. "We dunno what to do!"

"Yeh," Spud said, but without conviction. True to form, he looked more upset than the others, if that was possible; while she looked at him a single fat tear ran down his cheek.

She'd thought she was too dehydrated for tears herself, but apparently she wasn't. They filled her eyes. She tried to wipe them away before they overflowed, but she didn't manage it.

It was really happening. All of her things. Everything she'd kept at his place. It wasn't a small box, but then it wouldn't be, not with the contents of her drawers, the dresses in the closet, the hair products and toothbrush and . . . oh God, everything. He'd made them drive over there and remove every last vestige of her from his home.

He couldn't even wait until he got back from the hotel. Couldn't give it a couple of days and see if maybe time led him to believe again the things he'd started to say to her the night before about working it out. The things he'd started to say when he was interrupted, the things he'd never said.

And now apparently he never would.

She bit her lip, cleared her throat. The brothers looked ready to start sobbing. If she didn't pull herself together quickly, they probably would.

"Thanks, guys. I ap—thanks."

"Thought you was gonna come live wif us," Maleficarum replied. "Was it summat we did? We din't mean to, whatever it was, we can—"

"No! No, it wasn't, of course it wasn't anything you guys did. How could it be? You're—you're so great, all three of you."

Malleus wiped his nose on his sleeve. "If we're so great, how come you're leavin'?"

"We'll be better," Maleficarum said. "We promise. I din't mean to walk in when you was in the shower, t'other week. I know you don't like when I do that. I din't see nuffink, I swear it. I won't do it again, I was thinkin' you could put a sign on the door or somefing so I'll know—"

"It's your fault, then, Lif. She don't want you always peekin' in at 'er. I tole you before, ladies don't like when you see 'em naked. Why can't you quit bein' so rude?"

"Yeh!"

"You was the one who spilled a drink on 'er, Mal! An'

were you what ast her if she were menstratin', like it's any of your mind! No wonder she's leavin' us, with you pokin' your nose in—"

"She looked pale! I were only tryin' to 'elp! To show 'er I cared, like. Shouldn't I worry for 'er health?"

"Stickin' your big Mary's into 'er womb ain't helpin', ye gobshite! 'S personal business between her and Lord Dante! 'S all your fault!"

The sound of Tera's helpless giggling brought Megan back to earth finally. This was not some bizarre after-school special, and to stand and watch it in a half-sick, half-amused stupor as she'd been doing was not the best way to deal with it.

"Guys! Guys, please!"

"And what about Spud? He tried that new eyeshadow on 'er last month, an' it made 'er look like a consumptive! She don't want to go out lookin' like 'er lungs is about ter fall out!"

Spud said nothing, but his hands wrung faster than before.

"Guys!" She tried again. "Guys, shut up!"

Spud burst into tears. Malleus and Maleficarum simply looked injured; they huddled around Spud, with Malleus patting his back, and gave her baleful glances.

"I'm sorry. But this has nothing to do with you, okay? I promise. It's nothing you did, it's just . . ."

She resisted the urge to tell them that sometimes grown-ups just can't live together anymore, but they still loved each other very much. Well, she resisted the urge because she might have been able to start the sentence, but the thought of the last phrase made her ill. She didn't think she could manage to say it without crying, and Spud was doing quite enough of that.

From the depths of his black trouser pocket he produced an enormous white handkerchief and gave his nose a thunderous blow.

"We ain't gonna see you again," Maleficarum said. "Why can't you stay? Don't you want to be wif us?"

"This is so pitiful I may cry," Tera muttered. Megan ignored her.

"Of course I want to be with you." Now it was an after-school special on Coping With Divorce. Or it would be, if they were getting divorced, which they weren't, because one had to be married to get a divorce, and they weren't.

And obviously they never would be. She forced herself to ignore the stab of pain and focus. "But I— It's not that simple. There are some things I want out of life and some things he wants out of life, and we just couldn't find a way to make those things match up, is all."

"Don't make any sense." Malleus grabbed Spud's handkerchief—Spud didn't want to give it up, and they tussled for a second before Malleus won out—and dabbed his eyes with a clean corner of it. "If you love 'im, why can't you make them things match up?"

"I— We just can't. Look, guys, it's really— I really wish this wasn't— This isn't what I want, it's just the way it is." Her eyes stung. If she could just get through this, if she could just get them out of there, she could get into the shower and have her first solid cry of the day, the first of what she felt confident would be many.

"But 'e's miserable!" Maleficarum wailed. "Up there now, 'e is, starin' at nuffink! You go up there, m'lady, an' you sit an' you work this out. We need you, we do. Can't you just try it? For us, you know."

This was surely the most horrible morning of her life. Punishment for what she'd done to Nick; when she looked at it that way, she deserved this and more.

"I'm sorry, guys. I really am. But I can't. He needs to come to me if he wants to work this out. It's complicated. But trust me, I can't go up there."

Spud started sobbing anew. They stood there, the four of them with their interested audience—Tera had finally stopped giggling, but a quick glance showed Megan she was still smirking—for a long moment before Maleficarum finally nodded.

"Well. I guess if you say it can't be fixed, it can't be fixed. But m'lady, we're gonna miss you. Don't know what we'll do wifout you there."

"You can still see me." She knew it was lame even as she said it. Her heart hurt too bad for her to care. It had finally hit her. She wasn't just losing Greyson; she was losing them too. And she loved them, she really did. They drove her nuts sometimes, but they were family, and she wouldn't see them again. They were too busy to visit her even if Greyson would allow it.

Before he'd come to her room, she would have been certain he would. Now . . . probably not.

But she said it anyway. "You can come visit me anytime. I'd love to see you."

Then she did start to cry. The brothers crowded around her, patting her, stroking her. Spud offered her his handkerchief, which she declined. "I'll miss you, too, guys," she managed. "I didn't mean for this to happen."

They nodded. Malleus took her hand. "Got anyfing you want us ter tell 'im?"

Only about a million things but none she thought would matter or make a difference. "Tell him I'm sorry," she said finally. She couldn't fault herself for her reaction to the lies, to the work issue or anything else. But she could fault herself for trying to use Nick to get back at him. For hurting both of them. "Just tell him I'm really sorry."

# Chapter Twenty-four

The other Gretnegs were seated around the table when she walked into the dining room an hour and a half later. In deference to Justine the white candles had been replaced with black ones; the pale faces of the others rose solemn from dark collars.

Megan too wore black, not that she had much choice; a plain long-sleeved, knee-length dress she thought was subdued enough to look as if she cared. Which she did, at least for the most part. She cared that the angel—she had no doubt it was the angel—had attacked another demon and had succeeded this time. She cared that Justine was dead; despite her dislike of the woman, she was still capable of being sorry. Her gaze wandered to the empty chair where Justine had sat the night before, now draped in black fabric.

But she just didn't have room for any more sorrow. She was full.

Winston cleared his throat when she sat down. "So. We all know what's happened?"

There were a few general nods before Baylor spoke. "I'm not actually clear on the details."

"It was that FBI agent," Gunnar said. "She went crazy, it appears."

"It was the angel." Greyson shifted in his seat; Megan saw it out of the corner of her eye. She refused to look at him. Couldn't look at him. Just hearing his voice made her cheeks hot.

What the hell had she been thinking? To get back at him by kissing Nick? Well, no. That wasn't all of it. She'd wanted to be reassured that she was still . . . well, still desirable. And not only did she genuinely like Nick and care about Nick and not only, if she wanted to admit it, did she know Nick was "safe" somehow purely because of his friendship with Greyson—he wasn't going to want anything from her—but . . . Yeah. It was wrong, but the simple fact was that if a man who took home a different woman every night, a man who could have his pick of any woman he wanted, wanted her, it was an ego boost.

Plus, who wouldn't give a sex demon a try, if all she was looking for was a night of meaningless lust? It wasn't as if she was a total lunatic for thinking that if she was going to hop into bed with someone, the incubus with the intense sex energy was the one to hop. So to speak.

It didn't really matter, and it didn't make it right. Didn't make it less of the hideous mistake it had been. But her motive hadn't really been revenge, not entirely. At least there was that. She genuinely hadn't meant to hurt anyone, least of all Nick.

"Megan?" Winston's voice cut through her unhappy little haze.

"What?"

He raised his eyebrows. "Do you agree with Greyson?"

"I—" She glanced around the table, glanced at Greyson, who scowled and said nothing.

But agreeing with him was still probably pretty safe. So she nodded. "Yes."

Greyson's scowl deepened.

"But I don't understand what the agent was doing there," Baylor said. "If the angel murdered Justine, he could have done that on his own. He certainly wouldn't have needed to use some silly human to do it. And Justine was . . . I find it hard to believe the FBI agent would have been capable of that."

"What exactly did she do?" Gunnar asked again, and Megan was glad. She wanted to know—well, she didn't want to know, but she thought she ought to know—but didn't want to be the ghoul who asked.

Baylor confirmed this by glaring at Gunnar. "What the hell is the matter with you, Gunnar? Why are you so damned curious?"

Gunnar looked offended. "I'm not being disgusting. I think it's important that we know. What if it comes after us? I don't want—"

"She ripped her apart. Slit her open from stem to stern." Greyson looked at Megan. "Tore out her heart."

She looked away.

"The point is," Winston said, "that whatever this thing is—if it is indeed an angel, which I'm inclined to believe—it has now attacked Megan and murdered Justine. Our friend. Which of us is next, is what I want to know? How can we keep ourselves safe?"

"What do your Yezer say?" Baylor asked Megan. "Have they found any trace of it?"

Oh, shit, she hadn't even asked. Roc would have told her if they'd found anything, but still, she should have asked. Should have checked. "They're still looking."

"That doesn't do us any damned good," he replied. "This is ridiculous. I feel like I'm sitting in front of the firing squad. Like a lamb being led to slaughter. A sitting duck."

"A cliché waiting to be used," Greyson suggested.

"Yes, I—this isn't the time to make jokes, Grey."

"Well, it doesn't seem to be the time for much else. You all know how I feel about it, what I think we should do."

Megan looked at him, started to open her mouth. She didn't know what he wanted to do. Oh, she had some ideas—she imagined it had something to do with Reverend Walther, since he was the only connection other than Agent Reid they had—but if he'd talked about his plan, it had happened before she got there.

And of course, hearing his thoughts in this group situation was the only way she would hear them, wasn't it? No more late-night conversations in the dark. No more phone calls. No more evenings on the couch or long dinners or breakfasts or . . . anything else.

She stomped on her treacherous thoughts. This was not the time to mope and mourn. Or, rather, it was supposed to be a time to mourn, but the pitiful shreds of her relationship were not what she was supposed to be mourning. A woman had died. More of them could die. She didn't particularly want it to be her.

Or him.

"We can hardly leap into the middle of a crowd of humans and assault a public figure," Win said. "Really,

Grey, I agree he's our next best shot if the Yezer aren't finding the angel, but that fleabag hotel says he's playing his little games all day."

"The angel may be watching. He was yesterday."

"Yesterday he had Agent Reid to piggyback on," Baylor said. "At least according to you."

"And today there's a whole horde of believers over there. He can easily attach himself to one of them, if he hasn't already grabbed hold of the reverend. He did send Agent Reid over there as his first act once he'd nabbed her, don't forget. Clearly he's checking things out."

"Obviously that's his target," Gunnar said. "But he happened to find some demons in the area and has decided it would be fun to kill us off while he's at it."

Megan opened her mouth. Hadn't Gunnar and Winston been having *rubendas* killed for several weeks? That was the angel, wasn't it?

Something shut her mouth before the words could form, though. She didn't want to argue, didn't want to speak at all, really. But more than that, she simply felt as though it wasn't the thing to say. Something held her tongue, and that something was instinct, and she trusted it.

She couldn't resist sneaking a glance at Greyson, whose tilted head made her suspect he was thinking the same thing.

Winston said it, though. "He's been killing our *rubendas,* Gunnar. Why would he have just realized we're in town?"

"You don't know that. That's just Greyson and Megan's theory. We can't be sure."

"It's the only workable theory we have," Baylor said.

"If you have a better one, Gunnar, now's the time to mention it."

They waited. Finally Gunnar said, "He could have been after the exorcist for a while."

"Oh, come on."

The words triggered a memory in Megan. "No. He could have. The reverend suddenly got popular a couple of months ago, right?" She looked at Greyson, forgetting she wasn't supposed to. Forgetting, for one blessed second, that the day and night before had happened. "Isn't that what you told me? That he came out of nowhere in early June?"

He paused just long enough for memory to crash back in and her gaze to falter. "Yes. I did read that."

"So he came for us and latched on to the exorcist after," Winston said.

"So we should go over there," Baylor said. "The exorcist could have the key to the whole thing."

"The FBI agent could too," Winston said. "We could try to talk to her."

"Sure, Win." Greyson leaned back in his chair. "I'm sure the police and the feds would be happy to let you go in and question her. Privately."

"Justine could have done it," Baylor said. His tone wasn't sad so much as regretful. "She could get in anywhere. When will she be replaced? We need a sex demon for this."

"What about your friend Nick?" Win asked Greyson. "Would he do it?"

Megan just managed not to cringe.

Greyson's expression didn't change at all. "He's not full-blood."

"Oh, right. His father . . . what a mess. Still, do you think he's got enough incubus blood to do it? Has he ever—"

"No."

"Have you asked him? Perhaps he knows—"

Greyson stood up. His jacket draped over the back of his chair; he grabbed it and put it on as he spoke. "This is pointless. Megan and Asterope Green attempted to question Agent Reid yesterday, and she was apparently barely coherent then. Talking to her won't do any of us any good. The exorcism ends at nine. I think if we head over there then, we'll find the angel. Perhaps Megan could ask her witch friend to lend a hand with that as well."

He talked about her as if they hardly knew each other. She managed to nod. "I'll ask her."

"I suggest we skip the formal dinner this evening and meet up here around eight."

"Why?" Gunnar asked.

Greyson's eyebrows rose. "To go kill the angel."

"Do you really think that's a good idea?" Gunnar smoothed his hair, looked around him as if the walls were threatening to close in and he needed to keep an eye on them. "It could kill us all, Grey. I think you're being a bit—"

"Would you rather sit around and wait for it to pick us off, one by one?"

"I don't think—I mean, we don't know that it's after all of us."

Winston leaned away from Gunnar, peered at him through narrow eyes. "Gunnar, it's been killing our employees. Our *rubendas*. It attacked Megan and killed Justine. Do you think it's come to invite us to a tea party?"

Silence fell over the table—well, they'd all been silent anyway, but this was a deeper silence—while Gunnar's pale cheeks reddened. "No. I just don't think we should go running over to that hotel with our guns drawn. I think it would be better to stick together, all of us here, and wait for it to come to us. So we can ambush it and be prepared."

Baylor tilted his head. "That's not a bad idea."

"I'm for Grey's plan," Winston said. "So that's three for and two against. So we'll go over there tonight."

"Megan hasn't given her opinion," Baylor said.

Winston glared at him. "Of course she agrees with Greyson."

"But she hasn't said she does. You're just assuming."

Greyson sighed. A loud sigh, a sigh with purpose. "I'm going over there tonight whether the rest of you come with me or not."

"I'll go with you," Winston said.

Everyone looked at Megan. At least everyone except Greyson, who was studying the crown molding on the opposite wall.

"No," she said. "We'll all go. Greyson and Winston can't go by themselves."

"Good." Winston touched her arm. "Now, Megan, you beat the angel the night before last by yourself, correct? Because of your psyche demon side. I've never heard of such a thing happening, but . . . why don't you get together with Greyson's friend Nick, and the two of you figure out how to use those powers? He's part psyche demon, is he not?"

"Yes, he—he is," she managed. "But—"

"Grey, you tell Megan everything you think she might need to know, and make sure Nick comes along."

"Perhaps you should do that."

Win looked surprised. "Why?"

Greyson hesitated, glanced at her so fast she would have missed it if she hadn't been watching for it. "I just think it might be easier."

"Oh, no. I have a full afternoon planned." Winston stood up as well, picked up the notepad by his seat. "If we're going to battle an angel this evening, I want to make sure my affairs are in order. Probably a good idea for all of us, don't you think?"

# Chapter Twenty-five

His tall form didn't appear to be running down the blank white hallway toward the elevators, but he still moved too fast for her; she was practically jogging by the time she finally caught up to him and grabbed his arm. "Greyson, wait!"

She'd never seen his eyes that cold. He snatched his arm out of her grasp. "What do you want?"

"You said you'd tell me about the angel."

"Why don't you ask *Nick*?"

"I need to talk to you about that. About Nick."

"I really don't want to hear the details, Megan. Or should I say, any more details."

"But that's not—"

"He'll tell you whatever it is you need to know. I don't think you and I have much to say to each other at this point, do you?"

He didn't wait for her reply, just turned and started down the hall. She started to move too, then paused. Waited.

He hit the button, and the elevator doors opened; Megan slipped inside just before they closed.

A wave of cold blasted over her skin; he was pissed. That was fine, because so was she. When he reached for the button to open the doors again, she stepped in front of them, blocking them. "It wasn't Nick's fault."

"Yes, so you said. Thank you. It's so much more pleasant for me to picture you seducing him, rather than the other way around."

"Nobody seduced anybody. It wasn't—"

"Oh, of course. It was an accident. You fell, right?"

She closed her eyes for a second, took a deep, calming breath. This wasn't working, and it wasn't why she was there. "It wasn't Nick's fault. Think whatever you want about me. You're obviously going to anyway, you don't want to listen to anything I have to say. But don't blame Nick. He—he tried to stop it, he didn't want to—"

"Oh, for fuck's sake. This just keeps getting better. What's next, Megan? Will you describe it for me in detail? Maybe you can show me how you swarmed all over him like some hormonal octopus, wouldn't that be fun? Because what I really, really want, more than anything, is to get as complete a mental picture of this as I possibly can."

"Picture whatever you want, but nothing happened. He didn't even—we didn't—it was a couple of kisses, and it didn't mean anything. We were drunk. I was hurt and upset and angry. And, which I personally think is kind of important, you and I aren't together anymore. It's not like I cheated on you."

His face darkened. She didn't think she'd ever seen him so angry. The elevator around them shrank; the temperature dropped so low she shivered and wrapped her arms around herself. She was suddenly aware that they were alone together in a tiny room, suspended by wires. The night before he'd lost control, the first time she'd ever seen that happen. The first time she'd ever seen him come close to that happening. She didn't want to see it again.

"Yes. You're right. You left me before you seduced my best friend. I asked you to be my *wife,* and you said no, and then you seduced my best friend. Thank you so much for reminding me of that part. As if I could fucking forget."

"I didn't leave you so I could seduce anyone. I don't want anyone else. I . . ." *Shit.* She had no idea what to say, and her eyes stung. She rolled them up, hoping to keep the tears from falling. It worked but probably made her look ridiculous. "I was just so damn mad at you. How could you keep that from me? How could you—how could you hurt me like that, not trust me like that?"

For a long moment they stood there, while she tried to get herself under control and waited for him to yell again.

He didn't. Instead he sighed; she felt some of the tension lessen, felt his anger recede. "Does it matter? What difference does it really make, Megan? This is pointless. It's over. You said no. There's nowhere left for us to go."

The words fell with the finality of a medieval death-bell.

Not for the first time, the idea of simply giving in occurred to her. The way he'd said that, the fact that he'd come to her room the night before, made her think it was entirely possible she could end this stand-off, could end all of this absolute misery, just by giving in.

And really, she'd lost her job once before. Well, she hadn't lost it, she'd left it; her share in Serenity Partners, the therapy practice she'd been part of. She'd given that up. It had been sad, but it hadn't killed her, hadn't done this to her.

But she'd known she could start her own practice. She'd had her radio show.

And it had been her decision. *Hers.* Yes, it had been sort of forced on her, the day she fed off someone—the sister of a patient who'd died, and his death was her fault as well—but nobody made giving up the practice a condition of anything. Nobody had made it a condition of something that shouldn't have had any conditions. Nobody had deliberately hidden that information from her.

So she didn't make the offer. She couldn't. "Will you please tell me what I need to know? For tonight?"

He considered it, his eyes closed. Nodded.

"And please, forgive Nick. I know you don't want to hear it, but it was so innocent, Greyson, it really was. Seeing you leave with Leora—it hurt, okay? I just wanted to try to, I don't know, to forget about it. It was a mistake, and I'm sorry. He feels awful about it. We both do. Please."

He glanced at her but didn't speak.

"He's your friend. You know that."

"I'll try," he said finally.

"Thank you."

Pause.

His smile wasn't even a shadow of what it normally was, but it still made her heart skip. "Are we going to stand in the elevator all day?"

"What? Oh, no." She turned and hit the button for fourteen. And up they went.

It probably wasn't the best idea after all. Yes, there were things she needed to know. Yes, he was the best one to get the information from, especially if the others were spending the afternoon writing up wills—wasn't that cheery and optimistic?

But being there in the room again, talking to him, it was hard. Incredibly hard. Difficult to sit on the chair instead of beside him. Difficult not to smile, to joke. The chair felt wrong beneath her; she was cold without him at her side. Her hands felt too big at the ends of her arms, wanting to curve themselves over his thigh or around his chest. It was as if he wasn't Greyson. As if she was sitting speaking to a stranger who looked like him and sounded like him but was still a stranger.

They were both being so careful, so businesslike. As if their momentary ceasefire could crash at any moment like icicles over their heads and stab them.

Of course, if it didn't, the angel probably would. As time went on Megan stopped wondering about Gunnar and Baylor's reactions and started wondering about Greyson and Winston's. To willingly put themselves in that kind of danger . . .

"Of course," he said finally, leaning back on the couch

and closing his eyes, "this all assumes the damned thing hasn't been tipped off and isn't waiting for us. Which it probably will be."

"Tipped off? How?"

He stretched one long leg out and rested his foot on the coffee table. His eyes were still closed; Megan let her own do what they'd been dying to do all day and wander freely over every inch of him. Over the sharp bones in his face, the almost—but not quite—beaky nose; it wasn't a classically handsome face, necessarily, but at the same time it was. She loved to look at it, was all she knew. And with his eyes closed, when he couldn't see her, she let herself look, knowing it would probably be one of the last chances she would get.

He opened one eye and glanced at her; she quickly looked away. "Because one of them hired the horrible thing, and they've probably contacted it by now."

"What? But I thought it was here with the exorcist."

"Oh, it probably is. But if someone got wind of its presence here and knew this meeting was coming up—which, of course, we all did—it's quite probable he hired it."

"But why?"

"Think about it, *bry*—Megan." Oh, that hurt. "With the rest of us eliminated, the city belongs to whoever made the deal."

"But we all sort of control our own subspecies or whatever. I mean, would your demons accept me as a—"

He flinched. Oh, shit. Right. "I mean, would Winston's blood demons accept you, or Baylor, or me, or anyone else as their Gretneg? I thought it was, I don't know, a breeding thing. Wouldn't Carter, for example, simply take over your House if something happened to you?"

"It is a breeding thing, as you put it, to some degree. But it's also a money thing, and that trumps everything else. Carter couldn't take over right now. They'd never stand for it. But a Gretneg from another House, one who'd proved himself powerful enough? Who'd proved himself smart enough to eliminate the others? That's the sort of masterstroke they'd appreciate. It would prove his ability to control things, his dedication to controlling things."

It slipped into place then—well, not really. She knew. Maybe she'd always known and simply hadn't wanted to ask. "Like when you had Templeton killed."

He didn't move, and she knew she was right. "Yes."

Knowing and getting confirmation were two different things. Her head swam. It wasn't a surprise, and yet it was. It bothered her, and yet it didn't. She just sat, staring dumbly, unsure what to say or do or think.

After a moment he cleared his throat. "In my defense, he was trying to have me—us—killed first. The gun-toting witches, remember? The scene at Maldon's house?"

As if she could forget. "I remember. I just . . . that wasn't the only reason, was it?"

"I wanted to avoid it. It didn't work out that way."

"Why didn't you ever tell me? Before?"

He looked at her then, the old look, a half-smile and a faint gleam in his eye that made her knees weak even sitting down. "You didn't ask."

"Would you have told me if I had?"

The smile faded. "I've never lied to you. Not when you asked me a question outright."

Part of her wanted to argue that. It didn't really make much difference; lies by omission were still lies. But she didn't have the energy. Didn't want to.

She wanted it all never to have happened. Wanted to pretend, just for a minute, that it hadn't. And if that wasn't the healthiest thing to do, too bad.

"Justine did it for you, didn't she? That was the favor. That was what she talked about at Templeton's funeral."

"Yes."

"Do the others know?"

"I imagine so, yes."

"And they approve?"

He shrugged. "I don't really care."

Something else occurred to her then. Something she couldn't believe she'd forgotten, but she had; with everything else going on, it had faded away. "So do you think that *litobora* the other night, at my house, do you think one of my demons could have sent it? Roc, even?"

He shook his head. "No, I don't think so. I suspect we were right about that one. It's one of us here. Probably the same one. It makes sense, if you think about it."

"How?"

"You were able to escape the angel the other night. As a psyche demon—*part* psyche demon—you make the thing vulnerable. Psyche demons are pretty rare. Psyche demons that look human are even more so. When the wars were going on—we fought the witches on one front, and the angels decided to step in and see what they could do on the other—we didn't have too many, and most of them were only part psyche demon, most only about a quarter. They weren't as powerful as you are."

"But psyche demons are better against angels."

"Yes."

"Why didn't you just get the nonhuman-looking ones to help you? The ones people can't see?"

"Because they're very rare, as I said. Their populations are negligible, fractions of ours. They tend to be like Yezer. Small. Fragile. Or they're uncontrollable. They'd kill the angels, yes, but they'd also kill anything else they came across. And because of the way . . . well, let's just say most of them aren't really fans of those of us who pass for human."

"And someone knew this. They knew they'd have an angel here and that I could be useful against it."

"I assume so, yes. Especially since they assumed you'd—well, never mind. The point is you're useful, and that would be reason enough."

"Then it had nothing to do with—" She snapped her mouth closed. This was much bigger than Winston wanting to get her out of the way of the marriage he wanted or Justine doing it simply because she didn't want a human involved with demon business. If he thought that wasn't it, she believed him.

"What?"

"Nothing. You really think this is why?"

He nodded.

"Who's behind it, then?"

He shrugged. "I have my suspicions. Nothing concrete, but I'm fairly sure I'm right. I usually am."

"And so modest too."

"Modesty is overrated."

This time they were both smiling; their eyes caught and held for a second too long.

He stood up. "You should probably get back to your room and let Nick know what's happening. We'll need his help. Oh, and of course, don't let any of them in, okay? Don't open the door to anyone but me or the brothers or Tera."

If his voice changed slightly when saying Nick's name, she didn't comment on it. But she did have one more question.

"Greyson."

He was almost at the door. "Yes?"

"So—the ritual. The other night, when you said you thought it would protect me, you weren't—I mean, that wasn't just because of . . . us."

His hand rested on the doorknob; his eyes studied the floor. "No. Not entirely."

"Oh." Not that it made a difference, except to increase the pain levels in her chest. But she was glad she knew.

He still waited by the door. Her steps faltered as she crossed the room. "Okay, well, I guess I'll see you later, then. I'll call you after I've talked to Nick. Unless you want him to call."

"Sure. Whatever."

The door opened; she stood for a minute, not even

bothering to keep her eyes from greedily taking him in, studying him, trying to burn his face deeper into her memory than it already was. He wasn't looking at her anyway. "Okay. Bye, then."

He nodded. "Bye."

She'd just stepped fully into the hallway when his hand closed over her arm and yanked her back into the room, against the solid heat of his body. The door slammed shut behind her.

"You didn't really think I'd just let you walk away, did you?" His voice was low and urgent; his breath was hot on her skin; and before she could formulate an answer, his lips were on hers.

# Chapter Twenty-six

Her entire body went up in flames. Not literal ones, not like the ones already blazing near the ceiling and around the room. Not the ones flaring in her mind as the first rush of energy invaded her. But deeper ones, hotter ones, flames tinged with ice-blue edges of pain and sorrow.

She gave them back to him when his tongue slipped into her mouth, sending more sparks dancing through her veins, sharp hot bolts of pleasure and need racing down her stomach to pool between her legs and make her muscles tight.

For a second she thought she should stop this, push him away. It wasn't healthy. It wouldn't change anything. It would only make it harder.

But she couldn't. Not just because one hand had grasped her bottom and the other tangled in her hair, pulling her tighter to him. Not because kissing him made her feel alive again, safe again, for the first time since the horrible scene the day before. But because she didn't want to. She wanted him. She loved him. How could she say no to this, when she'd already said no to everything else, and that would haunt her until the day she died?

Instead she wrapped her leg around him, yanked his shirt up from his waistband, and shoved her hands beneath. This time the feel of his bare skin, of the spikes of his spine, didn't make her cry. She was too far gone to cry. She was already crying, somewhere deep inside herself, and she suspected—was terrified—that she would never be able to stop.

He kissed her harder, almost hard enough to hurt. His fingers left her hair to touch her face, tracing for a second the curve of her cheekbone before sliding down her throat and farther down again to cup her breast through the thin jersey of her dress.

She gasped. Her head fell back; he dipped down to kiss her throat, nibbling it, muttering things she couldn't quite hear. Things she was almost afraid to hear.

His skin beneath her palms was hot and covered with goosebumps. She couldn't decide which sounded more appealing, to run her hands over it and feel every inch of him or to dig her nails in, rip off his shirt, tug him to the floor because she didn't want to wait. His power simmered in her blood, and she was about to boil over.

Instead she shifted position as best she could, sought his mouth again, and pushed it back to him.

He gasped. "Meg. Shit, Meg."

Her feet left the floor. Her legs wrapped around his waist. They fell against the wall, cool against her back. It did nothing to soothe the fever in her veins or to calm the frenzied desperation of her thoughts.

His erection pressed against her; she didn't know what the sound that escaped her lips was called, and she didn't care. What she did care about was that in this position she couldn't reach the buttons of his shirt, and in her dizzied state she couldn't figure out how to get the damned thing off him. It was a crisp white barrier between her and what she wanted; she tugged at it, tried to pull it up over his head. Finally she gave up and dug her fingers into his hair, forcing him to kiss her harder still, until she tasted blood.

A rush of power came with it, even stronger. Somewhere she realized it was his. No time to think about it. No time to worry about it, because his hand was on her thigh, and it was not hesitant. It barely paused on the top of her stocking before continuing on, sliding beneath her bottom and forward to focus unerringly on the spot where she wanted it the most.

That one touch, coupled with her wild emotions and the power overloading her, was enough. Too much. She clutched at him as her back arched and her body shuddered, barely hearing her own voice or the low, thick sound of satisfaction he made in the back of his throat.

He swung her away from the wall, crossed the room in a few long strides, and opened the bedroom door. His mouth left hers; she felt him look up.

Malleus, Maleficarum, and Spud sat there, overflowing the small chairs that had been in the dressing area and at the corner desk. Their eyes were wide.

She probably should have cared that they were there, that her skirt was over her waist so her black silk panties were visible, that they'd probably heard her, and that they knew exactly what was going on. She didn't. That would have required too much energy, and she needed it all for him.

Greyson's voice was so close to a growl it was barely recognizable. "Get out."

The brothers moved fast when they wanted to. Or, in this instance, when ordered to; Megan had little doubt that they would have been happy to stay and watch. Not out of some voyeuristic need but because they wanted to make sure everything worked out okay.

Which it wouldn't. And which she couldn't care about just then either.

They raced out of the room. Greyson's lips met hers again before the door had closed.

Another shock. More flames, racing around the ceiling as if someone had sprayed the walls with gasoline. Flames tearing through her body as if she was made of gunpowder. She gasped, said his name. Said it again as he laid her on the bed, pushed up her dress.

She sat up, shifted position to kneel. Finally she had access to his buttons. Finally she could open his shirt, peel it back off his shoulders while their kiss continued, hard and hot. They broke off while he slipped her dress over her head and she did the same for his T-shirt, then found each other again as she tugged at his belt, working the buckle with fingers that felt swollen.

"My arms are like the twisted thorn," he murmured, quoting Yeats, breaking the last word off with a sharp gasp when she pulled down his zipper and reached inside, finding him swollen and slick. She curled her hand around him, stroked him, bathed in the hot orange light of the raging fire around them.

Her bra slid down her shoulders. His hands roamed over her breasts, over her ribs. Her skin leaped where he touched her; she almost lost her balance trying to lean forward, to push herself into his palms. Instead she fell against his chest, his bare skin tantalizingly hot and intensely gratifying. She kissed it, scraped her teeth over it. Curled her body down to kiss his stomach, down farther to take him into her mouth.

For the last time. She forced the thought from her head. It wasn't welcome. Instead she focused on the feel of him, the taste of his smoky skin. On his hands tangling gently in her hair, the sound of his breath catching in his chest and his voice saying her name.

She was just getting lost in it when he pulled her up, flipped her back. Her panties disappeared with one quick slip. He nibbled the top of her right thigh, urged it to the side with gentle pressure.

Her back arched. Her entire body buzzed and spun, her head cleared of everything but fire and smoke. Smoke drifting from her mouth, fire burning everything inside her, all the sorrow and misery and fear. It all disappeared when his tongue found her most sensitive spot, when he used the tiny cleft at the tip to tease and shift it and make her scream.

Her second climax roared through her, leaving her shaking with tears in her eyes. He didn't move away. Gave every impression of a man who intended to stay where he was for some time.

She grabbed him, twisting his hair in her fingers and urging him up. Enough. It was enough, it was too much, she couldn't wait any longer.

His lips traveled over her stomach, up her ribcage, and were joined by his hands. She shivered when they slid over her nipples, when he took them each into the heat of his mouth with a deliberateness that threatened to make her lose the last vestiges of her sanity.

"Greyson. Greyson, please—"

His lifted his head. Their eyes met; it hit her like an explosion in her soul. She couldn't look away, caught by him, held there as he rose and drove himself into her.

Her eyelids fluttered. She started to close them, to tilt her head back in a vain attempt to get more air. His hands stopped her, hard palms on each side of her face. She had no choice but to look at him, into his eyes, dark in the glowing gold of his skin.

One slow, careful thrust. Another. It was torture. She wriggled beneath him, trying to get him to speed up, she couldn't handle it—

He kissed her again. With that kiss came more power, more than she'd ever felt before. She wasn't just the flame. She was the *only* flame, burning, incandescent, swallowed by the heat, both of her hearts pounding frantically. It wasn't just the tiny fires sparkling high on the walls lighting the room, wasn't just the dull sunlight filtering in around the mostly closed curtains. She glowed. They glowed.

Maybe not for real, she couldn't tell, but something inside her was lit up like fireworks, and he shone so bright she couldn't look at him. Shone like the only light in a world gone cold and dark, and she was the moth desperately circling it, and somehow with that energy came a frantic, fluttering impression of his thoughts, and she realized he was thinking the same thing. Experiencing it the same way.

"Meg," he whispered, kissing her again, nibbling her earlobe. "Meg . . ."

She responded by grasping him tighter and giving it back. All of it. Everything she felt, every bit of power she possibly could. All of her love and sorrow and passion. She held nothing back, and he shuddered beneath her palms and sped his pace.

Faster and harder. The bed shook. She shook, meeting his movements with her own. His arms circled her, slid beneath her, crushing her against him. Pressure built, the energy in her, the pleasure, the need—

His mouth took hers again, one final time. Power roared through her, a forest fire, filled with everything she'd given him and more that was just him. The same emotions, magnified, run through with helplessness and regret and desire and love like she'd never felt before, and she came, crying, opening her eyes in time to see him do the same thing.

His head fell to rest on her shoulder. She reached up, intending to touch his hair, to stroke his nape, but he lifted his head again. His dark eyes searched hers, as deep and sincere as she'd ever seen them, pink and slightly wet around the rims.

"Marry me."

It would have been so easy to say yes. Easy because it was what she wanted. She wanted to, God how she did.

He must have seen her hesitation, her desire. "Megan, marry me. Please."

What was her problem? Was her job really more important than spending the rest of her life with the man she loved?

But why couldn't she have both, damn it? Why did she have to make this choice?

Not to mention giving up her humanity. That one she could have compromised on; she didn't necessarily want to do the ritual, but she did want children, and if that was the way to get them, she'd do it. She didn't even mind the idea of having them right away. The next day was her thirty-second birthday, and that seemed as good an age as any.

But why did she have to give up everything she'd worked for to be with him, in addition to her humanity? If she did that, she'd be . . . She didn't know what she would be. She wouldn't be equal anymore. She was proud of herself, of her achievements. Why did she have to give that up? If she did, what would be the point of having them to begin with, of all the work she'd done?

From the beginning she'd been aware of the disparity between them, the one thing she couldn't get over or past. She'd stopped worrying that he didn't really care about her, that she was just some infatuated girl, after the first few months. Once they'd both stopped seeing other people—or, rather, once he'd told her he wasn't seeing anyone else, that he didn't want to—she'd let that worry, that insecurity, go. At least as much as she could.

But she'd never wanted to have to depend on him in that way. Never wanted to find herself in such a position of weakness.

There were plenty of things she'd let him control. But her job shouldn't have been one of them. It shouldn't be a decision he made for her. If she let him do that, what was next? Would she have to ask for permission to go see Tera or Brian, to run out for an order of fries or something?

That was a bit ridiculous, she knew. But the principle was the same. She didn't want to be his dependent, and she didn't want him to think her life was his to control.

"I want to keep my job," she said.

He sagged above her, then pulled away in one quick movement that left her cold and alone in the center of the bed. "I'm not enough, is what you're saying."

"No! No, I don't mean it that way. Of course you're— Greyson, I just want, I need to feel like I get a say in this too. Like I bring something to this, more than just being some kind of brood mare or something. I need to be your partner, not your employee, don't you—"

"And you think that's what you would be? This isn't about— *It's too fucking dangerous.* How many times do I have to say it?" He slipped off the bed, yanked his pants back on, and tossed her clothes to her. She was grateful too. The only thing worse than arguing was arguing naked. "I'm not taking any chances with your life."

"But look at me now! I'm in danger because of my demons. Because of my position. It's nothing to do with you, right? So couldn't we—"

"Meg." His shirt snapped as he pulled it back on, not bothering to button it. "Either you want to marry me or you don't. If all these other things are so important to you that you'd rather have them than me, well, I guess that's my answer, isn't it?"

"I just want to be involved in the decision."

"And it appears you are." He covered his eyes with his right palm, rubbing his temples with his thumb and middle finger as if he was trying to crush his own skull. "It's not a complex question. It's nothing to do with equality, damn it. This is about your safety. It's about the safety of our children, when they come, and about how they'll be raised. I'm not going to keep asking over and over. Will you marry me or not?"

"I just want to have something for myself! Something I achieved on my own, something I can keep. Is that so hard for you to understand? You said last night we could work this out. Can't we?"

"Yes or no, Megan?"

She fastened her bra, pulled her dress back over her head, and stood up. "If we can't discuss this, if you can't stop pressuring me and trying to force me to do everything your way, everything you want, and you can't even listen to my side, then . . ." She couldn't say no. Couldn't bring herself to do it. "I think I should go."

Malleus had left his chair by the side of the bed. Greyson sagged into it, rested his head on his hands. "Fine. Go."

"I just think . . . we can talk about this later. After we've calmed down." It sounded so lame she cringed.

"Sure. Later. I'll just sit here and wait, shall I? While you decide if you want to be with me. If I'm more important to you than helping a bunch of strangers with their problems."

"That's not fair."

"Again. Life isn't fucking fair, Meg."

He still hadn't looked up. She stood there, fighting the urge to go put her hand on his shoulder, to sink to her knees and put her arms around him. Her fingers clenched and unclenched, hesitating.

Greyson raised his head just enough to expose hollow red eyes. "I thought you were leaving."

"We'll talk later," she repeated, and fled before she did something really stupid.

# Chapter Twenty-seven

Something attacked her the second she opened the door to her own room, a large beast with grasping arms that vibrated in her mind like a tuning fork.

Tera. Squeezing her.

Megan gasped and tried to disentangle herself. "Tera, what the hell—"

"Where the hell have you been? The meeting ended almost four hours ago. Nick and I were getting frantic. He's out searching the hotel for you right now. For the third time."

"Oh. Um, I was with Greyson. Talking. About the angel and stuff."

"And you didn't think to call and let us know? Nick's supposed to be guarding you. You were supposed to call him when the meeting ended so he could come down and get you. How do you think he felt when you didn't? What do you think—"

"I'm sorry, okay? I'm sorry. I didn't think. The meeting wasn't really very informative, and I needed to know some things, and I . . . no, I wasn't thinking."

Tera's expression changed; her expertly made-up blue eyes widened, her perfectly glossed lips lost some of their tension. "Did you guys work everything out?"

"No."

"Did he propose again?"

"Three or four times, I think. But he won't give in, and now he won't even discuss it with me. He just keeps saying if I really wanted to marry him, it wouldn't matter, and he won't even try to understand that it's not that I don't want to, it's that . . . oh, never mind. *You* understand. Why am I explaining it to you?"

They sat down on the edge of the bed. Tera reached into her designer bag and pulled out a couple of tiny bottles. "Here."

"What? Oh. Thanks." She suppressed a smile. Trust Tera to steal airline bourbon.

She knocked the bottle back in one throat-burning swallow, sighed as it blazed down into her stomach and loosened some of her tension.

Tera sipped from her own bottle. "Maybe he's right."

"What? How can you even think—"

"I just mean, maybe if you're digging your heels in this hard, it's because you really don't want to marry him."

"I do want to marry him. I love him. But I just don't see why he won't compromise with me on this. Why he won't even discuss it."

"Ha. So you do want to. I hate to sound like I know what I'm talking about here—I mean, you're the one who does this for a living, I just listen to your show sometimes—but don't you think maybe you're looking for excuses because you're scared of not being in control? Or because all those decisions you've been putting off are suddenly here, and you're freaking out, so you're trying to look for a reason not to do what—oh, shit, I don't know. What would you tell one of your patients?"

Megan stared at her for a moment, open-mouthed . . . and not a little ashamed. She'd never given Tera enough credit. "I guess you're right. Sort of. I mean, what would I be if I give up my job? Just some woman with a rich husband, who spends her days shopping and knitting or something. What if he . . . what if he got bored with me? Demons have mistresses, you know. They have their wives who sit home and their girlfriends who go out and do fun things, and . . . if we became that, and I couldn't even work anymore . . ."

"Megan, I've known him for a while, although not as well as I did before you came along. But he didn't even cheat on Lexie, and they weren't really doing more than having sex all over the place. And I don't want to get all mushy or anything, but the guy is crazy about you. Do you honestly think that if you got married, there'd be something you needed that he wouldn't get for you? Don't you think what he's waiting for is just for you to be willing to give all that stuff up, and once he knows you would, he'll make sure you don't have to? This is how he operates. Always has."

Her eyes were wet. She was going to have to take what little savings she had and invest it in Kleenex. "I thought you hated him."

"I've never hated him. It's just so much more fun to act like I do and watch him squirm."

Megan stared at her.

Tera shrugged. "You have your fun, I have mine."

"But that's— Okay, whatever. Yes, you're right. The

part about him thinking that way, not the part about you having your fun, you weirdo. It's still him giving me permission to have a fucking job."

"Or it's him trying to work with you so you can both be happy."

"Jesus, will you shut up? Since when are you all rational and wanting me to do this? I'd have to become a demon, you know."

"I know." Tera grinned. "But you're obviously never going to shut up about this particular topic until you just marry the guy, so you should go ahead and do it so we can move on already."

Too bad the little bottle in her hand was empty. Not that more was a good idea. She did have a life-or-death struggle on her schedule for the evening, so getting drunk probably wasn't the best idea. Damned life-or-death struggles, always getting in the way of a good drinking binge.

"You really think I should say yes," she said.

"I really think you should think about what makes you happiest and what you want out of life in ten years or twenty years or forty years and decide which option will—"

They both looked up when the door opened. Nick stepped through it, his face dark, until he saw her.

Then it got even darker.

"Where the fuck have you been? I've practically been dragging the fucking lake looking for you, and you're— and you!" He glared at Tera, reddish sparks shifting in his eyes. "You were supposed to call me if you heard anything. How long has she been back here? What the fuck were you doing, that you couldn't even let me know she was alive?"

"We were having mad, passionate sex," Tera replied. "Aren't you sorry you missed it?"

"I'm sorry, Nick. I've only been back for a couple of minutes, and I had to talk to her," Megan jumped in, hoping somehow to divert the violence telegraphed on Nick's face. "I'm sorry I didn't call. I was with—I was talking to Greyson."

"Oh." He subsided, but she hadn't missed the pained expression on his face.

She took a deep breath. "Tera, can you give Nick and me a minute?"

Tera looked for a second as if she was about to make a joke, and Megan's hand curled around the edge of the pillow at her side. If Tera said one word, she would smack her in the face with it.

She didn't. She just nodded and stood. "I'll be in my room. Give me a call, okay? To let me know what happened at your meeting and everything."

Megan nodded. The door closed behind Tera, and she still had no idea what to say. Okay. She'd better say something. Anything. "Nick, I'm really sorry."

He shook his head. "No, I—I mean, thanks, but it was my fault too. I should have stopped you, but . . ."

"You would have really hurt my feelings," she finished for him. "Thanks. I mean it, really."

"That wasn't entirely it. I mean, I didn't want to hurt your feelings, but it wasn't . . . Shit, Megan, I am a man. I'm part incubus. It wasn't pity or charity, is what I mean. But I still . . ."

"I shouldn't have put you in that position. I'm really, really sorry."

He nodded, his gaze cast down so she couldn't see his eyes. "Thanks. It's okay. It was just as much my fault, but thanks."

"I talked to Greyson." Why hadn't she asked Tera for another bottle before she left? That was stupid. "I told him again what happened and that it wasn't your fault and that he shouldn't blame you for it. He said he'd try. And once we're ready, you should call him."

He sank down on the end of the bed, a respectable distance from her but still, she could see, close enough that he could reach out to her if need be. God, he was so great. She'd never be able to forgive herself fully for hurting him. "So you talked to him."

"Yeah."

"And? I mean, you don't have to tell me, but did he—I mean, have you guys worked things out?"

She sighed and explained everything. Well, almost everything. She left out the sex, but she was pretty sure he knew anyway.

He shook his head. "What are you going to do?"

"I don't know. I know what I want to do, but I also know I don't want to start off a marriage—Jesus, I can't believe I'm actually talking about a marriage—with him thinking I'll just do anything he—"

The phone rang, and her heart leaped into her throat. It was as if he knew she was talking about him. Which would be more impressive if there weren't such a huge issue between them at the moment, but the point was the same.

Maybe he was calling to talk. Maybe he finally understood.

Except it wasn't him. It was Brian.

For a second the room actually seemed to tilt. Brian's voice belonged to another world, the one outside this fucking hotel. It seemed bizarre that he would intrude on the claustrophobic, miserable little stressball that what was supposed to be a relaxing week had become.

"Brian? What's up?"

"They won't let me upstairs until I have your room number, and they won't give me your room number. What is it?"

"What? You're here? Why?"

"Um, an FBI agent slaughtered a woman here early this morning, Megan. It's kind of a big story."

"Oh. Right." She gave him the room number and hung up, unsure why his presence bothered her so much but bothered just the same. He didn't belong here. This wasn't really the part of her life she shared with him. He knew about it, and he tolerated it, but they talked about her patients and work, about his work, about TV and movies and books.

If she stopped having that work, would she still have Brian?

Maybe that wasn't fair. After a few initial conversations he'd backed off; he didn't want anything to do with the demon part of her life, but he certainly didn't openly disapprove. He got along with Greyson in a grudging way despite distrusting him based on his demon-ness. But he clearly saw her as human. Wanted her to stay that way and saw it as if she were somehow cheapening herself by being so involved with demons. He never said it outright, but she knew he felt that way. Was a little disappointed in her for it.

It didn't matter, really. She certainly wasn't going to make an important life decision based on whether or not a friend of hers might disapprove. But she would have liked him to approve and would have liked to think it wouldn't matter to him. But it wasn't important, especially not then. She didn't have time to worry about Brian at the moment.

And she didn't have time to hang around with him either. Time creeped on, as time was wont to do; it was close to five, and she'd hoped to try to eat something and get a little rest before meeting with the others at eight. Not to mention letting Tera and Nick know what the plan was and trying to figure out who might be the one who'd hired the angel in the first place—damn it, she should have asked Greyson who he thought it was—and thinking of him opened a whole new can of worms, one she'd have to face soon.

Her mood didn't improve when Brian arrived. He wasn't alone. He'd brought Julie with him. Shit.

Oh, she liked Julie just fine. But that whole detective-with-FBI-connections thing set her pretty low on Megan's must-see list just then.

Best not to let that show, though. So she smiled and gave her a hug, admired the new way Julie wore her shiny shoulder-length chestnut hair. Julie had always looked to Megan as though rather than working as a detective, she should be milking cows somewhere; she had that healthy pink-cheeked openness that belonged in a shampoo ad.

Those wide brown eyes weren't smiling this time, though, despite the friendly greeting. Julie sat in the desk chair, leaving Brian to lean against the wall. "Megan, the murdered woman, Justine Riverside. You knew her, didn't you? She was part of this meeting thing your boyfriend came here for."

Shit. Shit. What did she know? Had Brian told her anything?

Okay. Honesty was going to have to be the best policy here, because she had no idea what Julie knew and didn't know. "I knew Justine, yes."

"Because Greyson has some business involvement with her."

There was a difference between being honest and being stupid, however. "Julie, am I being officially questioned here or something? What's going on?"

"No, I'm not questioning you." Julie sighed. "I'm just trying to figure out why Elizabeth would do such a thing. And I know she talked to you before you came here. So I wonder if she mentioned Justine or if they knew each other."

"Where is Greyson anyway?" Brian looked around. "I would have figured he'd spring for a better room than this."

For fuck's sake, could she have one conversation today that didn't involve someone asking her about Greyson?

"He's not here. Elizabeth didn't mention Justine to

me, Julie. And I didn't know Justine very well. So I really can't help you much, I don't think."

Julie frowned. Megan couldn't quite tell if it was a disappointed frown or an I-don't-believe-you frown, and she had no real way to find out. Trying to read members of law enforcement wasn't a good idea. She'd discovered over the years that they tended to have a little ability of their own, at least the good ones did, and got antsy if she read them. And even if she'd been tempted to try, Brian's presence made it unthinkable. He'd know. He'd be pissed.

"When will Greyson be back? I'd like to speak to him."

"I don't know. Do you need to speak to all of us? It seems like a pretty open-and-shut thing, from what I've heard. I mean, you know who killed Justine, right?"

Julie cocked her head, her gaze measuring Megan like Spud with a new lipstick he was thinking of trying on her. "Can I be honest with you?"

Oh, no. Questions like that never led anywhere good. But what could she say? No? "Of course."

"Elizabeth has been . . . she's been behaving very oddly. I spoke to her this morning, and she . . . It's normal for people who commit murders—I mean good, normal people who suddenly snapped or whatever—to be confused. Or even to say they don't remember it very well. I'm sure you understand what I mean."

Megan nodded. She did, very well. One of the benefits of her training and career.

"But Elizabeth is . . . If I hadn't worked with her before, didn't know her, I'd think she was just trying to set up an insanity defense. She keeps rambling on about beautiful white lights and witches and demons."

Megan and Nick didn't move, but Brian twitched. Luckily Julie didn't notice.

"This isn't part of an official investigation, which is why I'm telling you this," Julie went on. "Yes, as far as the case is concerned, it's done with. Elizabeth confessed. But she's making less and less sense. She's drooling. She's falling asleep. She's not on any drugs or anything, but she's totally out of it. And I just wondered . . . she mentioned you."

"Me?" Did that sound squeaky? She really hoped that hadn't sounded squeaky.

"She said you came to her room. At least that's what I think she said. And then she said something about another woman and then something about an army or something. She said guns. That guns were there, and they were pushing her to do it, and the light wanted her to do it. And she didn't have control—" Her cell phone rang. "Sorry, hold on a second."

Megan barely heard it. One of them. Not *guns. Gunnar.*

Elizabeth would have known who he was. Would have recognized him. And of course Justine knew him and would have opened her door to him. From there, Elizabeth, powering the angel or being used by the angel—a stroke of cleverness she wouldn't have expected from Gunnar, setting up a murderer so no suspicion was cast on him—could have walked in right after him and done the dirty work.

Gunnar, who'd tried to downplay the deaths of his

*rubendas.* Gunnar, who hadn't wanted to go to the Windbreaker and confront the angel. Gunnar, whom Megan had always considered the dullest and weakest of her fellow Gretnegs; the man collected fish, for fuck's sake.

She glanced at Nick, saw the same knowledge in his eyes. The same aching uncertainty of what to do, with Julie and Brian there.

"Oh God!" Julie's voice cut their eye contact but did nothing to still the panicked hammering of her heart. "And she's—oh my God. Yes. Yes. Okay."

She hung up and stood staring at the phone, her pretty face set in a deep frown.

"What's wrong, honey?" Brian took a step toward her, but Julie shook her head.

"Elizabeth is dead."

"Oh, shit, seriously?"

Julie nodded. "But . . . they said her body was all . . . She just died, but she's already decomposed. Like she's been dead for a couple of days instead of twenty minutes."

Knowledge hit Megan so hard she had to grip the bed to try to hide her shock. The angel had killed her. Killed her the other night, either right before or right after it had attacked Megan herself. That's where the blood came from. That's why Elizabeth had been so spaced out. The angel had either been inhabiting her body part of the time or using it, moving its limbs like a fucking marionette. The image made her stomach lurch; she put her hand over her mouth.

Luckily it wasn't too extreme a reaction to discussions

about decomposition anyway. Julie reached for her. "Megan, I'm sorry! I wasn't thinking—this must be really more than you want to hear."

Megan waved her off. Okay. It was Gunnar. And the angel hadn't just seen Megan, attacked her. It had seen her with Greyson, with Nick and the brothers, with Roc and—

Tera.

Tera the witch. Tera, whom, if Greyson was right, the angel would have just as much reason to go after as any demon would. Yes, as a witch Tera was better protected than the rest of them, but still. If it snuck up on her, alone? She hadn't sensed it at the exorcism, hadn't seen it the way the rest of them had.

Megan stood up, almost falling in her haste. "Hey, guys, I just realized the time. I've really got to get going. I'm—I'm meeting Greyson. And I need to go right now. Nick? Nick, we need to go. Can you call Greyson and tell him we're on our way while I freshen up? And tell him to meet us in Tera's room. And to hurry."

# Chapter Twenty-eight

When she emerged from the bathroom—her hair was tangled at the back, she looked ridiculous, and nobody had bothered to say a word—with her heart still hammering and her hands almost shaking, she expected to find Brian and Julie gone.

They weren't. Or, rather, Julie was. Brian wasn't.

"I asked her to go get us some Cokes," he said. "I wanted to talk to you."

She looked at Nick, but he was on the phone, his back to her. She hoped he was talking to Greyson. "Brian, this isn't a good—"

"What's going on? You look terrified. This is a demon thing, isn't it? Some demon possessed Elizabeth Reid and made her commit that murder."

"No, Brian, it isn't a demon. Really."

"Well, what did happen? Megan, I'm trying to help. Is something after you?"

"There's a . . . creature, yes. Something not human. It's after all of us. It attacked me the other night, it attacked Elizabeth and did something to her, and it killed Justine. And I think it might be after Tera right now. Or any one of us. So really, I need to go, I'm—"

"Can I help?"

"What?"

"Can I help? Is there anything I can do to help?"

She had no idea what to say. On the one hand, it's possible that, being psychic as well, Brian could be very useful. On the other, this was dangerous. And she couldn't bring him into it without telling him exactly what they were fighting.

But the offer brought tears to her eyes. All of her earlier worries about their future faded as she looked at his earnest face. He would always be her friend, no matter what.

"I—"

"Greyson's not there," Nick said. He looked more worried than she'd ever seen him, even more than he had the night before when Greyson knocked and interrupted their ill-fated and ill-advised makeout session.

Her heart fell into her stomach and started thudding so hard she imagined her entire body vibrated like a speaker on too loud. "What do you mean?"

"He's not there. Malleus doesn't know where he is. He went out this afternoon, after you left, I guess, and he hasn't come back yet."

"What about his cell?"

"No answer."

Her legs suddenly didn't feel strong enough to support her. He was fine, of course. Maybe he went for a walk or more likely a drive—he did that sometimes when he wanted to think—and saw where the call was coming from and just didn't want to answer. "Try calling from your cell," she managed.

He started dialing, while she tried not to panic. He'd said he was pretty sure he knew who it was. He wouldn't have blundered into Gunnar's room, or anyone else's, for that matter.

Good thing she hadn't eaten after all. She couldn't possibly hold on to food with this kind of fear making her body feel like an icy husk.

Okay. Time to focus. Time to call Tera and get her up there, make sure she was okay. And of course, Roc. She'd given him the day off, essentially, until they knew what was happening. She should have contacted him sooner. Should have reached out to him as soon as she got back to the room.

The little psychic cord connecting her to her demons vibrated when she sent a push along it, waited for the push to come back. Nothing. She sent it again. Nothing.

Okay, what the hell. If she hadn't known better, she would have wondered if they were planning some fucking surprise party for her or something.

One more time. This time it came back, finally, a little shiver that made her feel much better.

"Roc will be here in a minute," she told Nick. "Anything?"

He shook his head.

"What can I do?" Brian asked. "Just tell me."

They all turned when someone knocked on the door. Roc, Megan felt. But Julie too. Shit, she'd forgotten about Julie.

"You can't do anything, Brian. You have to get Julie

out of here. It might . . . it's probably not going to be the safest place to be around here tonight. So you really should just go."

Another knock.

"I'll take her home and come back." He put his hand on the knob. "Okay? I'll be back in a bit."

"I wish you wouldn't. It's not safe."

His brows drew together. "You're my friend. I'm coming back."

With Greyson gone—unreachable, she reminded herself; not gone, just unreachable—it fell to her to try to corral everyone, to figure out what was happening and what to do about it. She and Nick were the only ones aside from him who knew who was behind the angel.

Or they had been. Tera was mercifully safe, if a bit irritated to be interrupted in the middle of a manicure in the hotel spa. Roc was fine, if a bit irritated to be interrupted in the middle of feeding off a group of very bitter divorcees he'd found by the pool.

But none of her Yezer had found the angel. It wasn't traveling on the psychic plane, and it wasn't anywhere visible to them. Probably in hiding. Lurking. Waiting.

"So if you know who it is," Tera said, frowning at her half-painted nails, "why don't I just call Vergadering? They'll come get him. Once he's in jail, the angel probably won't come after the rest of you."

"You're assuming it would know. Or that it would care." Time wasn't helping Megan calm down. With every minute that ticked by, both of her hearts sped faster, and more horrifying images and thoughts buzzed in her head. If the angel had him . . . if he was gone . . . She should have been strong enough, focused enough, not to think about him. She wasn't. Embarrassing but true. "And it might not just be Gunnar."

That possibility had occurred to her not long after they'd found Tera. She was focusing on Gunnar, so sure it was him—and she was sure, she knew it had to be. But that didn't mean Winston wasn't in on it, or Baylor. This was business, if of a particularly twisted kind, and business made bedfellows just as unlikely—or unholy— as politics or anything else.

"I don't like the look of that Baylor," Roc said. "He looks shifty."

Coming from a tiny, wrinkly, bald green demon, that was saying something, but Megan didn't argue. "It could be any one of them."

"So what do we do?" Tera picked up the room-service menu and opened it. "How do we find out which one it is? Are you still meeting them all at eight?"

"Yeah, we've only got an hour," Nick said. Tera's room was larger than Megan's; Nick was at her side on the little settee.

It was a prettier room too, with crown molding and its own small balcony. Ordinarily Megan might have wanted to go sit outside, to try to think with the breeze on her face, but not then. Not when she felt as if sniper rifles could be trained on the room waiting for one of them to move.

Shit, an hour. Only an hour. She was due to walk into battle at eight with at least one traitor, and her death was apparently pretty high on that traitor's priority list.

But who could she trust? Aside from the people in that room, who could she call? Who could she warn?

Yes, Winston wanted to head for the Windbreaker and do battle. But he could have been looking forward to leading them all into a trap. He could have prearranged things with Gunnar, to throw the rest of them off. Or Baylor could have done the same. Or any one of them. The only way to know for sure who was behind it would be to track them somehow, or the angel, and see who—*holy shit.*

Nick and Tera were sniping at each other about some privacy law or something. They stopped when she snatched up the room phone and dialed Greyson's room—her old room.

"Megan, what—"

She waved them off, listening to the ring in her ear until Malleus answered.

"Malleus, he's at the Windbreaker, isn't he? Keeping an eye on the angel?"

Long pause. Long enough to let her know she was right. "I can't say where he's gone to, m'lady."

"Because he ordered you not to, right? But he is there, isn't he? Malleus, just say yes or no. That's not telling me, right?"

More silence.

Tears threatened—again, she was getting really fucking tired of all this damned leaking—and she let them come through in her voice, hating herself a little bit because she knew she was manipulating him. "Malleus, please . . . please just say yes or no."

He sighed. "Yeh."

"Is he alone? He's not alone, is he?"

"Aw, no, m'lady, Lord Dante can take care of 'imself, 'e can. Don't you fret."

"He's alone? You guys—"

"Spud's with 'im."

The air left her lungs in a huge, relieved rush, only to freeze again as it came back in. He was there, and he had Spud. But were the two of them together really any match for an angel? Neither of them had the abilities psyche demons had. Spud was strong and tough and relentless when it came to fighting and wouldn't give up until he won or died, but she didn't want to think about that either.

Besides, how the hell was he managing to hide? If Gunnar or anyone else walked into that hotel, they'd see him. How was that a good idea?

"Thanks, Malleus. Thank you."

"You din't 'ear it from me, m'lady. Don't want 'im gettin' mad at me. An' 'e will, if you tell 'im."

"I won't. I promise."

She said good-bye and hung up, turned to see them all looking expectantly at her. "He's at the Windbreaker. Keeping an eye on the angel. I guess he's looking for confirmation or whatever. So we need to go over there now."

"I thought everyone else was going at eight."

Megan, already scooping up her bag and slipping her shoes back on, nodded at Tera. "They are. But we need to go now. Because we might be the only ones who go at all, and if the angel finds him there first, or if Gunnar or someone in on this with Gunnar spots him, I—we need to be there. We need to go, now."

She looked at them all. Tera, in her casual fitted button-down and loose black pants, looking unconcerned as always. Nick, whose hand clenched and unclenched as if it was looking for his sword. Roc, picking at the cinnamon roll he'd brought into the room with him; the smell made her hungry and sick in equal measure.

And herself, five-foot-two, a hundred and seven pounds. No muscles to speak of. No real fighting experience.

But she had power. She had her abilities. Tera was a witch, and witches had managed to defeat demons and angels both. Nick was a warrior. And Roc . . . who knew what Roc could really do if he had to? More than that. She had the frantic adrenaline of the hunted, the panic of a woman who had to protect her loved ones.

It wasn't the greatest fighting team ever assembled, but it would have to do.

# Chapter Twenty-nine

The semi-good fighting team ended up in separate cars too, which wasn't really auspicious. Megan didn't have a car, having ridden with Greyson to the hotel. Tera drove one of those little red sporty things that barely fit one person, let alone two. Nick had cabbed it from the airport, and of course, Roc, being unable to see over a steering wheel and relying on psychic travel, had no car at all.

Which made Brian's return, a few minutes after Megan hung up with Malleus, much more of a relief than she'd expected. Not only was he there, but he at least had four seats in his little foreign jobbie.

Which would have fit all of them, had Megan not opened the door as they were about to leave to find Maleficarum standing outside. "Mal sez you plan on heading for the hotel. I'm goin' too."

"Okay, fine," she replied, and ignored the faint surprise in his black eyes. "You can ride with Nick and Brian. I'll ride with Tera."

He looked as if he was about to protest—she wondered how much of his appearance at her door was the desire to help and how much was the desire to badger her about why she was hurting Lord Dante so and what he could do to fix things—but subsided when she gave him the steeliest glare in her repertoire. "Right."

The drive to the Windbreaker didn't take long. It felt like forever. Not only was she worried, but she was starting to wonder if this was the best idea. Greyson may have been able somehow to hide in the crowd. He might even have found a way to conceal Spud, although one thing Spud did well was stand out, between his size and the general air of menace around him.

But to hide the rest of them?

A bridge to be crossed when she came to it. The simple fact was, there was a chance Greyson was in danger. And she could not let that happen. Especially not when things between them stood the way they did. If something happened to him and he thought she didn't— she'd never forgive herself. Never.

"Okay," Nick said, when they'd all gotten out of the cars. He did have his sword after all; she didn't want to ask how he'd gotten it through airport security, but she didn't really need to. "Megan, I think you're probably going to be the primary target if anything does go down here. Or, rather, when it all goes down here. So Maleficarum, you should stay with her."

Maleficarum nodded, a faint look of disbelief on his face. Megan understood. As if Maleficarum would do anything else.

"I'm going to stay with Brian. I know the thing doesn't know you, and neither do any of the others involved. But you are psychic, aren't you? Right. So you could come in handy here, and—forgive me—but I don't know how much fighting experience you actually have."

"I wrestled in high school and college."

Megan blinked. She had no idea.

"Okay, well, that could help. Still."

"What about me?" Tera cut in. "Don't I get some protection?"

"Do you actually need it?"

"Well, no, but it would be nice if someone at least thought I was worth protecting."

Nick smiled. "You stay with me and Brian, then. How's that?"

"Good."

"Okay," Megan said.

The Windbreaker loomed before them, larger in her eyes and mind than she'd ever seen it. Such a dull building, dingy gray walls, small windows in rows up the edifice. It looked more like a correctional facility than a hotel.

She checked her watch, the slim silver one Greyson had given her a few months before. He was in there, and she was going to find him, and they had about half an hour before they were supposed to meet the others back at the Bellreive. What would happen when—if—they didn't show up?

Not her problem. She squared her shoulders, paused a minute to pull what energy she could from the air. She could have taken it from her Yezer but wanted to wait until it was absolutely necessary. "Let's go."

The lobby was silent. Dead silent, way too quiet. She

should have heard moans and wails coming from the ballroom where Walther held his exorcisms. Instead the only sound was the low rusty grind of the air conditioner.

"Where do we go?" Nick asked low in her ear.

"I don't know. Hold on." If she were Greyson, where would she be? Where, in order to watch all the comings and goings, to keep an eye on the angel and anyone else?

Just as she turned to look for the security office, she saw him poke his head out from around the wall behind the front desk, the partitioned area where the desk clerk had been napping two nights before. His features were twisted in what wasn't quite a frown but was definitely not a cheerful welcome.

"What are you doing here? Shit, never mind. Get back here, then you can tell me."

That was the greeting she got? She'd brought the cavalry in to save his ass, and she got a grumpy—well, she guessed it was about all she could expect, given that a few hours before she'd turned him down. Again.

As one, they slid behind the counter and back to where he and Spud sat before a bank of security cameras.

"Did Malleus tell you where I was?"

"No. I figured it out. And I know who it was. It was Gunnar."

The quick flash of approval in his eyes made her heart leap. "But not just Gunnar. Do you know who else?"

She shook her head.

"Well. Come sit and wait, then, and get ready. I expect any second now she'll show up."

"She? But Justine—"

"Of course it's not Justine. Justine would never have had anything to do with an angel. I'm surprised—"

"Angel?" Brian looked stunned. "What do you mean, angel?"

Greyson rolled his eyes. "Oh, for fuck's sake. I didn't see you'd brought the True Believer along."

"Hi to you too, Greyson. What do you mean, an angel? You don't honestly expect me to—"

"Not that kind of angel," Megan said. "It's not a good angel. It's a—"

"Angels are kind of good by definition, Megan. You know, creatures of God, protectors—"

"Warriors," Greyson cut in. "Not protectors. Warriors. Who is it who ends the world in Revelations, Brian? Who carries a fiery sword? For that matter, what about Uriel as the Angel of Repentance? Is that a friendly image? Is it one you want to face?"

If Brian was surprised that Greyson knew what he was talking about, he didn't show it. "What about messages of great joy? What about protecting the infant Jesus from Herod? What about—"

"Again. This isn't that kind of angel. Think of it as a rogue angel, okay? One who's broken from God and works as a mercenary and stays out of Hell because he's just that sneaky. This is an abomination, Brian. Something that shouldn't exist. Like a Nephilim."

Brian shuddered.

Greyson nodded. "Right. That's what we're dealing with. It's not something that's going to touch you and fill you with heavenly light, Brian. It's going to rip off your head if it gets the chance. It's using all those people out there, feeding off their faith, taking their free will and their sanity. It used a woman to slaughter a demon. It ripped her from her throat to her abdomen and tore out her heart. It wants to punish, and at this point it doesn't care who. It doesn't care that we've made our peace with each other long ago."

Not entirely true. The demons and witches had wiped the angels off the face of the earth, if what Tera and Greyson had said earlier was to be believed. But there was little point in letting Brian know that.

Brian was silent. Greyson pressed him further. "It feels nothing. It doesn't care if you were an altar boy. It doesn't care about your religion. But it cares about— it would care about—your psychic abilities. And it will kill you for them."

"I can't . . . I can't believe this."

"Then you should go." Megan put her hand on his arm, tried to get him to look at her. "You should go, Brian, because we have to do this, or it will kill us all."

The silence stretched so long Megan began to wonder if it would ever end. Just a little while before, she'd felt certain Brian would be her friend forever. Now she wondered if he hadn't reached the breaking point.

But he nodded. He didn't look at her, but he nodded. "Okay. Okay, I'll stay and help."

"Excellent." Greyson turned back to the monitors.

"How did you get in here anyway?" Brian asked.

He glanced back. "I convinced the guards they were needed elsewhere."

"What, like—never mind. I don't want to know."

Greyson ignored him, his eyes fixed on the screens. Megan crowded up as close as she dared, close enough to smell his skin and his cologne and feel the sharp stab of pain those scents caused in her gut, but not close enough to touch.

"Any second now," he murmured. "Any second now, and we'll find out if it was one of them or both of them."

"Greyson, who—"

"Shh. You'll see. They're getting ready, can't you feel it?"

Now that she thought about it, yes she could. Could feel the emptiness spreading, a kind of thick blanket of dull silence spreading over everything. Not the silence of an empty building. The silence of the morgue, waiting for the dead to rise. The hair on her arms and the back of her neck stood on end.

"I do feel it," she whispered. "What is it?"

He glanced around at all of them. "They'll find us soon. Are you guys ready?"

Megan checked the monitors again, found after a moment's searching the one that showed her the ballroom. Walther's histrionics had slowed. He moved like a man fighting to run across the ocean floor, his feet sinking in the carpet, his arms pushing through the thick air.

The crowd moved slowly too, if they moved at all. Most of them sat wide-eyed, open-mouthed, like children watching the most fascinating cartoon ever produced.

Her entire body vibrated. Something was wrong. She couldn't feel them around her. Couldn't feel them in the building, not even when she lowered her shields all the way. Instead she felt them inside her, wriggling there, making her demon heart pound and squirm as if it was going to break through her ribs and throw itself against the monitors. She put her hand to it, feeling a little silly but wanting absurdly to add another layer of resistance.

Greyson watched her do it but said nothing.

The feeling kept going, traveling down to her toes, up into her head. She was stuffed with them, overflowing with them, their fears and sadness muffled by the kind of peace that came from heavy psychotropic drugs. They'd tried to give those to her once, in the hospital when she was sixteen and possessed by the Accuser. She remembered that heavy nod, that cotton-brain feeling, and set her other hand on the desk to try to steady herself.

Greyson turned around again. "Maleficarum, Nick. How fast can you guys get to the roof?"

"The elevator—"

"Can't use the elevator. You need to use the stairs, and you need to use them fast."

They glanced at Brian, who nodded. The three of them took off.

"Why the roof?" Tera started opening drawers, pulling out bits of paper and inspecting them.

"Because I have a feeling that's where he's going to try to take Megan when he gets her."

"What the hell do you mean, when he gets me?"

Greyson nodded at the monitor. "Because whatever Gunnar's goals are, I'm betting you're hers."

Megan looked. Leora Lawden was walking through the lobby doors.

Her mouth fell open. "No. It couldn't be her."

"Oh, I assure you it is. In fact, I thought it was her alone from the beginning. It wasn't until Justine was killed that I realized it was Gunnar as well."

"But why—"

"She didn't exactly want you in the picture, Meg," he said. "And I'm pretty sure Gunnar was using her to get closer to you. Who knows what he promised her, but it must have been good."

"But her father. She wouldn't have plotted against her own father?"

"She probably didn't even know what he had in mind. She's not the brightest child. I don't think she bothered to give much thought to anything else, as long as he was willing to give her a way to get rid of you." His mouth twisted. "Not every woman thinks marrying a Gretneg is a horrible fate."

"That's not—" she started, but the words were torn from her mouth when a blast of energy poured into her, through her, sending her to the floor in a vibrating heap. Her arms, her legs, were no longer under her control. Neither were her thoughts. She felt them all, felt above them that same horrible blinding white light she'd felt on the roof, the same light that had nearly destroyed her in Elizabeth Reid's room.

She was vaguely aware of Greyson's hands on her, of Tera's voice trying to talk to her or utter some sort of spell, or whatever she was trying to do. It didn't help. She curled up into a ball as tight as she could, tried to see through half-blind eyes a place to hide, a place to escape to.

And they were coming. Getting closer and closer. She felt the angel's triumph as the ballroom doors opened. Felt the entire crowd cowed by him, entranced by him, bathed in the kind of ecstasy only felt by lunatics and junkies. Felt the bloodlust they didn't even recognize. They thought they were on a crusade, and she guessed they were.

To rid the world of demons.

And she was first on their list.

# Chapter Thirty

Energy pulsed through her, thicker and darker and sweeter all at once. From Roc. From her demons. Some of the shrieking pain subsided. Somehow she was able to pull herself to her feet. "They're coming." She gasped. "They're leaving the ballroom, they—"

Greyson nodded at Tera. Each of them grabbed one of her hands. "Now," Greyson said, and Tera's voice filled the air, filled her ears. The room spun and swirled, and she felt herself turning into something unreal, something she'd only been once before a few days back. The world went blurry, and suddenly she was on the roof, beneath the darkening summer sky, its blue-gray glow still faintly orange at the edges.

And she could think again. "What are we doing up here? Why up here?"

"This is where it will come," Greyson said again. "This is where we have the best shot at beating it."

"But why? It doesn't make any sense."

"We can ambush it here. More important, it can't get hold of any more people up here. They're too far away. And it likes roofs. Angels like open areas. They're not happy indoors or anywhere with walls. This is going to be the place."

She didn't want to argue anymore. Especially not about something like that. He said it, he believed it. It was enough for her.

But there was one thing she could say, and she would. Energy still swirled and strummed inside her, making her feel as if her skin was about to fly off her body. She reached for him, tried to use that contact to calm her, but his hand just sat in hers.

"I didn't know where you were," she said. Tera was listening interestedly from a few feet away; Maleficarum, Nick, and Brian wandered around the door leading up from the floor below. Roc still hovered on her shoulder. But she didn't care who heard. "I thought— I thought maybe it had gotten you. That you were gone."

"And?" He wasn't pulling away, but he wasn't giving her much either. Well, she supposed she couldn't expect much else.

"I didn't—"

Shout. Screams. The door burst open, and a flood of humanity poured out onto the roof. Businessmen. Hotel employees. The sad sacks from the reverend's meeting. The reverend himself, his eyes literally blazing, his mouth open in a roar that sent fear shooting straight up her spine and into her brain.

And above them all rose the angel. Not the nondescript man she'd seen before, no. Not even the thing that had captured her on the roof. This was a beast, a creature of primordial rage and righteousness. Its eyes flamed, its skin glowed white, blinding white, searing its image into her retinas. In its hand it carried a flaming sword, blue-white flames, vicious and ravenous in her eyes.

Oh God how were they going to beat this how could they possibly beat this thing—

Roc's fingers dug into her shoulder; Greyson's into her hand. She heard Brian screaming, saw Nick—in typical Nick fashion—leap into battle with his sword raised and a look of unholy glee on his face.

But she waited. She didn't know what to do. Attack or hold back? Try to read the humans, see if she could break the hold on them, or would that take up too much energy?

The angel's flaming sword spun. He caught one of the people, a woman, with his blade; she fell, her shoulder and arm landing several feet away from the rest of her.

That was enough for Megan. She yanked her hand from Greyson's and stepped back, willing him to stand in front of her, to keep her from being seen just one second longer. She had no idea if this would work or if it would simply make her shine like a beacon, but she did it anyway.

She lowered her shields all the way and pushed her energy out into the crowd.

Oh God. The hold he had on every one of them, the way he subsumed them. They had no conscious thought. They had no free will. It was as if they had no souls.

She pushed at them, pushed with everything she had, calling every bit of strength she could possibly get from her Yezer, from the air, from everything else. Wind kicked up around her, stronger and stronger, the thing fighting back. She heard its voice like insects in her soul rising above the screams, braced her feet to keep from falling, and pushed harder.

The angel's hold—like a membrane, thick and semi-opaque—wavered around them. She caught a few thoughts, a few images, an overwhelming sense of peace and dark joy, the blissed-out happiness of the living, un-caring dead.

Greyson shouted something. She didn't know what, couldn't focus on him. His voice was a buzz in her ear, a fly she had to ignore. The membrane was loosening; it wasn't giving way, but she could feel it, could lift it away from some of the people. If she could set even a few of them free, just a few—

Greyson leaped forward. A scream, loud and femi-nine—Leora. Megan turned to look for the girl and lost her hold on the membrane.

Damn it. Leora was there, all right, and Greyson was heading for her, but it was too late. Brian already had a hold on her, gripping her by the neck and pulling her back. She would have smiled if she hadn't been so dis-tracted; Brian wasn't fighting the angel, but he'd take on anyone else, and clearly Greyson's heading for Leora had given him someone to focus on. Fine.

She switched her attentions back to the membrane, ignoring the way her hair whipped and stung around her face. It wasn't as easy this time; she was weaker, had used so much energy already. With a silent, guilty prayer of thanks that there were so many unhappy people in the world, she sent another call out through the invis-ible strand that connected her to her Yezer.

Energy roared back at her, so strong and thick it almost lifted her off the roof. There was the membrane again, sticky and grotesque. She pulled at it. Felt it weaken at the back—there! A few of them free. Just a few, but—

Something grabbed her from behind and threw her to the ground. Gunnar. Where the hell had he come from, how had—did it matter? No. Because his gun was loaded and cocked right in her face, and she had about two seconds to live.

Roc leaped forward, his spindly fingers clutching at the gun. The move startled Gunnar just enough for Megan to bring her leg up and kick him as hard as she could. Right in the groin. His shocked, pained expression might have been funny if the gun hadn't gone off.

The bullet hit the roof an inch from her face. Chips of rock and tar flew up at her, opening stinging cuts in her cheek.

Gunnar fell. Megan rolled away. Time to try again, time to—oh no, duh. "Roc, tell them to show themselves. Tell them to fight the angel, tell them—"

Roc shook his head. "They're gone," he said. "It chased them away."

"Then tell them to get the fuck back here!" How ironic was it that the only way she could hope to win was by making these poor people miserable?

Better than letting them die in this hideous state, all things considered.

Roc closed his eyes and shivered, sending the message. Yezer started to appear, blue and red and orange and yellow and green, like bizarre confetti strewn across the roof.

Gunnar got back up, the gun wobbling in one hand, the other pressed between his legs.

Tera shouted something. The gun exploded back at him. His hand disappeared; blood pumped from the end of his sleeve. His scream drowned out her next thoughts.

She felt her demons pushing, trying to get their humans back. Across the roof she saw Greyson binding Leora's feet with something, some kind of rope, while Brian held her arms behind her back.

Gunnar smacked her across the face with his good arm.

She fell back, too surprised to scream. Tera started to shout something else, and Gunnar jerked, but Tera's voice died. Megan managed to glance over and saw her friend sink to the floor.

Dark clouds appeared overhead and burst open with icy, stinging rain.

The angel set his flock loose.

They swarmed the roof, plowing each other down in their haste. Their haste to get to Megan. She craned her neck for one last desperate look through the haze of water and saw Nick, his face grim, swinging his sword like a scythe; in his other hand he held a gun, and the reports blasted across the rooftop and dulled her hearing.

Gunnar grinned. His arms closed around her, gripping her from behind, locking over hers so she couldn't move. Blood from his stump poured down her back, hotter than the cold rain. As she struggled and kicked at him, her feet sliding on the wet tar of the roof, she saw Maleficarum and Spud fighting their way toward her.

They wouldn't reach her in time. They couldn't, because the angel had seen her, and it was coming.

Its hollow black-fire eyes were trained on her. Its lips stretched into a grin, a grin she couldn't bear to see. It was red and white, too bright to exist, there on top of the building, and her demon heart shrieked and writhed inside her.

She struggled harder. Fought harder. It didn't work. She tore her gaze away from the angel's eyes and saw Greyson running toward her, waylaid by the reverend. He punched the preacher in the mouth and kept going, but the swarms of humanity were too strong, the rain and wind too thick.

At least too thick for him to get to her fast enough. Because the angel's hand was above her, strong and pale and glowing, and she watched it descend like a fly watching the swatter fall.

With all her might, with everything she had, she pushed against him. Turned her energy into a weapon as she had the other night and drove it into him.

That same blinding flash of light. That same power driving into her, making her scream. She waited for the sucking feeling, the sense of him weakening, fading—

It didn't come. The angel's laughter echoed loud and horrible above her. Screams echoed around her, all of the people, every one of them, screaming. Falling to the ground in agony, water splashing as they fell. Their thoughts, their images, flashing through her mind at an unbelievable pace, too much for her to handle; even the additional powers she'd gained back at Christmas weren't enough. Their memories, their feelings, burning into her, their agony tearing through her body. He was connected to them, and she was killing them.

Somewhere in the tiny part of herself that could still think, she knew she had to break the connection. Had to free them somehow so she could focus on him.

She pulled back. That was a mistake. The second she pulled her energy from him, his shot into her, wrapping around her heart and squeezing. She was choking. She couldn't breathe. Couldn't fight him off. Gunnar's grip on her remained tight; she felt it as if through layers of cotton. Her body was leaving her control, she was fading . . . her vision went black around the edges.

Fingertips like feathers touched her arm. Power flowed into her, enough for her to see again, at least.

Nick. Oh, thank God, it was Nick, and he touched her with one hand while his other swung back and knocked Gunnar down.

She fell with him. *Good.* Good because it gave her a second's respite from the angel's touch. She started to roll away, grasping for Nick, tugging desperately at the cord connecting her to her Yezer but not getting much back. Not enough. She needed more, needed to get more. Needed everything she could get.

The angel grabbed her, yanked her back. Its hands burned her skin, and she screamed, reaching for Nick.

The angel's arms fell away. Greyson was there. He'd jumped onto the thing's back. Smoke rose from his skin; flames erupted around the angel, untouched by the rain.

It laughed. Threw back its head and laughed, a beautiful, terrible laugh that made her want to cower on the ground with her hands over her ears. The people screamed again too, screamed louder, until she thought for sure the entire city could hear them.

Nick was still there, holding her back, because she tried to attack and fight, to pull the angel away from Greyson. It was smiling too brightly, Greyson's face was going too pale, for her to believe any good was being accomplished.

She had to do something. She had to end this now. Right now. She wasn't powerful enough to beat the thing, not when it had whatever it was taking from all those people; her demons fed on misery and sadness, but it was feeding off humanity itself, if what she'd felt was correct, and it was far more powerful than she was to begin with. She suspected she'd only managed to beat it the other night because she'd surprised it, if that had been a defeat and not simply a strategic retreat.

She needed more power. Greyson would die if she didn't get it. Nick, Tera, Maleficarum and Spud and Brian . . . all these people would die if she didn't get it.

"Roc!" The scream tore from her mouth, disappeared in the cacophony around them. She called for him psychically, saw him appear, and grabbed his bony fingers with her own. She didn't have the words to tell him what she needed, but he knew. She saw it in his eyes.

The scene before her slowed down. She saw every detail, saw Greyson getting paler and paler, his flames growing smaller. Saw Tera getting up and shouting, felt her spell brush past. It knocked Greyson off the angel's back. Knocked the angel to the side and down.

The angel got up. Greyson didn't.

She saw Malleus and Spud heading toward her. Saw Brian touching people in the crowd, saw him trying to break the connection. Saw him tiring. Saw her Yezer flitting in and out among the crowd, trying to do the same thing, beating their little fists and squirming and fighting. They needed her. All of them.

So she nodded, and Roc began to speak.

# Chapter Thirty-one

Roc's voice started low, growing louder, words in the demon tongue she didn't understand. Energy flowed through her, the thick, sticky-sweet energy of the Yezer, speeding her demon heart. Speeding both of her hearts.

Nick's hand clasped hers more tightly. Did he feel it? Did he know? She couldn't tell, but she hoped he did. And then she knew he did, because his energy pushed into her too, red with lust and black with anger. She opened herself to it. To all of it.

For a moment she floated on it like a dust mote in the sun, dancing lazily, twirling and drifting. Her shields were already down; she willed them to disappear, let the energy flow through her entire body. Let it become magic inside her while Roc's voice kept going and something wet touched her lips.

Roc's blood. Just a smudge. And then Roc's lips, and she started to jerk away when she realized he wasn't kissing her. He was breathing into her, and that was necessary too, and she flew so high she thought she was scattered in the stars.

Then the pain hit.

Everything went red. Her brain screamed. Her mouth screamed. Every muscle in her body caught fire. Her heart pounded, pounded, pounded; it was all she could hear, faster and faster, her blood rushing through her body and through her brain. That hurt too, her head throbbing, a migraine times a million, and tears fell down her cheeks, and sweat soaked her dress, and blood poured from her nose.

Her muscles snapped and stretched. Her stomach roiled. She threw up, and blood came with it. It hurt so bad, so much worse than she'd ever imagined it would. She didn't want this anymore and it was too late.

It felt as if her bones were breaking. It felt as if her body was breaking, curling in on itself. Somewhere in there she felt Nick's hand still in hers and realized she was squeezing it. Her organs rang like bells and that was Tera nearby.

She didn't know how long it went on, the pain. Deep beneath it something else was happening. A strengthening. A deepening. Her consciousness spread around her until she felt every person on the roof, every one of them, as a separate and distinct entity. Felt their connection to the angel. It was like grabbing each string between her teeth and snapping it; she was doing it, she could do it, and it seemed so much easier.

Her legs shook when she tried to stand. They wouldn't support her. Instead she leaned on Nick, let his strong arms hold her up as she turned again to the angel.

Tera had been holding it off, screaming spells, waving her hands, and shooting what looked absurdly like neon flares at it. She wasn't beating it, but she was distracting it.

Brian ran through the crowd; large portions of them had stopped screaming, were huddled together on the floor, crying. "What do you need? Megan, what can I do?"

She didn't reply. Instead she took his hand. His shock transmitted to her; he felt it then. Felt her new power. Knew what she'd done.

Time to worry about that later. Right now—Greyson still hadn't moved—she had some business to take care of. And if that was an overly dramatic way to think of it, she couldn't help it.

She drew on his energy as much as she could. Drew on what her Yezer were getting, which was so much more now that the angel's hold on the crowd had been broken. Took it from Nick.

And thrust it all, flaming, at the angel, as hard as she could.

The impact nearly knocked her over again. It would have, had Nick not been there to hold her.

The angel screamed. It was the kind of scream she never wanted to hear again, the kind that made her want to cry and scream herself. The pain and rage in that sound horrified her.

But feeling the angel's shock, its misery, feeling its power weaken and rebound into her . . . that elated her.

Maybe it shouldn't have. It hadn't been easy to deal with that feeling the first time. But this time? All she had to do was look at the people around them, at Greyson, and anger overshadowed any sense of shame.

It fought her, pushing back. She gritted her teeth. Kept going. Kept shoving at it, sending every bit of anger and rage, every bit of energy, every bit of pain into it.

It sank to its knees. Tera shouted something, and it convulsed. Again. And again. Its energy fading, it felt so weak . . .

Megan pulled back. She couldn't keep going, not anymore. It didn't seem so evil anymore. It seemed so helpless, so—

It shouted something, and Reverend Walther flew through the air at her.

"You will not—foul—" He shouted something else, but Megan didn't hear it. She was too busy trying to jump out of the way, because Walther held a knife in his hand, moonlight glinting off the edge of it, and it was aiming straight for her heart.

Her heart. Not her two hearts. Only one leaped; only one pounded. It was done.

No time to think about that. She jumped sideways. Nick and Brian grabbed at Walther and tackled him.

The angel screamed. Megan looked up in time to see Spud bring his own knife down and ducked before it finished falling.

Silence fell. The wind died. The rain stopped.

She peeked up through her fingers. People milled around, crying; some of them headed back down the stairs, some clutched at each other as though they'd never leave. Tera stood panting by the wall, edging away from the angel's body toward Nick and Brian. Spud got up and turned to look at—

Greyson. Not moving.

She moved faster than she ever had. Faster than she ever thought she could move.

He was warm. She thought he was breathing. She couldn't be sure, though, and her hand was shaking too hard to check his pulse.

"Greyson, wake up." He wasn't dead. Couldn't be dead, right? Did demons go into comas? Jesus, did they go into comas they never came out of? He looked so pale. He was warm, but he was pale.

She slapped him lightly. "Greyson, wake up!"

He stirred, coughed. Opened one eye and stared at her. And like a silly girl, she burst into tears.

"Now?" he croaked. "Now will you fucking marry me?"

She nodded. "Yeah. Yes, I will."


The afternoon sun shone beneath the thick curtains on the window by the time they woke up the next day. Megan didn't really remember going back to their hotel or falling, exhausted, into bed. She had a vague memory of Greyson helping her undress and another, much sweeter, of him pulling her close before her eyes fell shut.

She opened her eyes, rolled over, and found him staring at her. She jumped.

"Jesus, you scared me. What are you doing?"

"I was awake."

"So you decided to lie there and stare at me?"

"Well, actually, no. I got up, and I made some calls—I have a few things to tell you—and then I got back into bed and waited for you to wake up. How are you feeling?"

How was she feeling? That was a good question. "Okay. Kind of achy everywhere. And a little loopy, maybe. But other than that, okay."

He nodded. "So you did the ritual last night."

"Yeah. I guess I did."

"And . . . you're okay with that?"

"Yeah." She smiled a little. "I guess I am."

Their eyes met for a second, but he blinked and started to sit up. "I talked to Winston this morning. He and Baylor showed up just after we left and took care of Gunnar. So we're not sure who's going to take over his House just at the moment. He asked us please to let him deal with Leora. I told him I'd have to talk to you about it."

"What do you think?"

"I think we should let him. She's just a child."

She raised her eyebrows. "That's so generous of you. I'm surprised."

"You wound me. I've always been generous. In fact . . ."

He leaned over, giving her a lovely view of his bare back, the muscles stretching under the skin, and came back with a tiny wrapped package. "Here. Happy birthday."

"Oh, shit, I—it is my birthday, isn't it? I forgot."

"Well, you have had rather a lot on your mind."

"True." She tore open the thick silvery paper to reveal a small velvet box. Her breath caught.

"Last chance to change your mind," he said, but the smile didn't quite make it. "Still want to say yes?"

She nodded. "Yes."

He flipped open the box. Her eyes felt as if they were going to fall out of her head. It wasn't that it was a large diamond; it was, but not ridiculously so. It was just so . . . perfect. Just what she would have picked for herself.

"I've been carrying this damned thing around for a month and a half. How about you put it on now, so I don't have to anymore?"

Her hand shook when she held it out to him. She was elated. She was terrified. And she loved him.

The ring slipped over her knuckle, rested perfectly at the base of her finger. She sat mesmerized for a moment, watching it sparkle, unable to believe this was really happening. Had really happened.

"I've been thinking about your job," he said. "You know, there are a lot of demons who could use some counseling. Right at the Ieuranlier. There's plenty of room; you could have your own office in one of the wings if you like. If you hate the idea, we can talk about it, but I thought . . ."

It wasn't perfect. It wasn't counseling humans in her own practice. But how much of that would she be able to do now that she was fully demon?

And she didn't really feel any different. They'd been right about that, Roc and Greyson. She felt exactly the same. She'd just been afraid of change, afraid of moving forward.

It was time to stop being that way.

"I think it sounds great."

"And the radio show, if you want to keep doing it, we can work something out. You can take the brothers with you when you go, maybe. I'd rather you not do it. But I'd rather have you, period."

"You do have me," she whispered. She couldn't keep from looking at the ring, feeling its weight on her finger.

"I love you, you know. My little pilgrim soul. I really . . . I really love you, Meg."

"Is that where *bryaela* came from? That poem?"

He nodded.

"I never guessed."

"Yes, I was always rather surprised about that, but whatever. I suppose it's not your fault if you don't have my dazzling intellect."

She stuck out her tongue.

He raised an eyebrow. "Now . . . I believe I can't really see that ring very well. There seem to be all those clothes in the way. I think you should take some of them off, so I can get a good look. I spent a lot of time hunting for that ring, you know. I deserve to see it properly, don't I?"

She giggled and slipped the strap of her nightgown off her shoulder; they'd played this game before. "How's that?"

"Hmm. No, I think that makes it worse, actually. You'd better take that thing off entirely. It's in my way."

He reached for it, but she stopped him with her hands on either side of his face. "I love you."

His expression changed; a flicker of relief, of happiness, and he was his smooth self again. "It's a good thing you finally agreed to marry me, then, isn't it?"

"I think so," she replied, and slipped off the nightgown.

The rest of her life looked as though it would be awfully interesting. She couldn't wait to see what happened next.

# Megan's Peanut-Butter Cake

## Topping

  ½ cup all-purpose flour
  ½ cup packed dark brown sugar (dark muscovado sugar is best; Megan gets hers at a gourmet grocery store)
  ¼ cup peanut butter
  3 tablespoons butter or margarine (butter works better)

Stir together flour and brown sugar. Use a pastry blender to cut in the peanut butter and butter until mixture is damp and sticky, like wet breadcrumbs. Set aside.

## Cake

  2 cups all-purpose flour
  1 cup packed dark brown sugar (again, muscovado preferred)
  2 teaspoons baking powder
  ½ teaspoon baking soda
  ¼ teaspoon salt plus another pinch or two
  1 cup milk
  ½ cup peanut butter
  ¼ cup butter or margarine, softened

2 eggs, well beaten (this is a fairly stodgy cake; you
want to introduce a lot of air into the eggs to get it
really to rise)
2 tablespoons white sugar, approximately

In a large bowl, mix the cake ingredients. Beat these
with a mixer on high speed for three minutes, scraping
the bowl frequently.

Grease a 13-inch-by-9-inch-by-2-inch baking pan.
Pour the mixture into it. Sprinkle topping mix over the
top.

Bake at 375 degrees for about thirty minutes; test
with a toothpick for doneness.

Don't panic if it smells a little burned. It's the sugar
topping.

This cake is much better the second day. It's good the
first but excellent after it's had a chance to sit (covered,
of course) at least twenty-four hours.

# Bestselling Urban Fantasy
## from Pocket Books

### BENEATH THE SKIN
BOOK THREE OF THE MAKER'S SONG
**Adrian Phoenix**
Chaos controls his future.
One mortal woman could be his
salvation. The countdown to
annihilation will begin with his choice.

### THE BETTER PART OF DARKNESS
**Kelly Gay**
The city is alive tonight… and it's her job
to keep it that way.

### BITTER NIGHT
A HORNGATE WITCHES BOOK
**Diana Pharaoh Francis**
In the fight to save humanity, she's the
weapon of choice.

### DARKER ANGELS
BOOK TWO OF THE BLACK SUN'S DAUGHTER
**M.L.N. Hanover**
In the battle between good and evil
there's no such thing as a fair fight.

Available wherever books are sold or at
www.simonandschuster.com

POCKET BOOKS
A Division of Simon & Schuster
A CBS COMPANY

22185

# Butt-kicking Urban Fantasy
## from Pocket Books
## and Juno Books

**Hallowed Circle**
LINDA ROBERTSON
Magic can be murder...

**Vampire Sunrise**
CAROLE NELSON DOUGLAS
When the stakes are life and
undeath—turn to Delilah
Street, paranormal
investigator.

New in the bestselling series from Maria Lima!

**Blood Bargain**
Book Two of the
Blood Lines Series

**Blood Kin**
Book Three of the
Blood Lines Series

"Full of more interesting
surprises than a candy
store! —Charlaine Harris

Available wherever books are sold or at www.simonandschuster.com

POCKET BOOKS
A Division of Simon & Schuster
A CBS COMPANY

JUNO

22186

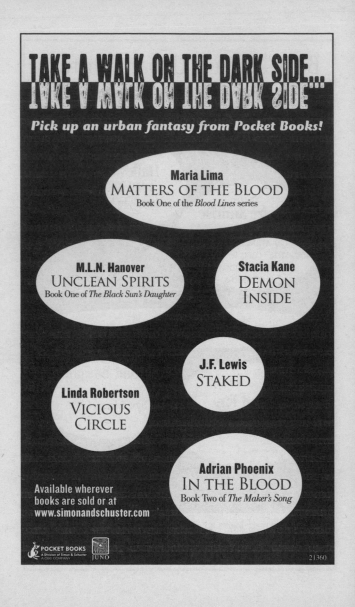

# TAKE A WALK ON THE DARK SIDE...

**Pick up an urban fantasy from Pocket Books!**

**Maria Lima**
MATTERS OF THE BLOOD
Book One of the *Blood Lines* series

**M.L.N. Hanover**
UNCLEAN SPIRITS
Book One of *The Black Sun's Daughter*

**Stacia Kane**
DEMON
INSIDE

**J.F. Lewis**
STAKED

**Linda Robertson**
VICIOUS
CIRCLE

**Adrian Phoenix**
IN THE BLOOD
Book Two of *The Maker's Song*

Available wherever
books are sold or at
www.simonandschuster.com

POCKET BOOKS
A Division of Simon & Schuster
A CBS COMPANY

JUNO

21360